SEAN McDOW ER

THE QUEST

A NOVEL

THE QUEST

A NOVEL

SEAN McDOWELL   BOB HOSTETLER

OUTRE⫟CH®

The Quest

Outreach, Inc., Vista CA 92081

Outreach.com

ISBN: 978-1-9355-4129-5

Cover design: Tim Downs

Editing: Marcia Ford

Printed in the United States of America

GODQUEST

"So I say to you:
Ask and it will be given to you;
seek and you will find;
knock and the door will be opened to you.
For everyone who asks receives;
the one who seeks finds;
and to the one who knocks,
the door will be opened."

—Luke 11:9-10

CHAPTER 1

I didn't answer when the call came. Not the first time. I saw who was calling and I let it go to voice mail.

I tucked the phone back into my jeans pocket and, instead of climbing the wooden stairs to my one-room apartment over the Stanfield Stationery store in tiny Oxford, Ohio, I stopped in to see my friend Artie in his two-chair barber shop. It's separated from the stationery store by only the staircase to my room.

"Emma!" Artie said, without getting up from the barber chair. He dropped the open *Cincinnati Enquirer* onto his lap. "What are you doing here? And where are the Young Republicans?"

Artie always had something like that to say. We'd been friends ever since he saw me moving into my apartment. He helped me carry everything up and even bought me pizza when we were done. We hit it off from the start, though he was easily twice my age. I quickly found out he could make me smile easier than anyone else. The "Young Republicans" was one of many ways he referred to Lincoln and Linden, three-year-old twins I cared for five days a week and sometimes on weekends, depending on the their college professor parents' schedules. Usually Artie called the boys Winken and Blinken or SpongeBob and SquarePants. He didn't seem to care that SpongeBob SquarePants was not two cartoon characters but one; I'm not sure he even knew that.

"Got the day off," I answered as I sat in the empty barber chair next to the one Artie occupied. Artie's shop was like something out of an old movie. Bottles of various shapes and sizes lined the counter in front of the mirror that occupied most of the wall behind us; old magazines were strewn haphazardly on the chairs and tables that lined the opposite wall, though I'd seldom seen more than one or two people in the shop at a time. "Their mom wanted to do something with them."

"So what are you doing out and about?"

I shrugged. "Nothing."

"She didn't tell you, did she?"

"What?" I asked, trying to play dumb even though Artie could see right through me.

"Why do you put up with it?"

"Put up with what?"

"You know what I'm talking about. Professor lady never even told you about her plans. She let you show up for work and *then* told you she didn't need you to watch the Fresh Princes today."

"She apologized." I avoided his gaze by pretending to study myself in the big barbershop mirror, in the space between the outdated hardware-store calendar on one side and the newspaper clippings and comic strips taped on the other side. I tucked my long red hair behind my ears.

"I bet she did."

"She did," I said. "She said she was really sorry and would make it up to me."

The phone in my pocket jumped to life, vibrating and playing my favorite song, "Think Twice," by the band One Off. I pulled it out, looked at it, and shoved it back into my pocket.

"Avoiding some guy?" he asked.

"You know better than that," I answered. "I haven't had a date since I started working at Common Ground." I'd taken a second job at a local coffee shop about four months earlier and still couldn't pay enough of my school debts to get the bursar to unblock my student account so I could take more classes. That's a long story; I'd been trying to pay my own tuition for the past year and a half. I told my dad—three weeks after his wedding—that I didn't want him to pay for my schooling anymore since he was married now and had a wife to take care of. We'd had a fight on the phone. As I said, it's a long story.

"What about that Randy guy?"

"You mean Ricky?"

"I know his name."

"He doesn't count."

"I hear that. So, who are you avoiding, if not some guy?"

It took me a second to remember how this conversation started. "Oh, that," I said, remembering the phone call. "My dad's wife."

He nodded slowly. "Don't they live—"

"In Israel, yeah," I said.

He kept nodding. "But you're not going to answer."

"I will," I said.

"When you're not so busy?"

Sometimes Artie could be a real pain.

Chapter 2

I glanced again at my phone. My stepmother had called twice and left two voice messages—that should have gotten my attention.

It wouldn't have been that unusual for my dad to call me. Well, maybe a little, since the wedding. Dad and I had always been super close. We had to be, since my mom died when I was too young to remember.

But in my sophomore year of college, he showed up one day outside my dorm, McCracken Hall. When I saw him, I ran to him so fast I dropped my books; they went everywhere. I left them lying there in the autumn leaves while I wrapped my arms around his neck and hugged him as tightly as I could.

"What are you doing here?" I asked.

"I want to take my blue-eyed beanpole to lunch. Is there anything wrong with that?"

So he helped me gather my books and drove me uptown to the Common Ground Café, where I ordered a turkey and cheese on toast, and he just had a cup of black coffee. I could tell something was on his mind—I always could read him like a book. But I was so happy to see him, I didn't mind waiting for him to get around to what he wanted to say. It didn't take him long.

"I've met someone," he said.

I waited. I thought it was just his way of starting a story, you know, like, "I've met someone, and he owns a New York art gallery, and he said he'd be willing to display some of your drawings," or, "I've met someone who flies a private plane back and forth from Ohio to New Jersey, and she's willing to fly you home for Thanksgiving and Christmas." But this wasn't *that* kind of "I've met someone." It was the other kind.

"Her name is Katya," he continued. "You're going to like her."

I immediately took a bite of my turkey and cheese and just nodded and chewed for a few moments. I had *not* expected this. I didn't know how to react. I didn't even know what I was feeling. I was feeling something, just nothing good.

"I feel like I have so much to tell you. She's a wonderful woman, Em. You're going to love her. She's warm, intelligent, sophisticated. She has a great sense of humor and is so much fun to be with."

"Huh," I said. It was all I could think to say.

"We met through an online dating service and we spent weeks exchanging e-mails before we had our first date at Little Anthony's in the theater district, in Manhattan. We talked for hours, Em, until the restaurant staff had to ask us to leave because they were closing!"

I tried to smile.

"And get this," he continued. "She's a writer. She's written more than a dozen books. That's pretty cool, huh?"

I nodded.

He produced his cell phone. "Here's her picture." He handed it to me.

I took it. Pretended to be interested. Handed it back. "She's pretty."

"Oh, she is. Absolutely gorgeous, five-ten, forty-one, and just four years younger than me. Beautiful in every way."

He looked so happy, smiling at me like a kid who's just heard the words "Disney World." I wanted to be happy with him—for him. So I tried, I really did. I asked him, "What kind of books does she write?"

"Christian books," he said.

"Christian books?" Had I heard him right?

"Yeah, like books on praying and faith and things like that."

"Christian books." I couldn't make his answer register. It felt a little like the way I felt when I used a word that Lincoln and Linden didn't understand. Their expressions would freeze. They would tilt their little heads and just blink at me.

Dad and I had never been religious. He raised me just fine without religion. He took me to the theater, the symphony, concerts, and art exhibits, but the only time we ever entered a church was for weddings and funerals. I couldn't picture my dad with a woman who went to church. I couldn't picture my dad with a woman, period.

He nodded. "I know it's shocking. But that's just the beginning, Beany." That's how he sometimes shortened his favorite nickname for me.

"What do you mean?" I asked.

"Katya has introduced me to God, Beany. She's changed my life. Actually, God's changed my life, but she's played a big part in that process."

"What do you mean, she introduced you to God? You don't even believe in God."

"You're right, I didn't, but now I do. I not only believe in him, I've come to know him … and love him."

I stood up—so suddenly that I knocked over my chair. It fell backward and hit the floor with a loud thud.

CHAPTER 3

KATYA'S JOURNAL

Emma's still not answering. Maybe she's busy with the children. Maybe she's avoiding me. I wish there was a way to let her know how urgent this is without leaving a message that will scare her. Maybe that's not possible. If she doesn't call me back soon, I may have no choice but to tell her that way. I hope it doesn't come to that.

I don't even know if I'm doing the right thing to call her now. It could still turn out to be nothing, but with each passing hour, that seems less and less likely. And I'm afraid I've already waited too long to contact her. But, really, what can she do? What can I do? What can anyone do, when we don't know anything yet.

I'm afraid, God, so afraid. It's been three days, and this isn't exactly the safest place on earth. I feel alone. I know you're here. I know that. At least I'm doing my best to know that. And there are others, like Tom and Stella, available to help. But Daniel's not here and I feel that emptiness so strongly. This little apartment is filled with his absence.

It's so hard to wait, so hard to not knowing, and so hard to think, or pray, even. I don't want to be

consumed by worry ... or fear. I want to trust you,
God. I know that trusting you is the only way I can
get through this. I'm sorry for all those times I've
ever responded to people who were hurting with glib and
easy answers about trusting you through tough times,
dark times. I know that trusting you is my only hope
and my only choice right now. I am grateful for the
blessing of faith and the benefit of prayer—when I
can pray. I don't know how people make it through,
otherwise. I don't know how Emma will.

But you do. You know all things. So I guess I'll
just leave it with you. So work things out, Lord. Let
Emma return my calls or answer the next time I try.
And somehow, somehow, get me through this night.

CHAPTER 4

I didn't even stop to pick up the chair from the floor. I had to get out of there, if only for a few minutes to catch my breath, so I locked myself in the women's restroom at the café.

It was too much. First, my dad tells me that he's met some woman and that she's a religious freak, and *then* he tells me that he's become some kind of religious freak, too? It felt like a betrayal—of what, I don't know, but Dad and I had always been so close. We did everything together, just the two of us most of the time. He was the best dad a kid could ever have. He taught me how to climb a tree, ride a bike, drive a car, ski, and dance. He taught me everything important, and he never taught me to believe in God. He used to say that religion was a lot like alcohol or drugs—it intensifies human personalities. You know, like if a person was generally good, religion sometimes made them better; but if a person was mostly bad, religion usually made them worse. But he always said I didn't need religion because I was already the best person he'd ever met.

I knew he was biased about me, of course, so I didn't take his words all that seriously. But it still felt awful for him to say he had a new woman in his life and that she had guided him to God or whatever. Didn't he know how that would make me feel? Couldn't he see how that was like a knife in my heart? The only way it could be any worse was if he—

The thought stopped my breath. I stared at my reflection in the restroom mirror. It wasn't possible. He had flown from New Jersey to Ohio to tell me that he had met some woman and that she was a religious person and now he was, too. Right? That was enough to drop on me in one afternoon, right? He couldn't possibly ...

I marched out of the ladies' room. I was so focused on getting to my dad's table that I would have knocked aside a girl headed in my direction if she hadn't stepped out of the way at the last second. I saw her shaking her head at me as I passed, but I didn't care. I reached the table as my dad set down his coffee and looked up, a concerned expression on his face turning to apprehension.

"Are you getting married?" I said.

He didn't answer immediately, which he would have, if the answer had been no. So I knew. It was true. He was getting married.

"Sit down, Emma. Please?" he said.

I sat. He reached across the table to grab my hands. I put them in my lap.

"I haven't asked her yet, but I'm going to. I haven't mentioned it to anyone else. You're the first."

"When?"

"I plan to ask her next weekend."

"I mean when are you getting married?" This was insane. It was too much, too sudden, too fast.

He moved to the chair beside me, leaned in close, and put his hand on my hands.

"I know this is a lot, Beany. I've wrestled with how to tell you. I wanted you to know, but I didn't want to tell you any of this on the phone. That just didn't seem right. But there's still so much to tell you, I've only just scratched the surface, and I know it's overwhelming, but—"

"When are you getting married?" I repeated.

He leaned back in the chair and withdrew his hand. "Emma, please don't be angry. I want you to be happy for me."

"I will," I lied. "I'll be ecstatic for you. Just tell me when you're getting married."

He shot me his chastened puppy-dog look that never failed to make me laugh … or cry. But this time it did fail. He inhaled slowly, then sighed. "I'm hoping we can do it while you're home for Christmas. A small wedding, just a few friends."

Just two months away. Not even that. Less than two months. Oh, God.

I stood again, this time keeping the chair from falling. I kissed his forehead—quickly, so as not to give him the chance to hug me. I knew I was being a jerk, but I didn't care.

"That's fine," I said. "I'll be there." I told him I needed to get my books out of his car because I had to get to class. He said he'd drop me off. I told him I'd walk.

From the Bloomfield Daily News

Hopkins/Seeger

Katya Marianna Hopkins and Daniel Drake Seeger were married Saturday in a ceremony at Bethany Community Church in Verona. The Rev. Robert Helwig officiated. The couple was attended by the groom's daughter, Emma and the bride's sister, Elena.

The bride, who will take her husband's name, graduated from Wesleyan University and is the author of 13 inspirational books. The bridegroom is a vice president for operations at Dressler Insurance in Manhattan. He is a graduate of Rutgers University and Fairleigh-Dickinson University, where he earned a master's degree in business administration. Mr. Seeger was a widower prior to his marriage to Ms. Hopkins.

The couple live in Bloomfield.

CHAPTER 5

I know I shouldn't have treated my dad so badly that day in the café. I apologized on the phone a few days later and things returned more or less to normal, at least as far as I let on to him. And I went to the wedding on December 23. It ruined my Christmas that year. Who am I kidding? It ruined my life.

I know that sounds like a drama queen, but it's not. I tried really hard to smile and act as if I was happy for my dad. I tried to like Katya. Dad was right; she is really beautiful, but that's just one more reason to dislike her.

She fell all over herself trying to be nice to me. She came with Dad to pick me up at Newark Airport; she insisted that I sit in front with him on the drive home while she sat in back. When I went up to my room to unpack, there was a gift box on my bed—a pretty birthstone bracelet and a note from her:

"Emma, thank you for accepting me into your family and for your kindness in being a part of our wedding. Your father has raised an exceptional young woman, and you have played a primary role in making him the man he is today! I am so looking forward to many happy years with him … and with you."

But the nicer she was, the less I felt as if I could tell her or Dad how hurt I was that I'd been replaced—and that Dad was so different from before. It sounds selfish, right? But all my life, Dad and I had had each other; now he had *her*, and I had … who?

THE QUEST

I didn't call Katya back, and I didn't listen to her voice messages. But when my phone rang again after I'd left Artie's and gone up to my apartment, I figured I might as well get it over with and I answered it.

"Emma, I'm so glad I finally reached you." The connection wasn't the greatest, but Katya's voice was clear enough.

"Yeah, sorry about that. I just got home." I sat down on my double bed, the largest piece of furniture in the room—which isn't saying much because the only other furnishings were an upright dresser with four drawers, a small easy chair that swivels and rocks, and an end table between the bed and chair.

"Thank you so much for answering."

"Sure," I said.

"I am so sorry to tell you this over the phone, but I can't think of any other way."

"What? Tell me what?" You know how people say "My heart skipped a beat"? That's exactly what happened. Only it was more like four or five beats. "Is it Dad? Is my dad okay?"

"Yes," she quickly answered. "I mean, I don't know."

"What do you mean you don't know?" I couldn't believe what I was hearing. It suddenly felt as if I was in one of those television crime-show episodes. "What's going on?"

"Your father is missing," she said. "I haven't seen him for three days. He left on Monday to go to a new community where we've been getting to know some of the people, and he never came home that evening."

"What? And you're just calling me now?" Six months after their wedding, Dad made another trip to see me in Ohio. I'd had to stop taking classes by that time and was renting the small walkup over the stationery store. He said that he and Katya had decided to move to Israel to be some kind of missionaries. They rented out the house in New Jersey to some friends, packed some clothes, and left everything else behind—me included.

"I didn't think much of it at first. Sometimes he can't get cell service or he has to stay overnight with someone if a border crossing closed."

I had no idea what she was talking about. Only that she had said my father was missing.

"But when he didn't call or come home the next day, I started to get concerned."

"Did you call the police?" I asked.

"Oh, yes, I contacted the police yesterday, and they promised to look into it, of course. I've also contacted our agency office, so they are doing everything they can for us—for him."

I sat down. Tears started to flow and my hands were shaking. "What—I don't understand." I fought to control my emotions. I was losing. "How could this happen?"

"Don't panic, Emma. I don't want to upset you. I wasn't even sure I should call you. I just thought it best to tell you."

"He must be hurt or—or something. If he was all right, he would call you."

"He would call me if he could, yes. But it's not always possible."

"Do you think he's okay?"

"I—I hope so. But I don't know."

"But what if he's hurt or—?"

"I don't want to think about that right now, and you shouldn't, either. I'd rather do everything I can to find out what's happened and leave the worrying for later."

"What am I supposed to do? I can't do anything from over here. You've taken him half a world away from me."

Katya was silent for a few moments. Finally, she said, "I'm sorry, Emma. I know this is hard. I hope I did the right thing by calling you."

It was my turn to be silent. I couldn't believe this was happening. I didn't know what to do. I felt so powerless—and alone.

Chapter 6

My conversation with Emma didn't go the way I wanted it to. But I suppose there's no good way to share that kind of news—or to hear it.

It's hard enough to be here in Jerusalem while my husband is missing. It has to be impossibly hard to get a phone call from half a world away and hear that kind of news about your father. Not knowing anything and not being able to do anything is the hardest part of it all. And for Emma, it is certainly much worse, infinitely worse.

God, I know that wherever Daniel is, you are on the job no less than you were before this current situation. But it doesn't feel that way. And Emma doesn't know these things. She is alone, miles and miles away from here, and I imagine she feels even more powerless than I do at the moment.

I don't know what I can possibly do for her from this distance, other than to keep her informed as much as possible. But I would love the opportunity, Lord. I would welcome the chance to discuss the things that really matter with her. If you would open that door for me, I would be so grateful.

In the meantime, Lord, please draw close to her. Surround her with the support of friends during this difficult time. Give her a strong friend, a faithful friend, to help her process all of this and cope with it. And supply what is lacking in her relationships, Lord, please. If there is no one in her daily life to give her spiritual counsel, send someone her way, place someone

THE QUEST

in her path, someone who can answer questions and give her hope.

Reach out to her in her fear and panic and bring her peace and comfort, whether or not she knows the source. Strengthen her for whatever the coming day—or days—may bring and while you're at it, please do the same for me. Amen.

CHAPTER 7

When I finished talking with Katya, I sat on the edge of my bed and let the tears come. I don't know how long I cried, but if anyone ever cried enough to be able to float away on a river of their own tears, it was me.

From as far back as I could remember, being in control of things was important to me—maybe more important than anything. When I was a toddler, I would arrange my dolls in a row on my bed, against the wall. It became a nightly ritual to take them off the bed and line them up carefully on top of the toy box in the corner, as well as in front of it. I don't know why it never occurred to me to find a place where they could stay in place. Maybe the comfort I felt from neatly arranging them over and over was the point.

In kindergarten, I did the same thing with crayons. I wouldn't start coloring until all my crayons were arrayed by color on my table. I liked the way they looked, all neat and colorful and ready for action.

Once I started driving, I always wanted to be—had to be, more or less—the one behind the wheel. Only on short trips would I let my friends drive me anywhere, and then only rarely. Sometimes I even said no to some party or get-together if it meant someone else would drive. Sounds silly, I know, but it really wasn't that big a deal. It didn't control me, if that's what you're thinking. I just felt better when I could control a situation. I still do.

So when Dad told me he was getting married … to a religious nut … and that he'd gotten religion, too, the most important thing about the situation was that I was losing my dad. But it also felt as if I was totally losing control. And then when he told me they were going overseas and wouldn't even be as close as New Jersey—as if I wasn't already far enough away, being in Ohio and all—well, there was nothing I could do about that, either.

But now, this was maddening. I was terrified. I felt alone. Powerless. Panic-stricken. And, maybe worst of all, I was—what? Six thousand miles away from my dad, and no one had heard from him in three days. I could do nothing, absolutely nothing, about it. Who could I call? Where could I go? What could I do?

From the Israel News Service website

Arnona Resident Reported Missing

✉ EMAIL 🖨 PRINT ＋ SHARE

An American citizen and resident of Arnona in southern Jerusalem was reported missing.

Katya Seeger, the wife of Daniel Seeger, filed a police report after Mr. Seeger had been missing for more than 48 hours. Mr. Seeger reportedly left home in his car, a white 2009 Hyundai Getz, on Monday morning and was expected to return that evening. On Wednesday morning, Mrs. Seeger filed a report with the missing persons bureau of the Department of Investigations and Prosecution at the Israel Police Central Headquarters.

Each year the police receive about 5,000 missing persons reports. According to police superintendent Yair Levi, head of the missing persons division, most turn up on their own and their names are removed from the list. However, 20 to 50 names remain on the list each year, causing the number of current missing-person cases to grow to more than 500.

Mr. and Mrs. Seeger are both employed by the Jerusalem branch of the Sar Shalom Institute.

CHAPTER 8

KATYA'S JOURNAL

It's becoming hard to sit down. Hard to focus my thoughts. I'm trying not to let fear take over. I'm trying to keep a handle on things, but it's not easy. I'm really struggling with the total loss of control I feel. Every once in a while, I feel panic gripping my heart, and I pray to keep the panic at bay, but I think even that focuses me on the wrong thing—on the panic itself, or the reasons for it.

I think what I need right now is to force my mind to think along other lines. Positive things. Things that are true, and noble, and right, as the Bible says. So I'm going to take a few minutes to list the things I'm thankful for, even in the midst of these dreadful hours and days:

Things I'm Thankful For
That I was finally able to reach Emma;
The fine friends and neighbors I have in my life;
Tom and Stella and their help finding the police station and filing the missing-person report;

THE QUEST

The other staff at Sar Shalom Institute;

Our kind neighbors, especially the Applebaums for lending me a car;

Our church family, small though it is. They have already been so supportive, so kind;

The Bible and the encouragement and strength that reading it brings to me;

The comfort of prayer and the knowledge that others are praying for me.

That's just a start. But I'm already feeling calmer and more hopeful. And for that, too, I give you thanks, God. Be with my Daniel tonight, wherever he is. Amen.

CHAPTER 9

I slept.

I don't know how I fell asleep or when, but I awoke with a start. I almost never remember my dreams, but I knew I had been dreaming about my dad and remembered only that he had been in danger. I didn't know if that was a premonition of some kind or just my fears showing up in my dreams.

I sat up. I knew I had to do something. I didn't know what yet, but I couldn't stand just sitting around waiting for news. I replayed the conversation with Katya in my head. She said she had called the police and their agency—the group they worked for in Israel—but all she really knew was that Dad hadn't called or contacted her since Monday. And now it was Wednesday.

I looked at the clock—12:54. I had slept a couple of hours. If it was almost one in the afternoon here, it would be—*what?*—maybe six or seven hours later in Israel, which would make it seven or eight o'clock in the evening there. If Dad had been kidnapped, wouldn't the kidnappers have tried to contact Katya by now? But that was stupid; why would anyone kidnap him? It wouldn't be for a ransom. He'd given up his job, income, home, and basically everything else to move to Israel with Katya; and the agency they were working for was probably some poor little Christian nonprofit. It's not as if they could pay any ransom.

But if he wasn't kidnapped, then what? I could feel my heart beating faster at the thought and my emotions started welling up inside me again. There were bombings and terrorist attacks to consider. I grabbed my laptop off the bedside table and accessed a search engine. My hands were shaking, but I managed to key in a few search terms to see if any terrorist attacks had happened in Israel or the Palestinian territories in the last few days. I scrolled down and scrolled some more. I clicked on a few links, but there didn't seem to be any news of recent bombings or attacks.

THE QUEST

I found an Israeli news site called Haaretz and scanned its homepage. *Russian President Cancels Israel Visit. Peace Talks Stall Again. Boycott of Companies Building Palestinian City Urged. Extradition Talks Collapse; Suspected Nazi Extradited from Kyrgyzstan.* But nothing about a terrorist attack. Not even any violence, as far as I could tell.

Yet Katya hadn't heard from Dad since he left their home on Monday morning. Could he have been arrested? Maybe he was involved in some protest or something like that. But if that was the case, wouldn't he have been able to at least call her to tell her what was going on? Do people in Israel get one phone call like people in America? Maybe not. Maybe they just throw them in jail to rot, and no one ever hears from them again.

I didn't know much about Israel and the Middle East, but I didn't think that sounded right. I still had to do something. I had to *learn* something, or I would go absolutely nuts.

But what could I do? I was in Ohio, thousands of miles away—I didn't even know *how many* thousands of miles away—from Dad, no matter where he was. I had no one to call, no one to turn to.

Well, that wasn't quite true. I had friends from school. Although, since I stopped taking classes, I hadn't seen much of them—not because they weren't good friends but because our lives just didn't mesh anymore, you know? They had their schedules of classes and study and parties and so on, and I had my schedule of—well, work. And not much else these days.

I had friends at the coffee shop, of course. But they wouldn't know any more than I did, would they? I thought of my employers, the Professors Reese, but they'd probably just say whatever they had to say to get rid of me quickly; even when I had to tell them about their own children, they seemed in a rush to get it over with and get on to something more important. But there was Artie.

There was always Artie.

When I entered Artie's shop, he was cutting some guy's hair.

"I need to talk to you," I said, my voice quivering. "It's an emergency." I passed him and the guy in the chair without pausing. I ducked through the black curtain and into the back room of his shop, which looked like someone had set off a bomb in a UPS store; boxes and paper were everywhere.

He stood patiently while I told him about my phone conversation with Katya. He listened without interrupting, still holding a comb in one hand and scissors in the other.

"What are you going to do?" he asked, when I finished.

"That's why I came to you. I don't know what to do."

He tapped the comb and scissors together for a few moments and then said, "Give me a minute."

He stepped back through the curtain and returned to the chair. I followed him into the shop, and after a few snips with the scissors, he turned the man around to face the mirror.

"All set," he said.

"What?" the man answered. "I just got here."

"Tell you what. No charge today."

"What's going on? I came here for a haircut."

"It's your lucky day," Artie answered. He set the comb and scissors on the counter, whipped off the barber cape, and lowered the man's chair. He grabbed a pen and a business card from the counter and scribbled a note on the back. "Your next cut will be free, too. But I have to close the shop."

Artie gave the man the business card, but the guy didn't move. He took the card from Artie and just sat there.

"*Now*," Artie said. "I have to close the shop *now*."

"You've got a funny way of running a business," the man said.

"You're not the first to tell me that. Have a nice day."

The man left, and Artie followed him to the door. He locked the door and turned the sign in the window so the "Closed" side faced out.

THE QUEST

Then he walked back to his chair and nodded for me to take a seat in the other chair.

"Okay, Red," he said. He called me that sometimes. He wasn't particularly original. "All you really know is that your stepmom hasn't heard from your dad since—Monday, was it?"

I nodded. "She said sometimes he's gone overnight, like if he can't get through a border crossing or something like that. And she said he can't always call because there's not always a signal for his cell phone."

"Right. But she thinks something's wrong."

"She told me not to panic. But ..." The tears started again, and I wiped them from my cheeks with my hand. "How can I not panic? I mean ... he's my dad. I'm his only daughter. What if something happens to him? What if something has *already* happened to him? What if I never find out?" I lost it then. I put my face in my hands and tried—I tried really hard—to keep from losing control, but I sobbed almost as hard as I had earlier, alone in my room.

Artie waited. He put a hand on my arm while I cried and just waited. I think every once in a while he said something soothing, but the words just got lost in my sobs.

Finally, I managed to wrestle my emotions under control. Or something like it. "I'm sorry," I said.

"Don't be. It's okay."

"I just don't know what to do or where to turn. I feel helpless."

"Well, you're not. Okay?" He made me look at him. "You've got me. I'll help you in any way I can."

"You don't have to do that," I said.

He got up out of his chair and stood in front of me. He took both of my hands into his hands. "Listen to me," he said. "You are my friend. And you're a good friend. I've seen you go out of your way to be kind to people. You're always putting others at ease by thinking first about what they might need. You got the kindest heart of anyone I know, and I know a lot of people. You're bright, you're beautiful, and you're responsible. And you're always taking care of other people. I know you don't take care of SpongeBob and SquarePants only for the money; you do it because you love them, because you care about people and you want to help. So let somebody else help *you* this time. Stop thinking you have to do everything yourself, and let me have the pleasure of helping you. Okay?"

I tried to smile. "Thanks, Artie." That really meant a lot to me. But almost immediately, I started thinking of my dad again, my hands started to shake, and the panic started to well up in me again. "I just feel like I'm losing control. I hate that. I start thinking about my dad and what might be happening to him, and then I think about how I don't know anything, and how I can't control anything. Then that makes me feel even more panic and it gets worse and worse from there. I wish there was a way to calm myself down, a way not to feel so helpless."

"Some people pray," Artie said.

"I don't pray," I snapped. "I don't even believe in God. I thought you knew that."

He nodded.

"I wouldn't even know where to start. I mean, how can a person pray if they don't even believe in God?"

He shrugged. "I don't know. I just know some people say it helps them. It brings them peace."

I felt the panic subsiding a little. Maybe just talking to Artie was helping, as if he was distracting me from the thoughts that were causing me to panic. "Maybe it doesn't matter. Maybe it just helps people to get their minds off their troubles."

"Could be."

We both fell silent. But at least I was calmer.

CHAPTER 10

I've slept so little in the past 48 hours, less than 2 hours last night. I know I need sleep. Whatever tomorrow holds, I'll be better prepared for it if I have rested as much as possible.

Tom and Stella called again. We spoke for more than an hour this afternoon. They have contacted the U.S. State Department and scheduled an appointment for the three of us tomorrow at the American Consulate in Tel Aviv. It doesn't seem real that anything like that is necessary. I keep expecting my phone to ring, and to hear Daniel's voice on the other end. He is constantly in my thoughts.

I can't stop thinking about Emma, either. Poor thing. God, I know that your ways are not our ways, and I'm sure your plans for me, and Daniel, and Emma, too, are good. But please have mercy on that girl, so far away from her father and so far away from you. I'm so sorry I did such a poor job of offering her comfort and hope in our phone call yesterday. Please be gracious to her. Comfort her and draw her closer to you. I know she doesn't believe in you, but of course I know you believe in her. Place someone in her path who will be an encouragement to her—someone who might even help her open up to you and experience your presence, support, and strength.

THE QUEST

And please be with Daniel, wherever he is. If he's cold tonight, wrap your warm arms around him. If he is afraid, send your angels to strengthen him. If he's injured, touch him and heal his wounds. If he's in danger, surround him with your protection. If he's hungry, send food. If he's thirsty, provide water. If he's sick, make him well. If he's lonely, fill him with an awareness of my love and prayers. Preserve his life, Lord, please. Keep him in your care. Sustain him with your Holy Spirit, and bring him safely home to me, in Jesus' name, amen.

From the U.S. State Department website

American Citizens Missing Abroad

Sometimes concerned relatives and friends call us when they haven't heard from a loved one who is abroad. We can help to pass messages to these missing Americans. Consular officers use the information provided by the family or friends of a missing person to locate the individual, and pass the caller's message. We check with local authorities in the foreign country to see if there is any report of a U.S. citizen hospitalized, arrested, or otherwise unable to communicate with those looking for them. Depending on the circumstances, consular officers may personally search hotels, airports, hospitals, or even prisons. The more information that the caller can provide, the better the chances are that we can find the missing American.

Privacy Act – The provisions of the Privacy Act are designed to protect the privacy and rights of Americans, but occasionally they complicate our efforts to assist citizens abroad. As a rule, consular officers may not reveal information regarding an individual American's location, welfare, intentions, or problems to anyone, including family members and Congressional representatives, without the expressed consent of that individual. Although sympathetic to the distress this can cause concerned families, consular officers must comply with the provisions of the Privacy Act.

PRIVACY | FOIA | U.S. DEPARTMENT OF STATE | OTHER U.S. GOVERNMENT INFORMATION

CHAPTER 11

Artie promised to make some calls and talk to some people to find out what he could about my options. He suggested I go see a friend of his the next day. A next-door neighbor, actually. He said he'd tell her to expect me.

She was a rabbi.

I felt really weird about talking to a rabbi and a woman rabbi especially. I told Artie I thought rabbis were all bearded old men. He said he used to think so, too, but this one was a woman, and he said she was pretty normal. He thought she might be easy for me to talk to and might even have friends in Israel.

I had to take Lincoln and Linden with me. I decided not to tell their parents about what was going on. I didn't want them worrying about whether I was paying close enough attention to their kids; I figured I could worry enough about that for all of us.

I showed up a few minutes early at the Hillel Center on the university campus and found the office of Rachel Cantor-Cohen, Artie's neighbor. She must have heard me come in because she came to the door, welcomed me, and invited the boys and me in. I apologized for having to bring them, but she didn't miss a beat. She showed them to the corner of her office where a kid-sized table was set up with a couple of chairs and some crayons and coloring books, and the boys sat down and started playing as if they were right at home.

Rabbi Rachel was a tall, thin, dark-haired woman, possibly in her forties. No makeup, but pretty. I told her, as quickly as I could, about my dad being missing in Israel and the talk Artie and I had yesterday. I told her why Artie suggested I see her, and that he thought prayer would help, but that I didn't even believe in God. I said I felt really foolish even talking about it.

"Well, don't. Some days I don't much believe in God, either."

I thought I hadn't heard her right. "What did you say?"

"Some days I don't believe in God."

"But ... you're a rabbi."

She nodded. "I'm also human. And that means I don't know everything."

"So you don't know that there is a God."

"No, I don't." She smiled. "I don't *know* that there is a God. Some days, I feel more faith than doubt. And some days I feel more doubt."

"Then why am I here?"

"Why *are* you here?"

I was starting to get confused. "I told you. Artie said I should talk to you, that maybe you could help me get through this."

Nodding again, she said, "If I remember right, you said you were wishing last night that you could pray, that prayer would meet a need you have."

"Yeah," I said. "But what good would that do, since I don't believe in God?" I thought I'd already said all that.

"So you feel like there is a need in you ... that maybe God—*if* he exists—could fill right now."

I blinked. I didn't know what to say.

"Isn't that why you came to see me?" she asked.

I stared at her for a few moments, then I started to nod ... slowly. "Yeah, I ... I guess that's right."

"In other words, at some level ... maybe down deep, but somewhere in there—" she pointed at my chest— "you are looking for, hoping for, and needing God."

My mind rebelled. "No," I said, but for some reason it felt like a lie.

"Why does it bother you to consider that you might be looking for God?" Rabbi Rachel asked.

"Because I'm not. I'm looking for my father. I just need a little help coping with his disappearance and my inability to do anything about it, to even know what step to take next."

"And if prayer could help, would you be willing to try it?"

"If I thought it would do any good, yeah."

"Even if you're not sure anyone is listening?"

"That's just it. I don't want to just play mind games, which I think is a lot of what religion is. No offense."

She smiled patiently. "Talk about that. Talk about mind games."

I felt like we were getting off track. "I don't think we can really know if there is a God or not."

"So, you're not an atheist so much as an agnostic."

Her words stopped me momentarily. I had never given it much thought. I just knew I didn't believe in God. "What do you mean?"

"An atheist is a person who believes there is no God. An agnostic wouldn't necessarily say that. An agnostic would say, 'I don't *know* if there is a God.'"

I thought about that. "I guess I'm an agnostic, then. I don't think we *can* know."

"You don't think it's possible to know whether there is a God or not?"

I nodded. "I think truth is out there, somewhere. I just don't think we can ever really know it."

"You don't think truth can be known or discovered?"

"No, I don't."

"Do you think that's a true statement?"

I blinked. "What do you mean?"

"What you just agreed to: 'I don't think truth can be known.' Do you view that as a true statement?"

"Well, ye-eah," I said slowly. Something didn't sound right.

She smiled and leaned forward in her chair. She didn't say anything, but looked at me like she was waiting for something.

It took a minute, but I finally realized what she was waiting for. "You're saying that if I think that's a true statement, then I've claimed to know something that is true."

She didn't respond. Just watched me as the wheels turned inside my head.

"You trapped me," I said.

"No," she answered, her tone soft and sympathetic. "I don't think so. I think you trapped yourself."

"By saying truth can't be known. I contradicted myself."

"It's called a self-refuting statement," she said.

"So … if I say that I can't know the truth, I'm making a statement I believe to be true. Which means I must believe I *can* know the truth."

Her smile became broader. "I think that really is what you believe, though maybe you've never fully owned up to it before. And I think it's true not only of your search for your father. I think it's also true in your search for God."

I shook my head. This was wild.

"Can I suggest something?" she said.

I nodded.

"What if you put some of your doubt aside for a while?"

"What do you mean?"

"Most people who claim to be agnostics put all faith on the shelf and leave it there. But they hold onto their doubt. That's never seemed quite fair to me. So what if you reversed things and put your doubts about truth and God on the shelf, at least temporarily and held onto faith, even if it's still very small?"

"But I don't have any faith."

"I think you do. You seem to at least have a little faith that truth can be known … or you wouldn't make any statements at all, would you?"

I rolled those words around in my head for a few moments while she waited. She seemed content to wait as long as necessary. "Maybe so," I said.

"That's a good place to start."

"Okay. How do I do that?"

"Give yourself permission to pray. It's okay that you're not sure whether God exists or not. At least you believe—at least I think you've discovered that you believe—that if he *does* exist, there might be a way to find him—to know him. Right?"

I bit my lip. "I—I guess so."

"Then why not proceed on the basis of that possibility? If God exists, then he might help you through this crisis. And if he *doesn't* exist, what has it hurt? And maybe you'll find some strength in prayer either way."

"But … wouldn't I be lying to myself?"

"I don't see how. At least until you confirm beyond a doubt that God does *not* exist, you're simply proceeding with a little bit of faith instead of only giving room to doubt."

I nodded slowly. "So you think praying can really help?"

She smiled and shrugged. "It helps me."

Chapter 12

"Simon and Garfunkel!" Artie exclaimed when I entered the barbershop with Linden and Lincoln in tow. "How are my favorite Young Republicans?" He leaped up from the chair and produced a couple of lollipops for the boys.

"You know their mom doesn't like for them to have sweets," I said.

"I know. That just adds to my enjoyment."

I summarized my meeting with Rabbi Rachel while the boys sat in the waiting area and concentrated on their lollipops.

"Are you glad you went?" he asked me when I finished.

I shrugged. "She was all right. But on the walk over here, I started thinking I mainly wasted my time. I should be finding out more about my dad or at least making some kind of progress in that area."

"Do you want to hear what I found out?"

"What?"

He snatched a piece of notepaper off the counter. "I talked to a friend who knows a lot about this kind of stuff. He knows a lot about everything, actually, and he said you should call your congressman and ask for help."

"I don't even know who my congressman is," I said. I'd never even voted. I'd always meant to get around to it someday, but I'd been in college since I turned eighteen and didn't see much point in registering to vote until I'd settled somewhere.

THE QUEST

"Gotcha covered," Artie said. He handed the slip of paper to me. On it was the name of Congressman Bob Brainerd and a phone number.

"What am I supposed to say?"

"Just explain your circumstances—that your father has gone missing in Israel, maybe in the Palestinian Territories, and you wonder if he can help."

"Do I ask to speak to him?"

Artie shook his head. "No, probably not. They have staff for this kind of stuff."

"What do you think he'll do?"

"I don't know. But it's worth a try."

I told him I'd call once I had the boys down for a nap. "Anything else?"

"Yeah. I told you the rabbi would be good to talk to. You should listen to her. Do what she says."

"Oh, okay, *Mommy*," I said.

* * *

I had no trouble putting the boys down for their naps—for once. They lived in a home on the quiet end of Vine Street, not far from the university campus. One of the reasons I took the job was because I could walk to it, which was pretty important since I sold my car to pay for part of my tuition last semester. Mrs. Reese loved to tell people all about the house, how it's a Colonial Revival built in 1893 and one of the oldest private homes in Oxford. I'd heard her go on and on about the house. I think she loved it more than she loved her kids. *Definitely* more than she loved her husband. And most people she told that to acted the way I did, as if they couldn't care less.

I fished Artie's note out of my pocket and dialed the congressman's office number on my cell phone. A woman answered after the second ring. I introduced myself and then tried to explain why I was calling. After a few moments, I stopped.

"I don't even know if I'm talking to the right person. Do you need to switch me to someone else?"

"No, not at all. I'm a staff assistant to the congressman."

"Okay," I said. I continued with my story and when I thought I had included enough information, I said, "So I guess I'm just calling to ask if there's anything the congressman can do to help."

"Certainly. We can contact the appropriate agencies on your behalf, such as the FBI, requesting that they look into your situation."

"The FBI?" I said.

"Yes," she answered. Her voice sounded very official, as if she was reading from a script. "The FBI is the lead agency for all kidnappings of American citizens, both in this country and abroad."

"Oh," I said.

"We also have connections with consular offices in overseas embassies, so we can inform them and enlist their help."

"Okay."

"However, we would need you to sign a privacy waiver before making inquiries on your behalf."

"What's that?"

"It's a simple form giving us permission to speak to various government officials for you."

"Oh. I guess that would be okay."

"The privacy waiver is on the congressman's website. Do you have access to a computer?"

"Yes."

"Good. Then all you need to do is complete that form and fax or mail it to our office. The mailing address is on the form. Let me give you the fax number."

"Okay. I can do that." She gave me the website address as well as the fax number and I wrote down the information. "Thank you," I said.

"You are most welcome. Is there anything else I can do for you?"

THE QUEST

"No," I said. "I guess not. Thank you very much." I started to hang up.

"Miss … Seeger?" the woman said.

"Yes?"

"I hope you find your father."

In that moment, the tears arose again, as if they'd been waiting for an outlet. I managed to croak, "Thank you."

CHAPTER 13

I'm so grateful for Tom and Stella! Such faithful friends and helpful advocates. They seem to always know the right thing to say and the best way to serve others.

They picked me up early this morning and we drove the 60 kilometers to the American Embassy in Tel Aviv. Stella brought along a Thermos of hot coffee and made the 90-minute drive a rich time of fellowship and catching up with each other.

At 9 a.m. we arrived at the Consular Affairs Office in the consulate.

It felt strange entering that office, as though we had just stepped out of Israel and into America. Everything about the space was distinctly American—not just the flags and the photos, but the accents, people, and seemingly the air itself. Certainly the way of doing things was American.

A no-nonsense American bureaucrat efficiently guided me through telling the story of Daniel's disappearance. I felt a bit out of sorts, as though I had to tell the story in a certain order dictated by his paperwork, as opposed to a narrative that seemed to make sense to me. But Tom and Stella assured me afterward that I did well. I hope so.

It took less than an hour and a half, all told. The man was kind and thorough enough. He thanked me for the report and seemed sympathetic to my plight. He told me that the consulate would immediately run Daniel's name by the local authorities to see if his name showed up at a hospital, jail, or on a police report. He also gave me some photocopied pages detailing how Israeli law and procedures differ from U.S. practice. He assured me that they would do everything in their power to find Daniel and return him to me. I couldn't help but wonder—silently, of course—whether everything in their power would amount to much at all.

In any case, I know, Lord, that all things are in your power. You hold this world in your hands. You hold my life in your hands. You hold my Daniel in your hands. Be kind, Lord, please. Watch over him. Bring my husband safely home. Unharmed—and soon. Please. Amen.

CHAPTER 14

I almost got fired from my job at Common Ground that night. I filled out the privacy waiver before Lincoln and Linden got up from their naps and used the fax machine in the Reeses' study to send it to the congressman's office. But then Professor Reese—the father—was late getting home, and I dashed the five blocks to the coffeehouse as fast as I could, but still, by the time I was tying on my green apron I was almost fifteen minutes late. Jackie, my manager, didn't say anything, but I could tell she was irritated.

Things got worse from there. I couldn't concentrate on anything. I kept getting orders confused and spilled half a carton of half-and-half—no joke. I was just opening a fresh carton and the thing slipped out of my hands and onto the floor. Jackie pushed me aside. "Get the mop!" she said.

Once the mess was cleaned up, she clamped a hand on my shoulder and said, "Get it together or get out. Got it?"

I nodded and tried hard to focus on my job for the rest of the evening, but it was a losing battle to try to focus on lattes and cappuccinos and macchiatos when all I wanted was for my phone to ring and to hear Dad's voice saying he was all right. But I needed this job to pay my school bills, especially if I ever hoped to get back into classes. So I couldn't give Jackie any more reason to fire me.

Then it got worse again. Jackie was standing right behind me when a customer brought his cup to the counter.

"Something's wrong with this," he said.

THE QUEST

"I'm sorry, sir," I said. "What's the problem?"

"It doesn't taste right. I don't think you put any espresso in it."

I took his cup. He was right. I had given him a steamer: steamed milk, syrup … but no espresso. It was an inexcusable mistake. The man had ordered an espresso drink, and I had forgotten the espresso! Jackie heard the whole exchange between us.

I apologized and got the man a new drink, but Jackie interrupted my next order by asking me to step into the back room.

"I don't know what's going on with you, Seeger, but you've got exactly no time to pull it together."

"I'm sorry," I said. She was normally a pretty good boss. We'd always gotten along great. But of course she had no idea what was going on in my head. "I just found out yesterday that—"

"I don't have time for excuses," she interrupted. She pointed to the line of customers. "You see that line out there? Either you make sure those customers walk away happy, or you might as well sign out now."

I nodded and dropped my gaze so she wouldn't see my tears. I felt as if I was on the verge of a total breakdown. That's when I remembered the rabbi's advice. I headed back to the counter and prayed as I walked.

It wasn't much of a prayer. It was basically just "God, help me; help me, please," repeated over and over in my head. But after a few moments, I felt my breathing slow, and the tears went back to wherever it is they hide in between crying jags.

For the next six hours, I prayed repeatedly. I asked God to take care of my father. I asked for help focusing on my job and for peace to replace my panic. At first, I felt like a big fat hypocrite. It seemed ludicrous to pray to a God I didn't even believe in. But after a while, it started to work. I could feel a sense of sanity returning. Calm, even. I honestly don't think I could have finished my shift without it.

I still thought it seemed kind of crazy to think that there was some higher being hearing my prayers and reaching down from heaven to comfort me and help me focus, and all the other stuff I was praying. More likely, I was just using a time-tested psychological trick that gave me a sense of control over my circumstances, which I sure needed right then. When it came right down to it, it didn't really matter to me. Whatever was happening, it was helping.

I was still a long way from believing in God. But maybe I could come to believe in prayer.

THE QUEST

BOB M. BRAINERD
CONGRESSMAN
Ohio

H-301 U.S. CAPITOL BUILDING
WASHINGTON, D.C. 20516
(202) 215-0978

WASHINGTON OFFICE:
177 LONGWORTH HOUSE OFFICE BUILDING
WASHINGTON, D.C. 20516

DISTRICT OFFICES:
10069 FRANKLIN TRACE ROAD, SUITE A
WEST CHESTER, OHIO 45069

47 SOUTH ORANGE ST.
DAYTON, OHIO 45401

Ms. Emma Seeger
34 W. High Street, 2nd Floor
Oxford, OH 45056

Dear Ms. Seeger:

Thank you for contacting me for help in locating your father, who is missing in the State of Israel or the Palestinian Territories.

I have contacted the appropriate agencies requesting they look into your situation and provide any information that might be helpful to you. As soon as I have something to share regarding my efforts, I will contact you immediately.

If I may be of further assistance to you in this or any matter, please do not hesitate to contact me. Please feel free to contact me at my West Chester District Office.

Sincerely,

B. Brainerd

Bob Brainerd

CHAPTER 15

I awoke screaming.

I sat up in my bed. It was still dark. I snatched my phone off the bedside table and looked at the time—it was 3:14. I looked around the tiny room for a moment and then realized I was sweating profusely. I turned in my bed and felt the sheets. They were damp with perspiration.

It had been a horrible dream. I was with my father. We were canoeing together. I think it was the Whitewater River, not far from here. I had been there with friends but never with Dad.

We were laughing and splashing each other with our oars when suddenly there was a fork in the river and I looked at Dad in the other canoe. The current was sweeping us away from each other.

I started paddling furiously, and he did, too, but the more we paddled, the farther apart we got. I tried to shout to him, to tell him to jump from his canoe and swim to me, and then he turned and looked behind him. That's when I saw the rapids. He was heading into whitewater, white peaks of water that grew larger and larger and would soon threaten to capsize his canoe and drag him into the dangerous swirling currents.

I jumped in and started swimming toward him, but every stroke seemed to take me backward, increasing the distance between us until I could no longer see my dad. I looked around and realized my canoe was gone. He was gone. I was alone. And I was losing strength.

THE QUEST

That's when I awoke.

I got up from bed and padded into the bathroom. I flipped on the light and turned on the faucet. I was still breathing heavily, my heart still beating rapidly. I splashed cold water on my face and reached for a band to tie back my hair.

A few minutes later, I sat in the only chair in my room and pulled my knees up to my chest. I doubted that I would get any more sleep this night. Before I knew it, I was praying again.

"Wherever he is, let him be alive," I said. "Even if he's hurt, just take care of him, please. If he's a prisoner somewhere, don't let him be hurt. Don't let him give up. Don't let him suffer. Just keep him alive. Keep him safe. Keep him strong, please."

I buried my face in my arms and let the tears come. I'd never felt this way. Not in my life. I'd had disappointments, sure, but I'd never had anything bad like this happen to me. Not even close. I never knew my mom, so I guess I never knew what I was missing. And, sure, I was ticked when Dad married Katya. But my whole life, all these years, I'd never suffered, really. I'd never even broken a bone. Never been hospitalized. Never gone through anything that could have prepared me for this.

I picked up a book from the table and hurled it against the opposite wall. "It's not fair!" I said, my voice sounding unusually loud in that little space. "I'm helpless here! I'm so far away, and there's nothing I can do! I can't do *anything* about it. I can't see him, I can't talk to him, I can't tell him I love him—" I choked back tears and gritted my teeth until the urge to cry was subdued. "I can't go there. I can't even look for him. I can't even sit on his front step and wait for him to drive up."

I kept speaking, as if someone was listening. "Do *you* think it's fair? Do *you* think it's right that I can't do anything about this? Do you *like it* that I have to just sit here and wonder where my dad is and if he's okay?"

It was weird. There was no answer—because I'm not *crazy* … yet. But just a few seconds after I said those words, I realized that I didn't have to just sit there. A thought occurred to me that was so obvious,

I can't believe it never occurred to me before. I wasn't powerless. I wasn't trapped. I didn't have to just sit there.

I could go to Israel.

I knew I had a passport; I just didn't know where. I only used it once, when my dad took me on a cruise for my eighteenth birthday. But I had no idea where it could be. I checked all my dresser drawers, under my bed, in the drawer of the little table by my bedside. Finally, after about forty minutes, I remembered: Dad had given me a small satchel of important papers when he and Katya left for Israel. It was on the shelf of the tiny coat closet just inside the door to my apartment. I checked, and it was there, among insurance papers, my high school diploma, and the savings bonds he'd given me every birthday since I was a little girl.

I opened the passport. It wouldn't expire for a long time yet. Then I pulled out the savings bonds, bound together with a rubber band. Why had I left these sitting here all this time? I could have used them to pay my school bills! I counted them. Nineteen. Each one said it was worth a hundred dollars, which would probably be enough to pay for a plane ticket to Israel.

I held them to my lips and kissed them. "Thank you!" I said, though I didn't know who I was thanking. My father, maybe. Anyway, I was so glad to find them.

I grabbed a pen and notebook and sat cross-legged on my bed. I needed to list the things I would need to do before going to Israel. I would have to cash in the savings bonds. I wasn't sure how to do that. Maybe a bank would cash them for me. In any case, they might be able to tell me how to get them cashed. So I would go to the bank as soon as it opened.

I would have to pack. That shouldn't take long. I had a duffle bag in the closet; I'd use that.

I would need to buy plane tickets. I should call Katya and tell her I'm coming. Maybe she would pick me up at the airport.

I'd have to quit my job taking care of Lincoln and Linden. It would break their hearts. Mine, too. I would have to say goodbye to the boys, and they would cry, which would make me cry. I shook my head. I couldn't stop to think about it right now or I might change my mind. I would have to deal with it later.

I'd give notice at the coffee shop, too. Maybe Artie would drive me to the Cincinnati airport. I wondered how soon I could get a flight.

My mind was racing by now, and I tried to force myself to focus on one thing at a time. It wasn't easy. What about my apartment? Should I pack my things and ask Artie to store them for me? I didn't have much, probably a few boxes. Should I try to get out of my lease, or would I be returning after a few weeks? There was no way to know.

I decided to ask Artie to talk to Mr. Stanfield for me. We both rented from him, and Artie would do a better job at explaining things than I would.

I balanced the notebook on one knee and looked at my list. It didn't look as bad as I thought it would. Maybe I really could do this. A lot would depend on the plane ticket—how much it would cost and what day I could book it for.

I started to re-number the things on the list in the order I would need to do them. First, call Katya. Then go to the bank. Next, buy the plane ticket. Pack. Quit the coffee shop. Tell the Reeses. Scratch that. I should tell the Reeses as soon as possible. I looked at the time on my cell phone: It was 4:53 a.m.

CHAPTER 16

There wasn't much I could do this early in the morning. The bank wouldn't open for another four hours, and I didn't feel comfortable buying my plane tickets until I knew for sure that I could cash in the bonds without too much trouble. Artie didn't open his shop until then, either. And I'd have to wait until after seven to call the Reeses. But by my calculations, it was about noon in Jerusalem, so I found Katya's number in my cell.

She picked up after just two rings.

"Hi, Katya," I said. "It's Emma."

"I'm so glad you called. I have been praying for you."

I didn't know what I was supposed to do with that, so I didn't respond to it. Instead, I said, "Have you heard from Dad?"

"No, I'm sorry. I still haven't heard anything." She filled me in on some of the things she'd been doing and learning, but I interrupted her.

"I want to come to Israel," I said.

A pause. "Are you sure?"

"Yes. I've already started making plans. I have some savings bonds I can cash in for the plane ticket, and—"

"What about your classes?"

THE QUEST

I had never really told Dad and Katya that I had to stop taking classes. "My dad is missing," I said, my emotions starting to rise again. "I have to help somehow. I can't do anything from here."

"There isn't much any of us can do," she said. "Except wait."

It felt like she was saying I shouldn't come. Maybe she didn't want me there. "Look, I can find someplace to stay. I don't want to impose on you."

"Don't be silly. Of course you can stay with me. We can get through this together."

I didn't answer. I wouldn't even know where to begin finding a place to stay in Israel.

"It would be lovely to see you," she said. "Do you need me to send you money?"

"No. I think I can manage." I hadn't given much thought to how awkward it would be to stay with Katya. This was going to be weird. We had nothing in common—except Dad.

"When will you be coming?"

"I don't know yet." I glanced at the time on my phone. "The bank won't open for several hours, so I can't get the money or book my flight until then."

"Of course," she said. She asked me to let her know when I booked the flight and told me she'd pick me up at the airport. Then she told me again that she was praying for me and promised to contact me immediately if she learned anything about Dad. Then we hung up.

The next three days were a whirlwind. I cashed in the savings bonds at my bank, but they amounted to barely enough for the plane ticket to Tel Aviv. Artie helped me arrange things with Mr. Stanfield; he said Mr. Stanfield would hold my room for me as long as he could—we'd take it a month at a time and so on. I packed up the place and stored the few boxes I had in Artie's back room.

Mrs. Reese pitched a fit when I told her I was leaving. Lincoln and Linden cried; and I did, too. I told them I'd send them a postcard from Jerusalem, which meant nothing to them. But when I offered to take them to McDonald's when I got back, they were willing to kiss me goodbye.

Jackie was surprisingly understanding when I quit the coffee shop and told me she'd hire me back when I returned. Artie drove me to the airport, and after pulling my duffle bag out of his trunk, he squeezed a wad of money into my hand. I started to protest.

"Just take it. I bet you don't even have money for a sandwich along the way, do you?"

"I do," I protested. "As long as it's a small one."

He smiled. He looked like he might tear up. "I thought so," he said. He pulled a small folded piece of paper from his pocket. "And do me a favor. They say you can put little prayers in the cracks at the Wailing Wall." He put the paper in my hand and folded my fingers over it. "Put this in there for me, will you?"

I hugged him hard and long, until he broke off the hug and lifted my duffle onto the curb.

"You sure you can carry that?" he asked.

I hoisted it over my shoulder. "Please. I may be little, but I'm as tough as they come."

He smiled. "Got that right," he said. He blew me a kiss, got into the car, and drove away.

I waved for a few moments before turning to go into the terminal.

God,

please help my friend Emma find the one she is looking for.

Sincerely,
Artie

CHAPTER 17

Lord, I know there are millions of travelers on the roads, on the seas, and in the skies today, and you love and care for them all. But please keep an eye on Emma's flights today and through this night.

Watch over her on the drive to the airport, throughout her flights, and in every layover.

Give her safety.

Pave the way for her and engineer the details of her flight schedule.

Escort her to every gate, help her to make every connection.

Protect her from coach cabin infections,

mechanical failures,

turbulence,

and delays.

Give her rest on the way and a companionable seatmate.

Let her luggage arrive with her.

And please see me safely to Tel Aviv tomorrow and home with her, in Jesus' name, amen.

THE QUEST

CHAPTER 18

The first leg of my flight was from Cincinnati to Chicago. After a two-hour layover, I boarded the flight from Chicago to Tel Aviv—with a stopover in Brussels, wherever that is—which meant almost fifteen hours in the air. I was not looking forward to it, to say the least, but it turned out my seat in row 22 was next to a really cute guy with short brown hair who was maybe a few years older than me. No wedding ring. He occupied the window seat, and I was in the aisle seat next to him. He looked up from his book and shot me a half-smile before going back to his reading. I sat down.

Once we took off, I looked around the plane and suddenly felt totally unprepared. People were reading books and using ebook readers; I even saw a couple of DVD players. I was glad several movies were scheduled to be shown, because otherwise I'd be facing a long boring flight.

The first movie ended and the guy sitting next to me was still reading his book. He had barely even paused when the flight attendants brought drinks.

"That book must be really interesting," I said. The next movie wouldn't start for a while yet, so I figured I might as well make conversation.

He blinked at me for a minute, as though he had forgotten anyone was sitting next to him. Then he smiled. Nice smile. "It is," he said.

A brief, awkward pause. Until I asked, "What's it about?"

THE QUEST

"Oh." He flipped the book closed and looked at the cover. "It's about intelligent design."

"Are you an architect?" I asked.

He flashed a look of surprise at me and then smiled. "No," he said. "It's not that kind of design. It's about the scientific evidence that suggests that nature—and human beings—are not a product of random forces but of intelligent design."

"Are you some kind of scientist?"

"No." I think he blushed. "I'm a teacher."

"Oh," I said. "I guess it just sounds a little too heady for me."

"It's really not," he said, again turning the book over in his hands and smiling sheepishly. "I mean, I don't know you, but—I tend to make things sound more complicated than they are."

I nodded. I wasn't sure I knew what he was talking about, and I didn't want to sound stupid.

"Let me try again," he said. "This book explains why it's reasonable to think that this world and everything in it—including us—is not the result of some evolutionary accident but is the result of careful planning."

"You mean like God."

He turned slightly in his seat to face me. "Some would say so, yes. But this book is saying that intelligent design doesn't start with any assumptions about God. It starts with a willingness to follow the evidence, wherever it may lead."

"But I thought evolution was proven fact."

He smiled again. Really nice smile. "Well, there's evolution … and then there's *evolution*."

"I don't understand."

His forehead crinkled up, as if he was thinking really hard. "Take natural selection. No one denies that natural selection takes place. You know, like the main food source of a certain species dries up and that species dies out, while other species that don't depend on that food source survive. But Darwinian evolution goes way beyond that. Darwinism is much more than a scientific theory these days; it's a worldview. For some, it's just as much a religion as Judaism or Hinduism—maybe more."

"Okay. But what about all the fossils? I thought the fossils proved evolution a long time ago."

He nodded. "I used to think that, too. Turns out, the fossil record is more at odds with Darwin's theory today than when Darwin wrote *The Origin of Species*."

"How can that be true?"

"Well, since Darwin's time, lots of fossils have been discovered that Darwin never even knew about. New ones are discovered so often that they can't even catalog them fast enough! And Darwin expected that new discoveries in the fossil record would close the gaps and fill in the missing links in his theory."

"Hasn't that happened?"

"No, the exact opposite has happened."

"But haven't they found, like, more forms of life between apes and humans?"

"That's what Darwin expected, but again, that's not exactly what has happened. Instead, new discoveries like Java Man or Lucy, which were initially thought to be something between apes and humans, were later recognized as one or the other."

"But that doesn't disprove evolution."

"No, absolutely not. But the general direction of the evidence would definitely be frustrating to Darwin, if he were around to see it."

I shrugged. "Okay, but none of that makes me think God had to be involved." I didn't particularly like where this guy seemed to be coming from. It felt as if God was stalking me, like maybe I had opened a can of worms by talking to Rabbi Rachel and praying in the first place. Now he was showing up in all kinds of inconvenient places, like the seat right next to me on a flight to Israel. That is, it would have felt like that if I had believed in him, which I didn't.

"Not directly, maybe. But the more you learn about fossils, the more you realize that the fossil record has been unkind to Darwinism— in fact, it's actually undermined his theories. So much so that it's spawned a theory called 'punctuated equilibrium,' which tries to repair the damage."

"Interesting," I said. But that wasn't quite what I was thinking. I was actually thinking, if what he was saying was true, then why wasn't I ever taught any of this stuff in school? Was it some big secret? It didn't make sense. Plus, I sure didn't want to get into a conversation involving anything called "punctuated equilibrium."

Just then, the next movie appeared on the screens. I picked up my headset and smiled politely. "It's been nice talking to you," I said.

"You, too," he answered.

I put the headset on and focused on the movie.

Chapter 19

I could have used a more entertaining movie. The second one was about an elderly woman whose children wouldn't talk to her, so she practically adopted a family of misfits and lunatics. They were all so odd it seemed ridiculous, but she was so lonely she learned to love them anyway. Blah, blah, blah.

I don't know if the film was all that boring or if my previous conversation with the guy in 22J was that interesting, but I found myself paying more attention to him than to the movie, even though he was doing nothing more interesting than turning a page now and then. Or maybe it was because he was so cute. I thought about this for a while and finally decided it didn't matter.

He was still turning pages in the book, so about halfway through the film, I turned my head in his direction and said, "Can I ask you a question?"

He looked over at me without lowering his book. "I think you just did."

It took me a second, but I got it. "I guess I did," I admitted. "Can I ask you another one?"

He smiled, even bigger—and more charming—this time. "You can ask all you want."

I realized he could have repeated the same remark about having already asked a question when I asked if I could ask him a question, but he didn't. I liked him for that.

THE QUEST

I asked, "Do you really think that all the scientists who agree about evolution are wrong?"

"I could ask you the same question about all the scientists who agree about the evidence for intelligent design."

"Yeah, but most scientists believe in evolution."

"You're right. But once upon a time, most scientists believed the sun revolved around the earth."

"Yeah, but that was, like, hundreds of years ago."

He nodded. "But my point is that scientific consensus changes all the time. In fact, when Darwin first proposed his theories, he was bucking the consensus."

"Yeah, but now everybody accepts it, right?"

He shook his head. "Hardly. In fact, if evolution is the consensus right now, it's a shrinking consensus. There are hundreds of scientists who say they are skeptical about the claims of evolution."

"But what else is there?" I asked. "I mean, for a person like me, who's not religious?"

"You don't have to be religious to see the evidence. Intelligent design is not about religious faith; it's about letting the evidence say what it says. There's a lot of evidence to suggest that the universe is a result of some kind of intelligent design."

"Like what?"

"Like the universe itself."

"Come again?"

"Let me put it this way. A prominent atheist philosopher named Antony Flew wrote a book some years ago about why he changed his mind and concluded there had to be a God. One of the reasons he gave was the 'friendliness' of the universe. He titled one of the chapters in his book, 'Did the Universe Know We Were Coming?'"

"I don't get it," I said.

"In other words, the universe we live in is so finely tuned to support life that it obliterates the possibility that it's a result of random forces, even over a long period of time."

The flight attendants were coming down the aisle to offer drink service again. I glanced their way and then turned my attention back to my seat companion. That's when I realized I didn't even know his name yet.

"Uh, before I ask my next question," I said, "what's your name?"

"That was your next question," he answered.

"What?" I said, but then immediately realized he was playing the same game as before. "Okay, you know what I mean. My name is Emma."

"Nice to meet you, Emma. My name is Travis."

We traded smiles, and then I said, "So give me an example of how this universe is so friendly to life."

"I'll give you three," he said, holding up three fingers. "The big bang, gravity, and the laws of nature."

"I thought the big bang was the ultimate proof of evolution."

"A lot of people think that, because they have been led to think that. But get this: The big bang, as it's called, had to be so precise that it boggles the mind. If I remember right, the precision had to be something like ten to the fifty-fifth power. That's ten followed by fifty-five zeros."

"Yeah, I remember. I went to school, too."

"Good for you," he said good-naturedly. It seemed that he was starting to enjoy this as much as I was. And I was starting to enjoy it. "What that means is, if the big bang had launched itself just a teensy bit faster, it would have expanded too fast to allow the galaxies and solar systems and planets to form. If its initial speed had been just a tiny bit slower, gravity would have forced it to collapse back on itself. Either way, if it had been just a tiny bit less precise life would never have formed."

"Okay," I said.

He held up two fingers. "Gravity. If the force of gravity were off just a little bit, stars would be either too hot or too cold for life to exist in the universe."

"You lost me there. What does gravity have to do with stars being hot or cold?"

"Okay, remember, I'm not a scientist. But I've asked the same question. A star is made up of gasses, and the gasses have to be held together in a certain density in order for fusion to occur—or something like that. But my point is, at least according to this book"—he still held it in one hand—"it says that if gravity were off by the tiniest bit—there would be no life in the universe."

He held up the last finger. "And last but not least are the laws of nature. Scientists know so much more about this stuff than anyone could have guessed, even just a few generations ago. There are very precise mathematical constants that govern the way our universe operates—you know, like the mass ratio of proton to electron in an atom. It never changes. It's constant; it's the same today as it was thousands of years ago. But if it was just a tiny bit different—"

"Wait, I think I can guess. No life in the universe."

He smiled and nodded. "Right."

Just then a flight attendant, a tall blonde woman with a very short haircut, reached our row with her list of available drinks. I ordered water; Travis asked for a Coke. Very politely. I was really starting to like this guy.

The arrival of drinks gave me a little breather from Travis' science lesson. Not that I was having any trouble understanding him. I just welcomed the opportunity to watch him for a minute. He was mildly good looking, except when he smiled. Then, his face seemed to transform into something a woman could dream about.

I sipped my water and wondered if he would start the conversation again or if I would have to. I waited and pretended to watch the flight attendant move on to the row ahead of us. I started to worry that this flight—which had seemed impossibly long before—might not be long enough.

"Are you getting off in Brussels?" I asked.

"No. You?"

I shook my head and tried not to show any emotion, though inwardly I was glad that we had all the way to Tel Aviv to talk.

"What takes you to Israel?" he asked.

I sloshed around the water and ice in my cup. "I'm looking for my father."

He seemed to be searching my face. "I thought so," he said.

"You thought so? What's that supposed to mean?"

He looked suddenly guilty, as though he had said something wrong. Which he had, from my point of view. "I—I'm sorry, I thought maybe you were talking about a … spiritual search."

"A spiritual search?" I echoed. "I'm not on any spiritual search."

"You're not?" he said.

"No, I'm not."

He shrugged. "I'm sorry. I didn't mean to offend you."

"You didn't—" I started, then stopped. I realized that my tone had been really testy, so maybe he *had* kind of offended me. But I wasn't sure why I felt that way. "Why do you think I'm on a spiritual search?"

He tilted his head to one side. "I think *everyone* is searching. Not everyone knows it."

That didn't make sense to me. How can a person be searching for something if they don't know what they're searching for? If they don't even know they're searching at all? It made no sense. "Okay, sure," I said, finally. "Whatever."

"Look, I'm sorry. I messed up. I really do want to know more about— about your father. You say you're searching for him?"

I took another drink of water and then proceeded to tell him almost the whole story: How I'd found out my father was missing, how I'd decided to go to Israel to try to find him, and so on.

THE QUEST

"Wow," he said when I finished. "I hope you find him. I hope he's okay."

Tears started to form in my eyes. I didn't want to cry. Not here, not now. I excused myself to go to the bathroom.

CHAPTER 20

An airplane bathroom may not be the best place to give in to a crying fit, but I didn't care. My conversation with my seatmate had brought all the worry and fear for my dad flooding back, and I needed to release it somewhere.

I wasn't like a lot of people who can't wait to graduate from high school and leave home. I had an enjoyable high school experience, and Dad and I had always gotten along well. It was hard to leave for college. I was excited about going to college and being on my own, but saying goodbye to him after he moved me into my dorm room that freshman year was the hardest thing I'd ever done.

After driving all the way across Pennsylvania and Ohio with me in a rented minivan crammed with my stuff, he had spent move-in day with me, unloading the car, carrying everything into my tiny dorm room, unpacking everything, assembling shelves, and even setting up my wi-fi for me. By the time my new roommate asked if I wanted to go with her to dinner at Hamilton dining hall, I was the only person in my hall who was totally unpacked. No one else was even close.

I told him I'd walk back to the car with him.

"No, Beany. I think I can remember where I left it."

I rolled my eyes. "That's not what I meant. Though you are kind of old. Are you sure you don't need my help getting down the steps?"

He smiled. His eyes glistened. "I have to learn to do for myself now, remember?"

THE QUEST

"Just remember, you can always call me if you need to. I'll even read you a bedtime story over the phone if you want me to."

He reached out and pulled me into his arms. I did my best to hold back the tears as he held me for a long time. Finally, he released me and we looked at each other through misty eyes.

"Are you starting back tonight?" I asked.

"I'll drive for a few hours before stopping for the night."

"Be careful, okay? Watch your speed."

He smiled, then pulled me into his arms again. He squeezed me tighter than ever and whispered in my ear, in a voice tight with emotion, "Just promise me you'll be okay."

I lost it. I managed to squeak out, "I promise," and then we sobbed in each other's arms, until he straightened and gently released his hold.

"Well, that's enough of that, eh?" he said.

I tried to wipe the tears from my face. "I love you, Dad."

"I love you more," he said. It was a little game we played, always claiming to love the other more.

He turned then and headed for the staircase, and I waited until I could no longer hear the echo of his steps before heading to the bathroom to wash my face.

Ten minutes later, my roommate Becca and I set out for Hamilton dining hall for dinner. On the way, I thought I saw Dad's rented minivan swerve into a parking space on the street a couple blocks ahead. Then I was sure, because I saw him step out of the car, cross the sidewalk, and disappear behind a building.

I didn't say anything to Becca, but we quickly came to the spot where I had seen Dad, and I noticed that he had parked right in front of a church. This was before he met Katya and got all religious, so I was surprised by what I saw next.

A sign in front of the church—in the shape of an arrow pointing toward the church—announced, "Prayer Chapel Open Daily." I slowed my pace, looked up the sidewalk in the direction the arrow pointed, and saw my dad through the open doors of the little chapel. He sat in a pew, staring straight ahead. Tears streamed down his face.

I don't know what Becca and I talked about at dinner that night. We soon became friends, though she transferred to another school after our freshman year. My thoughts that night, and for big chunks of the next few days, were filled with Dad ... and the sadness he never knew I saw.

Chapter 21

I'm awake. Wide awake. Lord, why? Are you saying something to me? Is there something you wish to tell me? Or is there something you want to hear from me?

Is Daniel awake? Is he hurting? Is he praying for me? You know all things, Lord. You know his need right now. Please help him, wherever he is and whatever his need.

Maybe you're calling me to pray again for Emma as she travels. She is on my heart, too, so why wouldn't she be on yours?

So, on her behalf, I call to you for help, Lord.

You are the One who made heaven and earth; you can do anything.

You hold onto me; hold onto her.

You never take your eyes off me; keep your watch over her.

You're never surprised,

never confused,

never overwhelmed

THE QUEST

Alert her to your presence, please,
watcher,
keeper,
shelter,
shade.
Keep her from all harm—
watch over her life;
watch over her moment by moment and step by step,
in Jesus' name, amen.

Chapter 22

When I got back from the bathroom, Travis was reading his book again, but he looked up and asked if I was okay. I nodded.

"Is there anything I can do for you?" he asked.

I smiled. "Maybe we should talk about something besides my father. I can't do much until I get there, anyway."

"Sure. That shouldn't be too hard. Tell me about yourself."

"What do you want to know?"

"Where are you from?"

I told him. I talked about growing up in Northern New Jersey and about my decision to go to school in Ohio.

"What's your major?" he asked.

"Art. But I had to stop taking classes at the end of spring semester. I'm trying to pay for it myself, so it's been really slow going."

"Good for you," he said.

I shrugged. "My dad remarried last Christmas, and I told him that after my sophomore year I'd pay my own way."

"Wow," he said.

"Yeah, it's been harder than I thought. I didn't know anything about financial aid or that sort of thing. But I'm learning fast."

"Are you still living on campus?"

THE QUEST

"No, I have a small apartment uptown. Or, I should say, I did. I packed it up to make this trip."

"Wow. So this is a really big step for you."

"You could say that. I had to quit both of my jobs." I told him about the coffee shop and taking care of the Reese kids, and somewhere in the course of it all, I mentioned Artie.

"Is Artie your boyfriend?"

I laughed. "No! He's just a really good friend. I don't think I'd be on my way to Israel without him."

"So … are you seeing anybody?"

I blushed. It wasn't the question itself that made me suddenly so self-conscious. It was the way he tried to disguise—unsuccessfully—the interest behind his question. I told him no, explaining that my last real date was in my freshman year.

"That's hard to believe," he said.

"Why?"

It was his turn to blush. Then he turned that smile on me. "I would imagine a girl as pretty as you would be going out all the time."

"Well, aren't you a smooth talker."

He smiled and glanced away. "Not really. If I was smooth, I'd have asked that question long before now."

"What about you? Are you in a relationship?"

He shook his head. "I had a serious girlfriend a couple of years ago, and we both thought it was going somewhere." He paused and looked at me again. "But it didn't."

I could tell there was more to the story than that, but he didn't elaborate, and I didn't ask him to. By the time we landed in Brussels for a two-hour layover, I had gotten to know Mr. Travis Richmond a lot better. He was from St. Louis, Missouri, and he was working on a master's degree in molecular biology at some university I'd never heard of. And he was flying to Israel to fulfill a life-long dream of participating in an archaeological dig. He was only twenty-six, but he talked about it as if he'd waited a long time..

We ate together in the airline terminal and then reboarded—same plane, same seats—for the rest of the trip to Tel Aviv.

I managed to sleep for the first part of the flight out of Brussels. About the time the flight attendant came down the aisle with drinks, we got back to the subject of the book he was reading—I can't even remember how. I was surprised at how interesting it all was and how fascinating I found it. The more he talked and the more I understood, the more intriguing things became.

He told me that —for him—a compelling argument in favor of intelligent design was the complexity argument. He talked about a man who had written a book a while ago called *Darwin's Black Box*, which talked about a concept called "irreducible complexity." The idea is that some complex systems require multiple, interworking parts in order to function, and the removal of just one part would cause the entire system to fail.

Travis gave several examples of this, but I found it really hard to track with him. He talked about a mechanism that looks like a single hair on some bacteria, which enables them to swim. He said that little hair—or whatever it is—contains all kinds of different parts that all have to work together or the whole thing would become useless. He compared it to a mousetrap, which seems pretty simple to me, but he said it's an example of an irreducibly complex system. That is, if a mousetrap were the result of a blind gradual process instead of intelligent design, none of the in-between steps before a functioning mousetrap—with a platform, spring, catch, the thing that trips the catch, and the part that smacks down to trap the mouse—would have worked. There would have been no advantage for some "species" of mousetrap to develop a catch and a spring unless they had the part that smacks down. And without a platform, none of those other pieces would work together, and so on.

THE QUEST

Travis went on to say that a lot of things in nature are like that mousetrap. When he started to talk about a new idea called "specified complexity," I stopped him.

"Slow down," I said. "Let me think about this for a minute. You're saying that some things in nature—like that hair-like thing on bacteria—could not have evolved because the evolutionary steps to get there would have been useless. Right?"

"Yes. It's called a bacterial flagellum."

"Whatever."

He smiled. "And the point is, the existence of such irreducible complexity in an organism violates the way Darwinism says mutation and natural selection work together. A bacterium that mutates in such a way to have a part of a flagellum that's on its way to becoming useful would have no advantage because of that particular mutation. It would be 'dead on arrival,' sort of. There would be no reason for the species with that mutation to survive, let alone wait around a hundred generations for the next mutation to improve on it."

"Okay, but there's no other way it could have happened. So it *had* to have happened that way."

He smiled even broader than before. "That's exactly the point. That's the only reason Darwinism can give for the development of irreducibly complex systems like the bacterial flagellum. It had to happen that way because Darwinian science has no other option to offer."

"Right," I said.

"That is why I say intelligent design is not about religious faith. It's about letting the evidence say what it says. Darwinism can't do that because it can't consider the possibility of intelligent design. Many Darwinists completely rule out the possibility of design before considering the evidence. So, in that respect, it is not scientific."

"But if a person considers the possibility of intelligent design …"

"Yes?"

"They have to sooner or later wonder where the design comes from."

"True," he said.

"Well, what other options are there, except for—" I stopped.

He watched me without saying anything.

I lowered my voice a tad. "Except for God?"

He smiled. "I know, it's a problem for someone who doesn't believe in God. But intelligent design doesn't have to answer that question. As a scientific discipline, it merely goes where the evidence seems to go. After that, the scientist's job is done."

"Well, that's just peachy," I said.

"You don't find that particularly satisfying." It wasn't a question, but a statement.

"No, I don't," I answered.

"What would you *like* me to tell you?"

"I'd like you to be straight with me and just tell me you want me to believe in God."

"I want you to believe in God," he said.

"Okay," I said, as if that settled everything.

"But that's not why I've been talking to you all this time."

"It's not?"

He shook his head but didn't say anything.

"Why, then?"

"Well, at first it was because you asked me. Remember? You asked about the book I was reading."

"Right," I said.

"But I also love talking about this stuff. I just find it so interesting."

I nodded. That much was obvious.

"But then, you're kind of interesting, too." He turned back to his book with a smile.

I blushed and lowered my eyes to the empty drink cup on my tray.

CHAPTER 23

Good morning, Lord. It has been a night of little sleep and much prayer.

You know how heavy my heart is right now for my husband. I thank you that you gave him to me, and I ask that you not to take him away from me so soon, please.

I miss him so much. I miss his voice, his deep voice. How I wish I had saved his last voicemails on my phone so I could listen to them now.

I miss his laughter and his sense of humor. The sly smile he shows when he's teasing. Was it really only a week or so ago that he made me laugh until I cried with his imitation of Martin, the shopkeeper in the Old City who never uses his glasses, though he's nearly blind as a bat without them? It seems like so long since I've heard his laugh. Since I've laughed myself.

I miss his faith. I know I trusted you long before he did, Lord. But I'll never forget that hike we took at Bear Mountain, when he took me to the overlook, put his arm around me, and told me he wasn't the man I thought he was. It makes me smile even now.

THE QUEST

I thought he was going to confess some deep, dark secret in his past, such as a drug dealing past or a career as a CIA hit man. But instead he told me how our long discussions about God, Jesus, and faith had challenged him and moved him. He said he had sought out my pastor and had met with him several times. And then he told me the news I'd been waiting months to hear that he had become a new man—a follower of Jesus Christ. It made a pretty day immeasurably beautiful. Ever since that moment, I've seen his faith grow, and he long ago surpassed me in his determination to trust you in everything. I could use some of his faith right now, when I seem to have so little.

I miss his strength, his confidence, his level-headedness, and his optimism. How I wish he was here to say, "One day at a time, Kat." Or "Remember you're one of God's favorite people." He's the one who holds it together when everything seems to be falling apart ... and now that everything really is falling apart, I don't know if I can be the one to hold it together.

I even miss his bed hogging. I never thought I'd get used to sleeping next to him, with his flailing arms and legs. How many mornings have I awakened in a tiny corner of the bed while he's spread-eagle on his back like da Vinci's Vitruvian man? And how charming it is that he is always so apologetic, so stricken, when I complain over lost sleep. I'll never complain again, Lord, if you'll just return him to me. I'll sleep standing up if I have to, just to have him back in my bed again.

I need to be leaving soon for Tel Aviv to meet Emma. Lord, help me to find the right words to say and the right things to do for her. It would be so much easier if Daniel was here for that. But then, if he was here, of course, Emma wouldn't be coming. But that doesn't make things any easier. I need him. I miss him. I beg you to bring him home to me and to his daughter. Amen.

CHAPTER 24

As the pilot announced our approach into Tel Aviv, Travis and I exchanged cell phone numbers, even though neither of us would be using our cells in Israel. I'd heard that roaming charges make it really expensive, and Travis said his phone wouldn't even work in Israel. Something about different technology. I didn't understand a thing he said and didn't really care to. He burst out laughing when I told him so, which made me very happy.

Bottom line, Travis made me happy. Even when he was talking about that book, I think I was interested because he was interested. I didn't always like the implications of what he was saying, but I liked hearing him say it. And he didn't seem threatened or upset when I disagreed with him.

He said that his favorite part of the book—he finished it while I took another nap on the Brussels-to-Tel Aviv flight—was the part about "specified complexity." Despite myself, I found it kind of interesting, too.

He showed me a page in the book with three lines of type. The first line was:

THETHETHETHETHETHETHETHETHETHETHETHETHE

He said that was an example of a pattern that is specific, but not complex. Then he pointed to the next line:

XGOENAODIWGTNHPLXCVWQIZIDLRETPTRMNSTEJKI

"It doesn't say anything," I said.

"Right," he answered. "That's a complex pattern. But it's not specific. It doesn't say anything, as you put it."

Then he pointed to the third line of text:

THIS LINE CONTAINS VALUABLE INFORMATION.

"This pattern is an example of specified complexity. It is not simple like the word 'THE' repeated over and over in the first line."

"Yeah, that doesn't say anything, but it's not random."

"Exactly!" he said. He seemed genuinely pleased that I was tracking with him. And I had to admit, I was pleased, too. "And that second line of text, while it is complex, it is just a random assortment of letters."

"But the third line is neither simple nor random," I said.

"That's right. It is obviously the result of some kind of intelligent design because it isn't just complex; it possesses *specified* complexity."

"Okay. I think I'm following you."

"Well, the author's point is that chance plus time—the Darwinist scenario—is enough to produce specificity, like the first line of type. It is also enough to produce complexity, like the second line. But specified complexity, which we call 'information,' is on display all through the natural world, especially in DNA. And it is beyond the reach of Darwinian processes. It can only be produced by intelligence."

"Wait a minute. What about the monkeys and the typewriter?"

He smiled broadly. "What about them?"

"I've always heard that given enough time, you could sit down monkeys at a typewriter and they'd eventually type out the works of Shakespeare."

He continued smiling. "Yeah, I've heard that, too."

"Well, what about it? I mean, given millions and millions of years, why not? Why are you smiling?"

"I'm sorry," he said, but he didn't stop smiling. "I just think that illustration's hilarious."

"Why?"

"Because of the internal fallacies in the illustration itself."

"Um, what? Can you make that a *little* simpler?"

"I'm just saying it's funny because to make the illustration work—or seem to work, actually—you have to picture monkeys sitting down at a typewriter. Which is itself the product of intelligent design."

"Oh," I said.

"Wait, that's not all. They'd have to be typing on—what? Paper, right? Which is the product of intelligent design. And, oh, wait a minute—there's ink in the typewriter ribbon—the product of intelligent design!"

"Okay, but it's just an illustration."

"I'm not done. The monkeys … do they possess intelligence?"

"Yeah, I guess so."

"So, say the monkeys produce the entire works of Shakespeare—something like thirty-some plays and a hundred-and-fifty sonnets—in, oh, I don't know, twenty bajillion years … it would still be the product of intelligence!"

I sighed. "I get what you're saying, but I think you're missing the point."

"What point am I missing?"

"That over the course of millions and millions of years, anything can happen."

"Anything?"

"Yes," I insisted. "Anything."

"So let's go back to the monkeys and the typewriters."

"Okay."

"Only, let's take the monkeys out, because they possess some intelligence. They at least know how to strike keys on a typewriter. And let's put something in their place."

"Like what?"

"Anything that can't exercise intelligence, or the metaphor will continue to be ridiculous."

"That's not fair."

"Why not? Why can't we place a worm—no, even worms have brains—all right, an amoeba in front of the typewriter? Oh, wait, we can't have the typewriter, either. We have to put an amoeba in front of some kind of swamp filled with natural ink. With maybe a broken reed to write with. Now … how many millions of years before we get Shakespeare?"

I felt myself glowering at him. "I don't think you're playing fair."

He shrugged. "I'm sorry. But I am. *I* am playing fair. In fact, I am insisting on playing fair, by simply asking that an illustration *designed to refute intelligent design* not employ products of design or creatures with intelligence in doing so!"

I wasn't particularly fond of my new friend at that moment. And I told him so. But he seemed to take it well.

"You don't have to take my word for it," he said, a mischievous glint in his eyes. "I'd be happy to lend you this book."

"Right," I said.

"Can I tell you the second reason I think the monkey illustration is funny?"

I sighed. But I decided I wanted him to keep talking. "Sure," I said.

He flipped the book's pages for a few moments, then he seemed to find what he was looking for. "A few years ago a university professor and some students actually staged the monkeys-typing-Shakespeare thing as an experiment. They sat down some monkeys in front of a computer to see what would happen."

"And?"

He started to laugh. "It says the first monkey whacked the computer with a rock! And some of the others defecated and urinated on the thing!"

I couldn't help it. I started laughing with him. "Did any of the monkeys type anything?"

"Yeah. Over the course of four weeks, the researchers managed to compile five pages of text the monkeys had pounded out."

"I've done worse on some school assignments," I said.

We shared a good laugh at that. "Not one word, though. For some reason, the pages were mostly 'S's,' with an occasional A, L, M, and J."

"Maybe the S's were them trying to spell Shakespeare."

He smiled at that. "Maybe, but here's what may be the best part. It says they put those pages into an actual book and called it *Notes Toward the Complete Works of Shakespeare.*"

CHAPTER 25

Our plane finally dipped below the clouds, and Travis let me lean over him to peer out the window. Through the moisture-flecked window, I could see a vast expanse of lights and buildings below. The city seemed to go on forever, spreading out from the blue Mediterranean. Then came a break in the cityscape, what looked like maybe a small airport, which we passed right by, flying over a ribbon of expressway already lined, in the early morning, by travelers.

Then more buildings, many of them taller than before. I spied a great green plain in the distance beyond the lights, a soccer stadium, a massive construction site, and then green fields and lighted runways. I saw the white stripe of our runway and then our wheels touched the ground.

The passengers erupted in applause and cheers. Suddenly my interest shifted from the sights outside to those inside the plane. Black-hatted men in the back lifted their hands in the air in celebration. Several women around them cried out in long, freaky, wavering, high-pitched sound, like they were saying "Lulu lulu," over and over. An old woman in a scarf across the aisle was actually crying. I'd never seen anything like it.

I turned to Travis. "What's going on?"

He looked amazed, too. "I think everyone's really happy to be in Israel."

It was amazing. I mean, I like traveling as much as anyone. And I used to love going home … before my dad met Katya. But their reaction seemed way over the top. One of the flight attendants came on the loudspeaker to welcome everyone to Israel—first in English, then in a couple of other languages—and provide gate information while we taxied to the gate.

Travis and I walked together as we exited the plane. I realized we would soon be separating and probably would never see each other again. He had made this long day of flying one of the best days I'd had in a long time.

The Tel Aviv airport was easily the biggest airport I've ever seen. It was gigantic. We picked up our luggage—Travis waited for me—and made it through customs with no trouble. The lines were long, but they went quickly. Everything was so modern, and so spread out … and so busy.

"Is someone meeting you?" Travis asked as we entered the welcome center, where men stood shoulder-to-shoulder holding signs with people's names on them. Some of the signs were written in Hebrew and, I assumed, Arabic.

I scanned the crowd. "Yes. My father's wife said she would pick me up." I wasn't even sure I would recognize her.

Finally, I spied a short-haired brunette wearing a sheer scarf waving her hand in the air. "There she is!"

The row of men with the placards blocked our way. Travis touched my elbow, put his head down, and steered us through the line of drivers.

"I'm so glad you made it!" Katya gushed, glancing back and forth from me to Travis.

He finally let go of me and extended his hand in Katya's direction. "I'm Travis," he said.

"Hi, Travis. I'm Katya." She looked back at me, clearly hoping for an explanation.

I enjoyed her confusion for a moment before speaking. "We met on the plane," I explained. "Travis is here for an archaeological dig."

"Oh?" she said, smiling warmly. "Where? Maybe I know it."

"Tel Hazor?" he answered.

"Oh, Hazor, yes," she said. "That's in Galilee."

"Katya, would you mind giving Travis your phone number? Neither of us have a cell phone on us, so we have no idea how to get back in touch if, you know, if we have the opportunity."

Her smile changed. A knowing smile, I thought. She addressed Travis. "Do you have a way to write this down?"

He produced a pen and wrote the number on the back of his hand while Katya rattled off nine digits. "The first number is the area code for Jerusalem."

Travis repeated it back to her. "Okay," she said. Then she turned to me. "Can I help with your bag?"

Travis and I looked at each other. It was an awkward moment. "I'm so glad I met you. I'll be praying that you find your father."

I felt like I might cry. I couldn't cry. I wouldn't. "Me, too," I said. I tried to smile. "Thanks."

"Wait," he said. For a fleeting moment, I thought he might hug me, and I didn't know how to respond if he did.

Instead, though, he dug in his carry-on and drew out the book—the one we had talked so much about. He held it out to me. "Here. You don't have to read it, but it's something you can remember me by."

I took the book. I felt tears filling my eyes. "Thank you," I said.

I turned to Katya. She flashed me a curious look and turned toward the doors. I waved at Travis and then followed her.

CHAPTER 26

Once in the car, I noticed that Katya immediately buckled her seatbelt, so I did the same.

"This car is a loaner," she said. "From the agency. Daniel—your dad—has our Hyundai."

She pulled into a line of cars waiting to pay the airport parking fee.

"How was your flight?" she asked.

"Good," I said. I knew she wanted more information than that, but I was suddenly feeling the effects of nearly two days of travel with less than an hour or two of sleep. As long as Travis was around, I guess the lack of sleep made me slightly giddy; now it was making me decidedly cranky. I leaned my head back on the headrest and closed my eyes.

"Did you get any sleep on the trip?"

I sighed and answered without opening my eyes. "Not much," I said.

"I'm so sorry," she said.

I nodded without opening my eyes.

"Travis seems like a nice young man," she said.

"Mm … hmm," I answered.

"Did you meet on the flight from Brussels?"

"From Chicago. Our seats were next to each other—from Brussels, too."

THE QUEST

"Both legs," she said, surprise in her voice. "How did he manage that?"

"It just happened."

"Oh." She sounded unconvinced.

I felt the car move forward and heard a woman's voice speaking another language.

"English?" Katya said.

"Fifteen seventy-one," the woman said, in a heavy accent.

I opened my eyes and watched Katya pay the parking attendant. As she started to pull into traffic, I leaned back again and closed my eyes.

"I'm so glad you're here. And so blessed that your flight was on time. It's such an answer to prayer."

"Look," I said, my patience running out. "I appreciate you picking me up at the airport, I really do. But I haven't slept in almost two days."

"Of course," she said. "Forgive me. I'm so sorry. You rest. I'll keep quiet. We'll be in Jerusalem in less than an hour, God willing."

"And could you do me a favor?" I kept my eyes closed and tried not to sound as testy as I felt. "Could you keep the God-talk to a minimum? I'm not here to talk about God, and that's all people seem to want to talk about lately, for some reason. I'm here to find my father. So if you don't mind, can we just focus on that?"

She was silent for a few moments. I was tempted to open my eyes, but I didn't. Finally, she spoke. "I promise to do my best, Emma. I can't promise I won't slip up from time to time, though, because God is so real and present in my life; he's a part of everything I do, every moment I'm awake. But you're right about focusing on finding your father and reuniting with him. I can't make any guarantees, but I will try to respect your wishes."

I forced a tiny smile, not knowing if she was watching my face or not. I knew I wasn't getting off to a good start with her. I would probably regret my behavior when I was feeling more rested. But that still felt like a long way off. I was so tired.

"Thank you," I said.

We rode in silence the rest of the way. I turned away from Katya, leaned against the window, and pretended to sleep. But there's no way I could sleep; my mind was a jumble of thoughts about Dad, Travis, and the sights that sped past the car window.

I don't know what I expected Israel to be like, but it wasn't this. The road was a modern divided highway, with cars, trucks, and buses of all different kinds. Exits and turnoffs were announced by blue and green traffic signs just like back home, except with Hebrew lettering and strange place names like Ben Shemen and Sha'ar HaGal. Trees and shrubs dotted the rocky hills on either side, and every so often sprawling towns of white stone buildings appeared on the hills.

Everything seemed so normal. Different, but normal. A produce truck drove by. Uniformed soldiers waited at a bus stop. People were just going about their day. None of them seemed to know that this was anything but a normal day. My dad was out there somewhere, and no one seemed to know where. He could have been in one of those stone buildings we passed. He could be close by.

My thoughts became heavier the longer we drove—uphill all the way. I wondered if that was symbolic of the journey I had undertaken.

Hamas Official Calls for More Kidnappings

Hamas leader Ahmad al-Akhdar appeared on video last night to threaten Israel with more troop kidnappings if the Lazar administration does not accede to the group's demands for the release of Palestinians held in Israeli prisons. Al-Akhdar emphasized that it was the responsibility of all Palestinians to use every effort at their disposal to free the prisoners. The video was delivered to several Arab and Israeli television outlets.

Three men from the Ramallah area were arrested last week and charged with conspiring to kidnap Israelis from various intersections around Ramallah. The next day, two more individuals were detained and charged with a plot to kidnap civilians and use them as hostages who could be exchanged for imprisoned Palestinians; they were apprehended at the Damya Bridge after attempting to persuade two Jewish civilians to enter their vehicle. All five men are in their early or mid 20s.

There has been no official response from the Israeli government.

CHAPTER 27

Dad and Katya's apartment in Jerusalem was smaller than I expected. We entered into a long, narrow combined living room and dining room. At one end, sliding glass doors opened onto a small yard that they shared with several other families. Several bookcases lined one wall.

The kitchen was very modern, but everything seemed downsized from what I was familiar with in the U.S. The range was the same size as a dishwasher, but they didn't have a dishwasher. The refrigerator seemed to be less than half the size of the massive stainless steel thing I remembered from the Reeses' kitchen. And the microwave on the counter was no bigger than a toaster oven.

Most importantly, there was only one bathroom—and one bedroom. My face must have registered the question that was in my mind as Katya was showing me around.

"I'll sleep in the living room while you're here," she said over my shoulder as I stood in the doorway of the bedroom.

I turned. "Oh, no, that's okay."

She shook her head. "I haven't slept much lately," she said. "So it's really for the best."

I felt the first flicker of camaraderie with her. We eyed each other sympathetically for a few moments, and then I dragged my duffle into the room and leaned it against the queen bed, flanked on both sides by built-in wardrobe closets. "I hate to take your room."

THE QUEST

"Why don't you rest for a few hours?" she suggested. "I'll call you for lunch, and we can talk more then."

I felt a twinge of guilt for treating her the way I did on the ride here, shutting her down the way I did, but quickly chased it away. I wasn't ready to make nice yet. But I was here. That was something. I was in Israel, a half a world away from Ohio. I was in Jerusalem!

I didn't know yet where my dad was, but for the first time in a long time, he was somewhere nearby. "Please let him be okay," I said. That prayer filled my mind as I drifted to sleep.

I could smell something cooking, but the bed was so comfortable that I hated to rouse myself, even though I had laid down on top of the covers in my clothes and shoes. Eventually, though, the combined urgings of my stomach and my kidneys won the battle, and I stumbled off of the bed.

When I finished in the bathroom, I found Katya in the front room, reading. Then I noticed what she was reading: a Bible.

"Something smells wonderful," I said. It had a thick, earthy kind of aroma.

"It's Jerusalem artichoke soup," she said. She set the Bible aside and walked back into the kitchen. "Fresh Jerusalem artichokes mixed with onions, celery, and garlic and thyme. I was just waiting for you to be ready before adding the last ingredient—heavy cream. It's one of our favorite dishes since we arrived, and I decided to try making it for you."

I wasn't even sure what artichokes were, let alone Jerusalem artichokes, but I joined her at the table, where glasses of water—no ice—waited. She set a loaf of Italian bread on the table and sat down. For the next few moments, she bowed her head over her steaming bowl of soup and prayed. I watched her until she raised her head, smiled at me, and picked up her spoon.

"Dig in," she said.

I stirred the soup for a minute, then I took my first bite. Something was wrong. The taste was acrid. Neither of us spoke for a few minutes. I tried a few more bites, then I put my spoon down and reached for the bread.

"It's not very good, is it?" Katya said.

"It's fine."

"No, it's not. I'm sorry," she said. She had stopped eating, too.

"No, really—"

"I really didn't think I could mess up soup, but I must have burned it or something." She reached across the table and picked up my bowl.

"I'm probably just not used to it."

"You don't have to make excuses, really. I'm not a very good cook." She stood up from the table and picked up her bowl, too. "I may not be the worst cook in the world, but I'm in the running."

A few moments later, she came out of the kitchen with a couple of jars of jam and clean spoons and suggested we enjoy the bread, at least.

"Your dad's been very patient with my cooking, and I think I've gotten a little better. But I still have more failures than successes in the kitchen. I can make a good tomato sandwich, though."

"That's all right," I said. "This is good." I began to look around the room and saw that the other end of the table and the open closet beyond it had been turned into a sort of command center. A photo montage of Dad was at the center, hanging from the middle shelf in the closet. All around it were stacks of papers, notebooks, newspaper clippings, various forms of correspondence on government letterheads, and more. On the table was spread a map of Israel and Post-It notes all around with cryptic notations and questions jotted on them.

"You've been busy," I said, between bites of jam and bread.

She smiled. "It helps me think. I suppose on some level, it helps me cope, too."

I remembered what the rabbi had said about prayer—pretty much the same thing. But I wasn't going to tell any of that to Katya. "What is all this stuff?"

"Oh, a little bit of everything." She went on to explain at great length what each stack of paper and notebook and clipping was. As she talked, I studied her. I didn't hate her, but I did resent her—not just because she was so beautiful, even as old as she was. Though, sitting next to her, with her dark hair and tanned skin and insanely full lips, I felt like a rag doll.

I probably could've gotten over my envy of her beauty if she hadn't stolen my father away from me and talked him into going to a dangerous country on the other side of the world. I know he would never have done that under normal circumstances.

"Can I get you anything else?" she asked. "Some cheese?"

I told her no, but I ate most of the bread while she talked about her little command post. She slid a brown loose-leaf binder to me. "I thought it might be helpful for you to know as much as possible about your dad, our work, and the things I've done so far to …" Her eyes welled with tears. She swallowed hard. "To try to find him."

I opened the binder that she had made especially for me. Section dividers bore the labels "Sar Shalom Institute," "Appointment Book," "Official Contacts," "Radical Groups," "Possible Avenues," and so on.

"Wow," I said. "How did you do all this? It's only been a week."

"Eight days," she said.

"I can't believe you did all this."

She shrugged. "Like I said, I haven't slept much."

Chapter 28

Katya suggested that I take some time to review the notebook, and then she and I would start making our plans together.

I went back into the bedroom, sat cross-legged on the bed, and opened the binder. It was all so neat and organized; I couldn't help but be impressed.

In the "Sar Shalom Institute" section, she explained that *sar shalom* is Hebrew for "Prince of Peace," and included the group's mission statement, a paragraph that said Sar Shalom Institute exists to forge lasting, constructive relationships between Christians and Jews worldwide.

"However," she wrote, "your father and I have discovered that our mission is a very difficult task. Many Israeli Jews, both religious and secular, see any Christian organization as a threat. Even our best Jewish friends see any Christian effort to introduce Jews to Jesus as offensive.

"To be fair, throughout history, our Christian predecessors have done a great deal of harm, and I find it hard to blame my Jewish neighbors for being suspicious of Christians. To complicate matters, the term 'Christian' can mean a wide variety of things to the Jewish populace, from the radio and television ministries of Pat Robertson and others, to the Orthodox denominations that fight bitterly over the tiniest issues relating to the holy places they oversee."

She went on to describe how her and Dad's work focused on what she called "living in true community" with their Jewish neighbors.

They share their joys and sorrows, become a part of their lives, never deceive anyone about their faith in Christ, but try to be true friends to them—praying and waiting for the moment when some of their neighbors might express an interest in Jesus the Messiah. She said most of their ministry focused on visiting with neighbors; hosting dinners, coffees, and book discussions; and finding ways to serve them, like babysitting, driving Orthodox Jews to the hospital on the Sabbath, and so on. She said they eventually planned to present occasional lectures and ongoing classes on various topics, but that they hadn't begun to implement those plans yet.

The "Appointment Book" section had several photocopied pages of her calendar, showing appointments she'd had at the U.S. Embassy, Israel Police, and so on.

In the "Official Contacts" section, she listed the names and contact information of people in the Israeli and U.S. governments, the Sar Shalom Institute, and other organizations she had been contacting.

She also had a listing of "Radical Groups" in the notebook, under the headings: Palestinian, Islamic, "Jewish—Left," "Jewish—Right," and "Miscellaneous groups."

There was only one page in the "Possible Avenues" section. It looked like a page full of doodles—shaped like a spider web—with my dad's name in the middle and lines emanating from it. Other lines branched out from those lines. When I looked closer, I saw that Katya had tried to brainstorm possible answers to the question, "Who could possibly want to hurt Daniel Seeger or take him hostage?"

The last couple of sections had very little information in them. There was one page of notes in the "Strategies" section, and none in the "Discoveries" section. There was a final section labeled "Miscellaneous," but it held only a half dozen sheets of blank notebook paper.

I spent a few more moments leafing through the notebook then I returned to the front room, where Katya sat in an easy chair, reading.

Orthodox Jewish Youths Burn Christian Texts

A group of more than 20 Haredim youth set fire last night to hundreds of Christian texts, including copies of the New Testament, in a violent protest against Christian missionaries who proselytize among Jews in Israel. The incident took place in the ultra-Orthodox West Bank town of Modi'in Ilit.

The protest was encouraged—by some accounts, initiated—by the town's mayor, Aron Schlomowitsch, who said the demonstration was a response to Christian missionaries recently entering the town of 48,000 to distribute Christian materials and gain Christian converts. However, Schlomowitsch said that he was not present during the demonstration, which he said arose spontaneously.

Schlomowitsch's claims were disputed by David Bendavid, an attorney who represents "Messianic Jews," Jews who worship Jesus as their Messiah. Bendavid said the incident was planned. "Mr. Schlomowitsch drove through Modi'in Ilit and used a loudspeaker to urge residents to turn over all Christian texts to a well-organized group of yeshiva students, who then assembled in a lot near the synagogue to start the bonfire," he said. Bendavid called on Israeli authorities to bring charges against the mayor and any others who instigated the book burning.

"There is no excuse for such behavior as this," said Rabbi Elchanan Davis of Mikveh Israel Synagogue. "The burning of books—of any kind—ought to be abhorrent to all Jews, who not so long ago endured the hideous sacking of synagogues and burning of our holy books in the Holocaust. It is a shameful thing to emulate such behavior."

Missionary activity aimed at Jews is legal in most cases, but is considered inflammatory by many in government and among a large percentage of the public.

Israel Police had no comment as of press time.

CHAPTER 29

Again, Katya was reading the Bible. I waited. After a few moments, she turned the page and looked up.

"I'm finished looking through the notebook," I said.

She closed her Bible and set it aside, indicating the chair next to her. "Did you find it helpful?"

"Oh, totally," I said, taking a seat. "Thank you."

"I'm glad. I wanted you to have something to bring you up to speed as quickly as possible."

"What … what do we do now?" I asked.

"I've been praying about that." She shot me a self-conscious look. "Thinking a lot about it. Ever since you called to tell me you were coming, I've been preparing for your stay, in between my efforts to find your dad. Now that you're here, I think it depends on what you want to do."

"I want to find my father," I said, a little impatiently.

"I want that, too. But it seems to me there are two ways we could go about this."

I didn't say anything, but my body language indicated I was listening.

"We could stick together—you know, go to appointments together, and so on, or we could split up and try to share the workload that way."

"We could accomplish more by splitting up."

THE QUEST

"Well, yes, in some ways. But since you're not familiar with the area, the customs, or anything like that, it wouldn't be a good idea for you to go out alone—"

"That's what I came here for. I came to find my dad!"

"But not alone, Emma. We only have one car. I'd have to give you directions to everywhere you go and you might still get lost, which is very easy to do, especially in Jerusalem. You don't know the language, or the currency, and you're a beautiful young woman in a strange place."

"*You're* beautiful." I meant it as a counter argument, but it made her smile.

"Thank you. But—" She hesitated. "Israeli men can be very forward. And they seem to really have a thing for redheads."

"Really?"

"You'll find that out soon enough. Your red hair, blue eyes, and porcelain skin—you'll turn heads everywhere you go. My point is, if we were to split up and try to go different directions, you would be the one stuck here at the apartment making phone calls or writing letters—that sort of thing."

"No," I said emphatically. "I could have done all of that back in Oxford. I came here to actually look for my dad. I pictured … I don't know … actually going places and talking to people. I just have to believe that he's somewhere nearby and that maybe, if I get close enough—" Here came the emotions again. I did not want to cry in front of Katya.

She edged forward in her chair and took my hand. "I know. I have those same feelings."

I tore my hand out of her grasp. "No, you don't," I said. "Not like me. He's my *dad!*" I was struggling for control, but it felt like I was losing the battle. "He's all I've got!" The dam broke and the tears flowed. I buried my face in my hands and let loose with great sobs and moans that shook my whole body.

At some point, Katya must have sat on the arm of my chair and wrapped her arms around me. I don't know how long I cried, but after awhile the tears subsided, leaving what felt like jagged ruts in my face … and my soul. She set a box of tissues on my lap and we sat like that for a long time, the silence broken only by the sound of my sniffles or my attempts to blow my nose. When I finally looked at her face, just inches from mine, there were tears on her cheeks, too.

Katya broke the silence. "I am so sorry," she said.

I shook my head. I didn't know what to say.

"We can do this any way you like."

I continued to shake my head. "No, I can see your point."

"I didn't want to upset you at all. I was trying to say I think our best choice would be to get through this together. I didn't say it very well."

I swallowed. Sniffed. "I don't care about anything but finding my father. That's the most important thing in my life. Nothing else even comes close."

She studied my face for a moment before speaking. "I agree," she said. "I agree." She jumped up from her chair and walked to the open closet by the dining table. For the next hour or more, she explained each of the charts, diagrams, and stacks of paper. I had to marvel at her organizational skills. It all reminded me of a scene from one of those detective shows on television.

"I've been in almost daily contact with the Sar Shalom Institute, the Israel Police, the U.S. Embassy, and just yesterday, the FBI called on me. Did you contact them?"

I shook my head. "I called my congressman's office. And they said they'd be contacting whatever agencies should be contacted. I think they even mentioned the FBI. But I never talked to the FBI myself."

"That might have been it, then. Or the U.S. Embassy."

"What did they say? The FBI, I mean."

"Not a whole lot. I did most of the talking. They asked questions; I answered them. One of them made notes. I got the impression that the reason for their visit was to get the information they needed to fill out a report back at the office."

THE QUEST

"Did they say they'd get back to you?"

"No. They did say that area hospitals, police, and jails had been contacted, and nothing about Daniel had turned up in any of those places. So I guess that means that he hasn't been hurt or arrested, as far as we know."

"As far as we know," I said.

She nodded solemnly. "It's something, at least."

"I guess."

"Right now, I'm clinging to anything I can find out. There's so much I don't know, so many questions and almost no answers. I'm grateful to at least know something—no matter how small it may seem. You know?"

I bit my lip, thinking. "We know something else, too," I said.

"What's that?"

"We know the FBI is not out there looking for Dad."

She shot me a solemn look. "You're right."

CHAPTER 30

KATYA'S JOURNAL

Oh, Lord God, how my heart hurts for Emma.

Is it fair for you to let me hurt for her, on top of my hurt for my husband … and myself? Or is that a way of being merciful? Is it a way of drawing me out of myself and granting me grace by giving me someone else to think of?

Maybe if Emma weren't here, I'd be more apt to break down. or even fall apart. Maybe preparing for her arrival has kept me from going completely crazy.

Whatever you're up to, Lord, please help us both. Help us through this.

Keep watch tonight over Daniel, help him to sleep.

If he is hurt in any way, heal him.

If he is in danger, deliver him as you delivered Daniel in the lions' den.

If he is afraid, strengthen him.

If he feels alone, surround him with your presence.

Hold him in your arms, constantly, until I can hold him in mine!

Keep him from making risky decisions. Give him a vision of his return to me. Help him to feel the effects of the many prayers that are being prayed on his behalf.

And help me and Emma to feel the effects of prayer, too—his prayers, even. And the prayers of my friends at the institute and at church.

And bring him home, Lord. Safely. And soon, please.

Until then, give me grace to sleep tonight and to face another day tomorrow. Amen.

THE QUEST

From the Israel News Service website

Freed Activist Urges More Kidnappings

✉ EMAIL   🖨 PRINT   + SHARE

Freed Hamas activist Ali Abdul-Samad spoke out a mere three hours after his release from an Israeli prison to urge fellow Hamas members to abduct more Israeli soldiers.

Abdul-Samad spoke at a press conference today in Beit Hanoun after 21 months of imprisonment. In addition to his call for more kidnappings, he urged Hamas not to free kidnapped Israeli soldier Anah Martin.

Abdul-Samad was considered one of the highest-ranking activists incarcerated in Israel. He was convicted for the 2010 bombing of a Tel Aviv café, in which Miriam Kahn and her three-year-old daughter, Abigail, were severely injured. His wife, who was tried as an accomplice in the attack, served one year in prison.

"My mission will not be complete until all Palestinian prisoners of the racist and oppressive Israeli regime are reunited with their families and their people," Abdul-Samad said. He reiterated claims that he was abused at the hands of his Israeli guards and prison officials, and he promised that his abusers would pay for their crimes.

Israel has released more than 400 Palestinian prisoners in recent months, a move seen as an effort to boost the prospects of moderate candidates in the upcoming elections in the Palestinian territories. Hamas is considered likely to win a majority in the Palestinian Parliament, placing some doubt in the future of peace negotiations. Israel's government has refused to negotiate with Hamas, preferring the more moderate Fatah leadership. Fatah has been steadily losing influence in the last few elections.

Abdul-Samad concluded his press conference by saying that, while activists should target Israeli soldiers, "the people of Israel are all complicit in Israel's crimes. Any distinction between active military and Israeli citizens is a false distinction."

CHAPTER 31

Our first step the next morning was to buy a cell phone for me, a process that reinforced to me that I was not back home. Katya argued with the man about the price. They went back and forth, back and forth, several times, getting louder and louder until finally she placed some money in his hand and he handed her the phone. He kept talking loudly even as we walked away.

"What was that all about?" I asked.

"What?" she answered. "Oh, that? That's just how things are done here."

"Was he really mad at you?"

"No. The more I make him work for a sale, the prouder he is. It's a game."

"But he acted like you cheated him or something."

"It's all part of the game. The tougher the customer, the better he feels about making the sale."

I just shook my head. When we got into the car, I turned on the phone and added just two numbers to it, with Katya's help: her cell and the Israel Police. I thought of Travis and wished I had a number for him I could add to the phone, but he had not yet called Katya's number, and until he did, I had no way of getting in touch with him— until we both got back to the U.S. and could use the numbers we traded on the plane.

THE QUEST

Our next stop was in a modern business district. As we drove there, Katya pointed out some of the sights to me, like the walls of the Old City and the ancient City of David, which she said was the whole city back in the days of King David. She pointed out the Mount of Olives, the gray dome of the Al-Aqsa Mosque, and the Valley of Hinnom, which she said was a burning garbage dump in Bible days.

Soon we arrived at our destination and entered the offices of something called CID, which Katya said was a private security firm in Jerusalem that provided security for private businesses to discourage terrorist attacks, among other things. It was one of many, she said, which underscored the danger in and around the city.

A pretty woman with olive skin met us in the lobby and ushered us into a small conference room, with potted plants in three of the four corners and a large framed road map of Israel on the long wall behind the conference table. The room smelled strongly of cigarettes—or cigars, or both—and the only objects on the conference table were three glass ashtrays. She offered to pour us coffee from the carafe in the center of the table, but Katya and I both declined. She smiled and said Mr. Avraham would join us shortly.

When the woman left us alone in the conference room, I asked, "Why are we here, again?"

"Sar Shalom Institute suggested that I hire these people to help search for your father."

The next instant two men entered the room and introduced themselves to Katya and me as Michael Avraham and Adi Yadin. Avraham was a burly man with a shaved head, probably in his fifties. Yadin was younger, in his twenties, I thought, with a full head of curly black hair and piercing blue eyes.

After exchanging a few pleasantries, Avraham invited us to sit down and he asked us to explain what brought us there. Katya told the story from the moment Dad got out of bed on the last morning she saw him, including my arrival the previous day, up to our activities until we arrived there. Her account was straightforward and sequential; it reminded me of the orderliness of the "command center" in the apartment.

When she finished her account, Avraham produced a cigarette and offered it first to Katya, then to me. We both shook our heads. He gave a slight shrug, then lit the cigarette and took a long drag, blowing out the smoke very slowly.

"You have not been contacted?" he asked.

"As I said, the FBI has contact—" Katya started to say.

"I mean by someone who has your husband in their custody."

"No," she said. "We haven't heard a word."

"It is not so unusual." He glanced at his young associate and said something to him in Hebrew. The younger man leapt up from his chair and left the room.

"If he's been kidnapped," I asked, "wouldn't someone have contacted us by now?"

He continued smoking for a moment. Exhaled. "Not definitely. There may be reasons."

"What reasons?" I asked.

He gave me a measured look, then turned it on Katya. "He may be wounded. He may be giving them information. They may be determining what he is worth to them. Shall I go on?"

"No," I said.

Katya asked, "What could anyone possibly want from Daniel? We have no money. We own next to nothing."

He shrugged again. "You are Americans. That is enough, for some."

"I still find it hard to believe," she said.

"What did you say is your husband's job?"

"The same as mine," Katya answered. "We are both Christian aid workers with Sar Shalom Institute."

"What is this 'Prince of Peace Institute'?" he asked.

"It's a nonprofit organization. We try to promote good relationships between Christians and Jews."

"What do you do, exactly?"

She hesitated. "We try to be good neighbors—visit people in their homes, host them in our homes, and try to find ways to serve them."

"You are paid for this?"

She smiled. "We receive an allowance from the institute to live on."

He turned to me. "What is your job?"

The question surprised me. "I—I'm a student."

"Where do you study?"

"In the United States. In Oxford, Ohio, at Miami University."

"Miami is not in Ohio."

"It is not named for the city of Miami in Florida. Both the city and the university are named for a tribe of Native Americans that once lived in the area. Sometimes we call it 'Miami of Ohio' to distinguish it from the Miami University in Florida."

He didn't seem interested at all. He turned his attention to Katya. "Have you encountered any difficulties since you arrived in Israel?"

"Difficulties?" she asked.

"Arguments."

"Oh," she said. "No. None at all."

"Have you been on the television or radio, or have any newspaper reports mentioned you or your husband?"

"No."

"Have you met anyone new?"

"Have I—" Katya frowned. "Yes. Everyone! All our friends are new."

He paused. "In the last six months, then."

Her frown deepened. "We've made many new friends in the past six months."

"Can you write down their names for me?"

"You want a list?"

"Please."

She blinked. "I—I suppose I could do that."

"That would be helpful." He turned to me.

"What?" I asked. He obviously intended for me to speak, but I didn't know what he wanted me to say.

"Have you met anyone new in Israel?"

"No," I said. "Well—"

"Yes?"

"Does on the plane count?"

"It counts, yes."

I glanced at Katya. "I met a guy."

"A guy."

"We sat next to each other all the way from Chicago to Tel Aviv. His name is Travis. We just talked."

"Tell me about Travis."

I told him—at least as much as I knew. He smoked slowly as he listened, every once in a while inserting a question. Then, suddenly, he seemed to tire of listening to me talk and he turned his attention back to Katya.

"Since his disappearance, have you been watched or followed by anyone?"

"No," she answered. He looked at me, and I shook my head.

"Have you received any unusual phone calls—when you answered, did the caller hang up?"

"No," she said.

When he looked at me, I said, "I left my cell phone at home and just got a new one this morning. No one has my new number."

He addressed Katya. "Have you received any packages in the mail?"

"No."

"Have you seen any strangers around? Perhaps near your home or place of work?"

"No."

Yadin came into the room and slid a file folder onto the table in front of Avraham. He opened it. Inspected it. Flipped up the corners of a couple of pages.

After another drag on the cigarette, Avraham said, "He does not seem to have appeared in any hospital or police station in the area."

"Yes, the FBI told us that," Katya said.

"About the FBI," Avraham said. "They are not going to be helpful to you."

"Why not?" Katya asked. "They're American."

"Yes," he said. "That is why. They are limited to information gathering. They cannot arrange meetings, they cannot negotiate, they cannot deliver ransom money, arrange for the release of prisoners, or anything like that. Basically, they do nothing that would resemble negotiating with terrorists."

"But we don't even know any terrorists are involved," I said.

"It does not matter. In order to find a man missing in Israel, you need the help of Israelis. You need us."

"How much will it cost?" Katya asked. "As I said before, we don't have any money."

He stubbed out his cigarette in an ash tray and then pulled a single sheet of paper from the folder. He slid it across the table to her.

She read the paper while holding her head in her hands. "I don't know how we can possibly pay these charges."

He studied her. "Do you want your husband back?"

Her eyes brimmed with tears. "Yes." It was a tiny sound.

"Then you must find a way."

Private Security Companies Flourish in Israel

✉ EMAIL   🖨 PRINT   + SHARE

JERUSALEM—Suicide bombings and other terrorist attacks in Israel have declined significantly as the West Bank security barrier has drawn closer to completion, but the public's demand for safety has not. The growing desire for security has sparked a boom in the establishment and growth of private security companies.

Michael Avraham, 56, founded the Jerusalem-based company, Comprehensive Intelligence and Defense (CID), in 2002, just weeks before the start of construction on the security barrier. "At the time it was not at all clear that the barrier would be constructed or that it would have the desired effect," he said. "Though the barrier has prevented the entry of would-be terrorists into Israel," he said, "it will not eliminate the need for caution and vigilance on the part of Israel's businesses and citizens. There will always be a need for private security to aid in both prevention and recovery efforts. It is a reality of life."

Avraham says his firm cannot keep up with the demand. CID employs more than 500 people, and is constantly recruiting—a task made more difficult during times like the present, when the government has called up more than 25,000 reservists for active duty. The majority of CID's security force have military or intelligence-service experience.

A former member of an elite counter-terrorism unit himself, Avraham provides security forces for large and small businesses. CID also aids in the recovery of hostages and kidnap victims, as well as supplementing government forces for special security details on some occasions.

Industry analysts estimate that the private security business is one of the fastest growing in the national economy. Avraham declined to divulge CID's annual income, but it is ranked as one of the 10 largest Israeli companies in the field.

CHAPTER 32

"Are you sure about this?" I asked Katya. Mr. Avraham and Yadin had left us in the conference room, telling us that someone would come soon with the necessary paperwork for Katya to sign.

"No," she said, shaking her head.

"You don't even know if you can trust these people."

"They come highly recommended by the institute." She turned her head and fixed her eyes on me. "Besides," she said. "What else can I do?"

All I could do was blink at her. I had no answer. There didn't seem to be any alternatives. We could shop around for a cheaper company, but did we really want to go to the bargain bin for something like this? And any time we spent shopping around for help was lost time, time that could have been spent actively looking for Dad.

The olive-skinned woman came in a few moments later with a stack of papers and showed Katya where to sign on each sheet—a series of procedures to follow if we should be contacted by someone claiming to be holding Dad, a commitment not to contact the media and generally avoid publicity, a checklist of points on how to interact with the Israeli government, and so on. When she was finished signing, she pulled out her checkbook and wrote a check for the deposit. She handed the check to the young woman and asked, "When will they start?"

The words weren't even out of her mouth when Mr. Avraham swung through the open doorway. "We already have," he said. He spoke in

Hebrew to the young woman, who apparently responded satisfactorily, and swept out of the room.

"Haviv will return with your copies. And then I would like you to come with me."

"To where?" I asked.

He showed me a tight smile. "An errand."

I looked at Katya. I was liking this guy less and less.

Moments later, Katya had the paperwork in her pocket, and we sat together in the back seat of Mr. Avraham's Range Rover. Yadin was in the front passenger seat.

Avraham drove like a madman, weaving in and out of traffic as if he was running from someone. He even parked the Range Rover with violence, slamming to a stop and jumping out in one fluid motion. We followed him as closely as we could to the door of a white stone building. Yadin trailed behind us.

Suddenly Katya stopped and grabbed my arm. I looked at her, but she was looking straight ahead. She stared at a sign over the door—a sign that read "Givat Sha'ul Morgue."

"Oh, Emma," she said.

Mr. Avraham had kept walking when we stopped, and the double doors closed behind him. Yadin circled around us and opened one of the doors.

"Please," he said.

Katya didn't let go of my arm. I felt my throat tighten. Somehow we walked through the doors into a long hallway with sickly green walls and flickering fluorescent lights that droned like lazy insects. Every step down that hallway took enormous effort, as though I was walking in sand.

Mr. Avraham had walked ahead of us through another door, which Mr. Yadin opened for us. It led into a dimly lit room where a row of four gurneys awaited. A large woman in a white frock stood next to the gurneys, and Mr. Avraham waited next to her. Katya and I stopped, simultaneously, as if we had encountered an invisible barrier just outside the room. I closed my eyes. I remembered a time when I was no more than four or five years old. I had been sick for weeks, and our family doctor thought I might have lyme disease. Dad took me to the hospital, where they drew blood. The needle hurt, and I cried. Dad wrapped his arms around me while I lay on that hospital gurney, put his lips against my ear, and sang "Itsy Bitsy Spider" until it was all over. The tests turned out to be negative, but I'd had a fear of needles—and hospitals—ever since.

This was more than fear, though. This was terror. I opened my eyes and looked at Katya. She gripped my arm even tighter and together we crossed the threshold.

Mr. Avraham spoke to the white-frocked woman, who pointed at the gurney farthest from us. He walked ahead of us and stood there, waiting. We inched forward.

"One unidentified man fitting your husband's description has been reported since the day of his disappearance. I must ask you to tell me if this is him."

He lifted the sheet, and I gasped. Katya buried her face in my shoulder.

Mr. Avraham placed the sheet over the bruised and bloodied face, and snapped out some words to the morgue worker. Then he turned to us. "It is him?"

I shook my head. "No," I answered. "No, it's not him."

We were exhausted by the time we returned to the apartment late that afternoon. I offered to help Katya fix dinner, but she said we could think about that later. Neither of us felt much like eating.

I went to the bedroom and lay down. The face of that poor man on the gurney was so hideously battered, I couldn't imagine what it would have felt like if it *had* been my father. I was angry at Mr. Avraham for showing it to us. And I was even angrier at his business-like way of doing so, as if he could spare no emotion or compassion, for a wife and a daughter who were already on edge.

THE QUEST

I needed to sleep, but I didn't want that man's face to haunt my dreams. So I did something I hadn't done for a couple of days now, at least. I prayed.

"God," I said, "if you're even there, and if you're paying attention at all, you can see that we need your help. *I* need your help. If you are who everyone says you are, then you know where my dad is. You know where we need to look or who we need to talk to, so please give us a hand. Give us a sign or signal—at least a clue. Because right now, I feel like we don't have a single one."

When I awoke and padded into the living room, Katya was—again— reading her Bible. I don't know why, but it irritated me a little bit. I sat down opposite her.

"Why are you always reading that?" I said. I didn't mean for my tone to sound accusing, but I could hear it in my voice nonetheless.

She inserted a bookmark between the pages and closed it. "It's a refuge for me."

"How?" I asked. "How can you even believe all that stuff?"

"All what stuff?"

I hadn't intended to go down this road, but I'd already stepped on the gas, so I decided I might as well steer straight and see where it ended up. "I don't know, like all the stories and stuff. Isn't it all just kind of hard to believe?"

She actually stroked the cover of her Bible as she answered! She said, "No, I don't think so. I don't think it's hard to believe at all."

I shrugged. "Okay. I guess it's easier for some than for others."

"How much of it have you read?"

I opened my mouth. Then closed it again without speaking. I swallowed. When I finally spoke, it sounded stupid to my ears. "None."

"None?"

I shook my head. She had me.

"You mean you've never even tried to read any of it?"

"No," I said, a little defensively, I admit. "I never saw a need to. Why would I?"

She nodded, slowly, rhythmically. "So, where do your impressions about the Bible come from?"

"What do you mean?"

"Your impressions that the Bible is hard to believe. Where did you get that idea?"

Her question surprised me. "Where did I get that idea," I echoed. "I don't know. I never really thought about it. I just—I guess I just kind of assumed that's what everybody thought."

"Everybody," she said. "You mean friends? Or professors?"

"I don't know," I said, a tone of irritation entering my voice. "I guess the people I've known have dismissed it as just a bunch of myths and fables. I mean, there's all kinds of religious books out there, and they're pretty much all just made-up stuff. Stories of, I don't know, angels and miracles and stuff like that. I mean, isn't that what it is, mostly?"

She inched forward until she was perched on the edge of her chair, the Bible propped on her knees. "Do you really want to know?"

This was weird. How did I get myself into this discussion? I didn't want to give her the satisfaction of saying yes. But I had to admit, I was curious. I shrugged and tried to make my answer sound dismissive. "Sure. Why not?"

Maybe this would take my mind off my dad.

CHAPTER 33

Katya's eyes twinkled like those of a child walking into a toy store. She placed her Bible on the end table next to her chair, then she stood and walked over to her command center. "Why are we doing all this?"

"What?" I said. I had no idea what she was talking about.

"This," she said, waving at the charts and posters and stacks of paper. "What is the purpose of all this work we've done, the notebook I gave you, the forms we've filled out, the pictures I've posted at bus stops and other spots around the city? What's the purpose?"

"You never told me about posters at bus stops."

She waved a hand. "I guess I forgot. Sorry." She strode back to her chair and sat down. "But tell me … why are we doing all this?"

She was really starting to freak me out. "What are you talking about? We're doing it to find my father!"

"Exactly," she said. She leaned back in her chair. "To find your father."

I watched her, feeling completely lost. I didn't get her point.

She leaned forward again and placed a palm on her Bible. "This is much like that notebook I gave you. I compiled that notebook to bring you up to speed—to give you as much information as I could about what had happened and steps I'd taken, and so on—so that in a relatively short time, you could know as much as you needed to know to fulfill your purpose—to find your father."

THE QUEST

She picked the Bible up and held it in both hands. "This is much more sophisticated than my notebook, but with the same idea behind it. People from all walks of life—farmers and kings, musicians and philosophers, you name it—wrote down their stories and songs and letters, all for the same purpose we're pursuing here: So people like you and me wouldn't have to start from square one, but could be helped to find what every human heart longs to find, whether we know it or not."

"What's that?" I asked.

"Our Father," she said.

"Oh, okay. But still, it's all a bunch of human writings, right?"

"Yes," she said, nodding. "At least to some extent. Every word in here was recorded by a human being using a pen and ink, basically. But every one of them, writing hundreds of years and thousands of miles apart, wrote with an amazing unity of purpose and perspective. They all pointed the same direction, to the same person, with the same longing."

"To God." I knew that was where she was going.

"Yes. More specifically, to Jesus, God's Son."

"Okay, yeah, but still … it's just what random people said. I don't get why I should believe it."

"Well, you shouldn't," she said, which surprised me for a few seconds.

"What?"

"You shouldn't believe it. You shouldn't believe *anything* without reading it."

"Oh, I see what you did there. You're going to try to get me to read it."

She smiled. "I might."

"Well, good luck with that."

She set down the Bible and held up her palms in a display of perfect innocence. "I'm merely saying that you're totally right in not putting faith in something you haven't investigated."

"You think you're pretty slick, don't you?" I couldn't help smiling, though I resisted the urge as well as I could. It felt like we were getting along with each other and I wasn't feeling quite ready for that.

She laughed. "No, I just believe anyone who approaches the Bible in a fair-minded way won't remain a skeptic for very long."

While Katya fixed dinner and I set the table, we talked mostly about CID. We were both still upset by Mr. Avraham's stunt in the morgue. Whether he thought that poor man in the morgue was Dad's body or not, it was a horrible thing to do to us.

"He could have at least tried to prepare us," I said, placing a cloth napkin beside each place setting. I'd already noticed that Katya's kitchen was smaller and her cupboards emptier than any I'd ever seen. She didn't rely on paper products or microwaveable dishes like we did back home; when she brought the plates to the table, there was a lamb kabob and a generous helping of fresh cucumbers, tomatoes, and peppers on each plate.

"Don't worry. It should all be edible," she said.

"It looks good."

She shook her head as she sat at the table and turned the talk back to CID. "I just don't understand; they come so highly recommended by the institute. I think I'll call Tom and Stella in the morning and—I don't know—make sure they know what they're talking about."

She bowed her head to pray, as she had each time we'd eaten together. I waited, hungry as I was. Neither of us had given any thought to food while we were out, and the lunch hour had passed us right by. My stomach had been growling ever since Katya started cooking the lamb.

When she finished praying, we both started eating. "Do you think they'll do us any good?" I asked.

She chewed for a few moments and swallowed. "I hope so. They know people. They know the area. Even though Mr. Avraham handled it horribly, I am a little reassured that they checked out a lead at the morgue so quickly."

I considered that. I guess she had a point. I didn't know what I would have done if it had been Dad. I tried to shake the thought. Katya seemed to read my mind.

"It may not be the last time we have to do that," she said.

THE QUEST

I answered without looking at her. "I know."

We ate in silence for a few minutes, until I asked, "How are you going to pay them?"

"Who?"

"The security company. You said it was expensive."

"It is—very expensive." She impaled a juicy piece of lamb on her fork. "I've been thinking about that. When I talk to Tom and Sheila in the morning, I'll ask about any help the institute can provide. And maybe there's some help available through the insurance; we carry a small accidental death insurance policy through the institute."

"You think that will be enough?"

"No. The next step will probably be calling and writing family and friends back home to ask for donations toward expenses. I really hate to do that, though."

"I could try contacting some people, too. I don't know how much good it would do, but I guess it can't hurt."

"Thank you, Emma, that's sweet."

We fell silent again, and ate for a few minutes, until Katya started giggling softly.

"What?" I asked. "What's funny?"

She demurred at first, but I insisted she tell me. "Oh, it's silly," she said, finally. "I was just thinking: If Daniel has been taken hostage, those poor people—whoever they are—don't know what they're up against! Won't they be shocked when we start the negotiations by asking if they accept coupons!" She started giggling again. Maybe it was all the stress finally finding some release, but I started laughing too. I couldn't help it.

"I know," I offered. "I've got a brand new cell phone I could try to sell on eBay!"

By the time we finished eating and cleared the table, our circumstances hadn't changed, but our moods were a little lighter.

CHAPTER 34

I showered after dinner and took my time brushing my hair. Katya said that the next morning she would have to spend some time on the phone, talking to people about the funds we would need for CID. Then, in the afternoon, she said we might do a lot of driving and walking, distributing some flyers she had produced, talking to people, asking if they had heard or seen anything that might help. She said gossip and rumors were a major form of entertainment in Israel, so even with CID conducting their own investigations, there was a chance we could find out some things just by asking around.

As I was stepping out of the shower, I heard a sound I'd been intending to ask Katya about; it was coming into the apartment from outside. It sounded like a man, but I couldn't be sure. It was a half-singing, half-wailing sort of a sound. It only lasted a few minutes each time I heard it, but it seemed like it happened several times a day. Once my hair was finished, I went into the living room to ask Katya about it.

She sat in the same chair, in the same position as before, reading her Bible. I sat down opposite her.

"What is that sound I keep hearing outside?"

"Sound?" she said.

"Yeah, I heard it when I was getting out of the shower. I've heard it several times now. Like a man moaning or wailing or something."

"Oh, that. That's the Azan, the Muslim call to prayer."

"Oh," I said. I guess that answered my question, but I didn't feel any better informed.

"Five times a day, a man called a *muezzin* climbs up into a minaret, one of those tall pointy towers you'll see all around town, and calls faithful Muslims to prayer. The Azan is basically a call to get ready, and then a second song, the Iqama, is the cue for them to line up for the beginning of the prayers."

"And this is five times a day?"

"Five times a day," she said.

"And everybody has to drop what they're doing and go to the mosque, then?"

"No, not necessarily. Those who are able go to the mosque, but if a person is at his place of work and can't leave, for example, he'll just stop what he's doing and pray right there in the shop. You'll see it when we're out and about."

"So all that noise is just one guy in a tower?"

"No," she said, smiling. "You'll see loudspeakers on the minarets these days. So it's a recording. At least around here."

"And that doesn't bother you?"

"Bother me? Why would it bother me?"

"I don't know, I guess because you're not Muslim and you still have to listen to it."

She shrugged. "It's part of living in Jerusalem. A lot of non-Muslims get to the point where they don't even hear it after awhile, sort of like car alarms in New York City, I guess. Most of the time, though, when I hear the call to prayer, I use it as my own little reminder to pray. I don't put out a prayer rug like they do, but I'll often pause in the midst of whatever I'm doing and spend a few moments talking to God."

I realized that I'd walked right into that one. But for whatever reason, her words didn't bother me this time. Maybe because I didn't feel like she was preaching at me. She was just answering my questions.

A thought occurred to me. "This call to prayer can be heard anywhere? Everywhere?"

"Anywhere there's a mosque. Which around here is practically everywhere."

"So … wherever Dad is, he can probably hear it."

"I think so, yes."

I'm not sure why, but that brought me some comfort. I didn't know where he was, but if he and I could both hear that weird sound several times a day, it made him seem closer somehow. I even said a quick prayer that he would realize the same thing and feel closer to me and Katya, even though he had no way of knowing I was in Israel.

I felt that momentary comfort start to evaporate and had to think about something else before a wave of sadness overtook me. I pointed to Katya's Bible.

"What are you reading tonight?"

Katya seemed to study my face for a few moments before answering my question. "Thank you for asking. I follow a daily reading plan for much of my Bible reading. So every day, I read an Old Testament portion, something from the Psalms, something from Proverbs, and a New Testament portion. And I'm often amazed at how a specific day's reading applies perfectly to my situation on that day."

"What do you mean?"

"Well, this reading schedule I'm following was not planned out with your father's disappearance in mind, to say the least. There's obviously no way I—or anyone—could have known what my circumstances might be when I sat down to read today's passages. But part of today's reading is Psalm 18, which talks about God protecting and sustaining me, and watching over my every step. It reminds me that he is in control, even when it doesn't feel like it. And it ends with a reminder of his unfailing love, something I really needed to remember tonight."

"Huh," I said. I wasn't sure what else to say.

"I'm sorry. I shouldn't have gone on like that."

"No, it's okay, really. I just …"

THE QUEST

"What? What are you thinking?"

I hesitated.

"Go ahead, say what you're thinking. I really want to know."

"I think it's great. It's really great that reading that stuff makes you feel better."

"But?"

"I don't understand how you can believe it. I mean, I know I haven't read it, okay? And maybe I will. But still, it's just a book. It's what people long ago thought was true, right? But they were still just people. What makes what they wrote down worth believing?"

She turned and looked out the sliding doors. The sun was down and darkness had fallen. A tiny sliver of a moon hung in the sky. She spoke without turning back to look at me. "Do you really want to know?"

I felt a little offended by her words. What kind of question was that? As if I would ask a question I didn't really want an answer to. Then, for some reason, I suddenly thought of Travis and our discussion on the plane. How he had more or less offended me by assuming I was on some kind of spiritual search. "*Everyone* is searching," he'd said. "Not everyone knows it." Was he right? Was I searching? Did I really want Katya to answer my question?

"I don't know," I admitted.

She smiled, as if my answer delighted her. "Wow," she said. "Thanks for that. That's an honest answer!"

I guess it was. I think part of me wanted to know, and part of me didn't. Part of me was afraid she'd make sense. And part of me was afraid she wouldn't.

Chapter 35

We were both silent for a few moments. I could tell that Katya was thinking, processing—maybe even sorting. But I wasn't doing any of those things. I was waiting for what she would say next.

"Okay. I think I can answer your question, at least as it pertains to me, and the reasons I find it not only possible to believe the Bible, but very nearly impossible *not* to." She had that glint in her eyes again.

"I hope I'm not sorry I asked," I said.

"I hope so, too," she said with a chuckle. "But I probably should warn you: I'm not sure I can explain it briefly. It may take me a while."

"That's all right," I said.

"And keep in mind, no one's really asked me that question before, so I may ramble a bit. But I think I can boil it down to—" she paused, thinking. "Four main things. Four basic reasons I trust the Bible."

"Okay," I said.

"I've already told you about how amazing I think it is that the Bible was written by such a variety of people, in different times and languages, and yet they all pointed the same direction."

"Right," I said. "So is that number one?"

"No," she said with a smile. "That's just kind of laying the foundation. The first reason I consider the Bible trustworthy is all the evidence indicating that what it says really happened. I guess you could say it's an accurate record in the first place."

"Like what?"

She looked out the window at the crescent moon for a moment before turning to me. "Like the fact that many of the biblical writers claimed to be eyewitnesses of the things they were reporting. Or, they claimed to have gotten their information from eyewitnesses.

"See, many ancient writings adhered only loosely to the facts of the events they reported. You probably remember names like Herodotus and Thucydides."

It was my turn to smile. "If you say so."

"Oh, come on. Maybe you've forgotten them, but I bet you came across their names in a world history or ancient history course at some point. My point is: Many highly regarded authors of the ancient world, like those two guys, reported events that took place many years before they were born … in a place they had never visited! And while their writing may be largely factual, historians today understand that some of their accounts have to be taken with a grain of salt because they really weren't anywhere near the events they recorded. So basically everyone would admit that writers who were closest to the events should be given more weight. Follow me?"

"Sure," I answered. "I get that."

"Okay," she said, picking up her Bible and flipping the pages. "So, with that in mind, notice what the New Testament writers claimed." She apparently found what she was looking for. "A man named John talked about the 'things we have heard, and seen with our eyes, and touched with our hands—these are the things we proclaim.'"

She flipped a few pages again. "And a man called Peter told people, basically, 'We did not make up clever stories about Jesus, but we were eyewitnesses of all the amazing things he said and did.'"

She turned more pages. "And Luke refers to 'many' accounts that had been handed down from eyewitnesses, and says his goal was to thoroughly investigate everything from beginning to end, in order to write an orderly account. And those are just a few among many."

"Okay, yeah. But anybody can claim to be an eyewitness. That doesn't mean they were."

"Right, but when you take those claims and put them alongside the documentary evidence, it presents a pretty compelling picture."

"Whoa ... wait. You're losing me."

She took a breath. "Sorry, it's easy for me to get carried away with these things. Let me back up a little bit." She cleared her throat. "A hundred years or more ago, there were a whole bunch of scholars who claimed that none of the New Testament writings could have been written before the second century, long after Jesus, his followers, and every eyewitness would have died. But more recent scholarship has basically blown those claims out of the water."

"How?"

"One example would be a papyrus fragment of John's Gospel—the fourth book of the New Testament—that surfaced in the first half of the twentieth century. It's a tiny piece of manuscript, but it is clearly a part of John's Gospel—and it has been dated to within twenty to fifty years of John's lifetime. And that's a book that scholars generally believe was one of the latest New Testament books to be written. That discovery has caused many to rethink their position and makes it all the more likely that those claims to being eyewitnesses are true."

"But not for sure," I said.

"No," she said. "Not for sure, but I'm just getting warmed up."

"What I've seen time and time again in my lifetime is supposedly smart, highly respected 'scholars' taking positions that seem to say the Bible can't be trusted," Katya continued. "Then before too long, a new discovery is made that shows their previous position was clearly wrong. It happens all the time."

"For example ..." I prodded.

"I'll get to that. But let me try to stay on track right now. I'm talking about the first reason the Bible is trustworthy: Because all the evidence concerning what it says is what really happened in the first place. Right?"

"Right."

"So the first thing is the claim to proximity."

"The what?"

"Never mind—the claim many biblical writers made of having seen or having been close to the events they describe. That's just part one, though. Part two of the reason the Bible is accurately recorded is the fact that biblical writers not only said, 'We saw this,' or 'We heard that,' but they were also confident enough to say, 'Check it out,' 'Ask around,' and 'You know it as well as I do!'"

She flipped the pages of her Bible as she spoke. I watched the pages go by and marveled at her obvious familiarity with the book, which seemed to me, looking upside down as I was, almost like a code. She really seemed to know what she was doing.

"For example," she said, finally, "when Peter preached on the Day of Pentecost—soon after Jesus' resurrection and ascension—he told the crowd of several thousand that Jesus had performed miracles, wonders, and signs among them, as they were well aware.

"And just one more quick example: Paul once wrote a letter in which he talked about the numbers of people Jesus had appeared to after his resurrection, adding that most of those people were still living."

"I'm not sure I'm getting what you're saying," I said.

"It's like this. A liar will insist on the truth of what he's saying, right?"

"Yeah."

"But only a fool will invite you to investigate what he knows can be quickly proven false."

"Okay."

"That's what the biblical writers did, over and over again. They said, 'Check it out.' When Peter said, 'As you yourselves know,' someone in the crowd could have shouted, 'I know no such thing! I've never heard of this guy Jesus!' And when Paul wrote about Jesus appearing to hundreds of people who were still alive to that day, he was saying, 'They're still around; go, ask them.'"

"Oh, okay. I get it."

"So that's part two. It's not just that the biblical writers claimed to be very close to the events they reported—and we have good reason to believe they were. They also invited investigation into their claims, which only a fool would do if he were lying; especially if, like Peter, he was making his claims in the same location where these things were supposed to have happened. But also—are you ready for part three?"

I shrugged. But I was more interested than I wanted to let on.

"Part three, really quickly, is this: The scarcity of apparent contradictions."

"What does that mean?"

"In other words, one of the reasons I think the Bible describes what really happened is that there are so few contradictions."

"I've always heard there are all kinds of contradictions."

"I know; a lot of people believe that."

"Are you saying there aren't any?"

"No," she answered. "I'm not."

CHAPTER 36

I couldn't believe what I was hearing. Katya had just admitted there were contradictions in the Bible. "How can you believe it," I asked, "if you admit there are mistakes in it?"

She sighed. "I didn't exactly say that."

I narrowed my eyes. I wasn't going to let her wiggle out of this. "I think you did."

Again that smile. "To be fair," she said, "there are apparent discrepancies and contradictions."

"Apparent contradictions," I repeated.

"Don't give up on me yet," she said. "There are some things in the Bible that, when you first read them, look like a glaring inconsistency. Like the death of King Saul."

"Who?"

"He was the first king of Israel. And the first account, in 1 Samuel, I think, says that when Saul saw that he had lost this very important battle and was likely to be taken prisoner, he asked his armor-bearer to kill him—but the armor-bearer refused, so Saul fell on his own sword."

"All right," I said.

"But then the account continues and says that a man came to David and reported Saul's death. When David asked how Saul had died, the man said, 'He asked me to kill him, so I did.'"

"Okay, I get it. So in one account, Saul killed himself, and in the other, someone else killed him."

"Right. Seems like a contradiction, right?"

"Right. But you're going to tell me it's not."

"No, I'm not going to tell you that. But I am going to tell you that the Bible makes no attempt to explain it, even though the seemingly contradictory stories were part of the same account."

"So?"

"So, if you were making up a story, wouldn't you make sure to avoid apparent contradictions?"

"Sure."

"I would, too. But if you're writing history, you might not. You might just let the facts speak for themselves. You might record that the fact of the matter is that Saul fell on his own sword. Then someone came to David, who had been running and hiding from Saul because Saul wanted him dead. So this guy comes and when David asks how Saul died, he says, 'I did it,' perhaps expecting a reward from David, maybe a position in the new government. The Bible doesn't tell us that was the case; it seems to be simply reporting the facts. Which makes me believe it all the more."

"So," I said, processing what she was saying, "you're saying all the contradictions in the Bible are like that?"

"No." She shook her head. "I'm not saying that. There are a handful—seriously, just a handful—of seeming contradictions or problem areas that make me scratch my head. I can't reconcile one with the other, but those parts I can't explain are so far and few between, I never spend a second worrying about them. Not a single one affects or confuses what the Bible tells me is true. And to me, it's absolutely mind-boggling that the writings of forty vastly different human beings could be assembled into one book and not be a total mess of contradictions and inconsistencies. That itself strikes me as a miracle—or something close to it. And, as someone who's read all sixty-six books of the Bible numerous times, I've got to say, that's one of the reasons I honestly believe I can trust it."

We'd been talking a long time. I didn't know how long, but I didn't care. I actually wanted to hear more. Katya seemed to read my thoughts.

"Is it okay to keep going?" she asked. "I know I've been talking for quite a while. I hope I'm not boring you."

I shook my head. "No." I didn't want to appear too anxious, though, so I just said, "I'm okay for now."

She told me not to let her monopolize the conversation because she tends to do that when she is enthusiastic about a subject; and the Bible was something she was very enthusiastic about. Then she said, "What do you think so far?"

"What do you mean?"

"Well, am I making sense? Or are you just humoring me?"

"No, you're making sense. But—" I hesitated.

"But what?" she said.

"You're talking about the Bible you have today." I glanced at her Bible on the table between us. "But that's, like, thousands of years old, right? There's been time to change stuff and add things over those years. There's no way it can be the same as when it was first written."

She didn't answer immediately. "Hold that thought. I'm going to get a cup of tea. Can I get you something?"

I said no. She went into the kitchen, and I reached for her Bible and started turning the pages. It didn't look like any book I'd ever read, though some of the pages reminded me of a Norton poetry anthology I had at home. It was the text for a course I took a year or two ago on English poetry.

As I thumbed through, it fell open to a bookmark—a photograph of Dad and Katya on the deck of some house. It wasn't our home in New Jersey, I could tell that. Their arms were wrapped around each other, and they looked so happy. *He* looked so happy—at peace.

I couldn't tell if the photo had been taken before they got married or after. But it belonged to a different time and place, that was for sure. I studied his face until my eyes clouded with tears. When I heard what sounded like a spoon clinking the sides of a teacup coming from the kitchen, I closed the Bible and returned it to the table. A moment later, Katya returned with a steaming cup of tea.

"Earl Grey," she said. "It always helps me think."

I waited while she settled again in her chair and took a sip of tea.

"Okay. So your impression is that the text of the Bible has been changed—maybe even corrupted—over the years."

I struggled for a moment to return to the conversation. It seemed unreal that we were talking so much about this stuff when Dad was still missing. But at this hour, there wasn't much we could do but wait for a new day to dawn tomorrow. I wrestled my thoughts back to Katya's statement. "Right. How could it not? It's been copied and recopied so many times. And," I continued, pointing to her Bible on the table, "if I tried to copy that whole thing by hand, like they used to do before the printing press, how many mistakes would I make? And then, add to that, I might come across some things I don't like or don't agree with, so maybe I'd change them or leave them out—or put in some of my pet ideas. If you multiply that over and over again for thousands of years, there's no possible way it could be the same as it was when it was written. And it might not be anywhere *close* to what the original writer actually wrote down."

She took a long sip of tea before answering. "I probably should say a thing or two about how the Bible came to be in the form we have today." She took another sip, then set her cup down and picked up the Bible, holding it in front of her, one hand under it and one hand resting on top. "What we call the Bible is a collection of books that were written over the course of sixteen hundred years or so. A few hundred years after they were written, the church began to think about what books enjoyed pretty much universal acceptance as being true, authoritative, and trustworthy. By the third and fourth centuries after Jesus, this collection of books as we have them today became generally recognized as the Word of God."

She set the Bible down, picked up her tea again, and took another sip. "By the time that happened, there were hundreds, maybe thousands, of scrolls in synagogues and churches all over the civilized world."

"Right. So there could have been hundreds or thousands of different versions floating around, until no one could be sure what the original said."

She smiled. "Actually … it's exactly the opposite."

"What do you mean?"

She studied her tea cup for a few seconds. "Did you have to study Homer's *The Iliad* in high school?"

"Yeah," I said. "Hated it."

"I did, too. But what did you think about the text?"

"What do you mean?"

"The actual words you read on the page. Did you worry about how close those words were to the actual words Homer wrote down?"

"No."

"Neither did I."

"I don't get it. What's your point?"

"Homer probably wrote *The Iliad* around 800 BC, smack in the middle of those sixteen hundred years during which the books of the Bible were being written."

"Okay. So?"

"The copies of *The Iliad* that we read today are based on a little more than six hundred ancient copies that go back to about four hundred years after Homer's time."

I shrugged. "Okay," I said. But I still didn't see where she was going.

"I want you to remember that: six-hundred-some manuscript copies, and the earliest copies were from four hundred years after Homer's time. All right?"

"Sure."

"Those numbers make *The Iliad* the most reliable document of the ancient world."

THE QUEST

"Whoa, wait," I said. "What?"

"In other words, scholars today can be more confident that when they read *The Iliad* they're reading what Homer wrote, more so than anything written by, say, Julius Caesar, Plato, or Aristotle. Because they can compare hundreds of ancient manuscripts to each other, and because there's only four hundred years between the time Homer wrote and the oldest manuscript they have."

"*Only* four hundred years? That's a pretty long time."

"To you or me, it is. But when it comes to the literature of the ancient world, it's a very short time. The earliest manuscripts of some writings that we have today date to more than a *thousand* years after the time the original was written!"

"Wow."

"So, can you see how relatively impressive it is that we have six-hundred-some copies of *The Iliad* and the earliest manuscripts are a mere four hundred years from when he wrote?"

"Sure."

"So," she said, placing her tea cup—still half full—on the table, "you want to know how the Bible compares to that?"

I finally saw where she was going with this. Duh. "Sure," I said.

"More than *five thousand* Greek manuscripts and fragments of the New Testament exist today ... compared to six-hundred-some of *The Iliad*. Add in other versions and translations over the centuries and the number swells to more than twenty-four thousand! So as reliable as *The Iliad* may be, the New Testament is many times more so! And the earliest manuscript fragments from the New Testament date to less than a hundred years of the time those books were written, compared to four hundred in Homer's case."

"Those manuscripts are like the Dead Sea Scrolls? I've heard about them."

"No, some of the Dead Sea Scrolls were Old Testament Scripture, but there were no New Testament manuscripts among them. However, that does bring up another fascinating point. The Dead Sea Scrolls were discovered in 1947 in some caves not far from here. Until then, the oldest complete manuscript of the Hebrew Scriptures dated to about AD 1000, roughly thirteen hundred years after the last Old Testament prophet wrote. But the Dead Sea Scrolls were dated to about 125 BC. So the Dead Sea Scrolls were more than a thousand years older than the manuscripts scholars and translators had been using up to that time. Follow me?"

"I guess so," I said.

"But get this: Once the Dead Sea Scrolls were translated and compared with modern versions, the Hebrew Bible proved to be identical, word-for-word, in more than 95 percent of the text, and what differences they did find were mainly spelling variations. What that discovery did was to show that after more than *a thousand years* of copying, the text as it appeared in modern Bibles was almost exactly the same, letter-for-letter and mark-for-mark, as it had been three thousand years ago!"

Katya's tea was probably cold, and my energy was flagging. She looked as fresh as when the conversation had started, but I didn't know how much longer I could keep my eyes open, so I told her I thought I needed to turn in.

"I'm sorry. I'm sure I've bored you into a stupor."

I shook my head. "No, I'm just really tired."

She smiled, really warmly, I thought. "Can I get you anything?"

"No. Thanks."

"Good night," she said.

"You can tell me the rest tomorrow."

"I'd like that."

As I turned toward the bedroom, she was opening her Bible—again.

I closed the bedroom door and sat on the bed. I looked around the room. It was such a simple room, sparsely furnished. A double bed in the center of the room. Shelves on the wall over the bed. A wardrobe closet on each side of the bed. A single window. A chair in the corner. A low bookcase on the opposite wall. One picture hung on the wall,

THE QUEST

a pose from Dad and Katya's wedding. I was next to Dad, and Katya's sister stood next to her. Everyone but me was smiling.

I went to the first of the two wardrobe cabinets and opened it— Katya's clothes. I closed it and went to the other side of the bed.

As soon as I opened the wardrobe, the subtle scent of Dad's cologne enveloped me. He'd worn the same fragrance as long as I could remember. I reached out and touched one of the suit jackets on a hanger. I closed my eyes and clung to the jacket sleeve—and sobbed.

CHAPTER 37

What a roller coaster ride this day has been. If this is what the days are going to be like, I don't know how I'll cope, how I'll survive.

God, I pray, please don't let the face of that poor man in the morgue haunt my dreams tonight. I'm so grateful it wasn't Daniel, but it was such a nightmare nonetheless. How could Mr. Avraham be so insensitive? Mr. Yadin was much kinder, but how could they have escorted a wife and a daughter into a situation like that without any effort to prepare us? It makes me wonder if these are the kind of people I want to work with. But ... what choice do I have?

Worst of all, I can no longer escape the possibility that Daniel may not be okay. That body in the morgue wasn't him ... but what if it had been? How could I go on? How could I survive? How could you ask such a thing of me, God? You know I am no stranger to sorrow. You know I have had my share of grief. But that—that would be asking too much. I can't imagine that you would give Daniel to me only to snatch him away so quickly.

THE QUEST

And what about Emma? I can see the first fragile tendrils of faith springing up in her, Lord. She seems to be moving in your direction. Please don't let the tender shoots of faith in her be stamped out by unimaginable suffering. It is agony enough to not know where her father is or what he is going through right now; please don't let worse news come to her ... and to me.

God, I know you are not shaken, as I am right now. I know you did not tremble in that morgue, as I did. Help me. Help me not to lose faith. Help me to remember that you are in control. Help me to believe in your goodness. Help me to trust you through this night and through tomorrow, whatever tomorrow may bring, in Jesus' name, amen.

CHAPTER 38

I pulled that suit coat jacket off the hanger and wrapped it around me while I lay in the bed and tried to sleep. It felt like him and smelled like him. I felt as if it brought him closer. I lay in the bed a long time, crying and remembering.

I could never remember what it was like to have a mother. She died before my fourth birthday, but I have no memories of her. When I started going to school, I felt different from the other kids in my class. Some of my classmates lived with both parents, of course, and some lived with a single mom. Some only saw their fathers on weekends. But I was the only one who didn't have a mom.

I had a babysitter named Esther who would pick me up from school, walk me home, and stay with me until Dad got home from work. One day, some kids had been really cruel to me, and I ran home on my own. I crawled under the back porch and hid there. When Esther found me, I refused to come out.

When Dad got home, I expected him to be mad but he wasn't. He didn't scold me or punish me. He crawled under the porch with me, in his business suit. He took me in his arms and let me tell him all about the mean kids at school. He yelled for Esther, who didn't immediately come, so he asked me to help him and we both screamed her name at the top of our lungs until she came out of the house and poked her head under the porch to ask what was wrong.

"We're hungry," Dad said.

Esther told him that dinner had been ready for some time.

THE QUEST

"We want to eat it out here," he told her.

"Here?" she said, her tone clearly communicating her disapproval.

He winked at me. "Yes, ma'am. Would you bring us a plate? Please? We promise we'll eat everything on our plates. Won't we, Beanpole?"

Esther stomped back into the house and brought us our dinner, which we ate under the porch. It turned a terrible day into an adventure. Esther never mentioned that day again, as far as I know, but I never forgot it.

Lying in bed that night, with his jacket wrapped around me, I could almost close my eyes and imagine that he was there with me, in his business suit, holding me close and helping me get over a horrendous day.

I was not ready to wake up when Katya came into my room the next morning.

"I got a call from the security company," she said. "They want us to come to a meeting this morning."

"Why?" I asked, sitting up and squinting against the daylight streaming in through the window. "What's happening?"

"They wouldn't say; they just said they might have new information."

"What kind of information? They're not going to take us to the morgue again, are they?"

"No, definitely not that. I asked them about that," she said, irritation creeping into her tone for the first time since I'd arrived. "But we do need to get moving. We have barely enough time for some breakfast before we go."

I dressed in record time and joined her in the kitchen. She tried several times to start some casual conversation, but I wasn't feeling very cooperative.

We arrived at the CID offices seven minutes before the time Katya had agreed to. The same olive-skinned woman ushered us into the same small conference room. We waited. And waited some more. I had just opened my mouth to tell Katya I would go see what the delay was when Mr. Avraham and his assistant—what was his name again?—entered the room.

Avraham dropped a file folder on the table and shook our hands with exactly zero warmth. The assistant smiled and said, "Good morning," but he didn't offer his hand.

They sat down and I tried my best to be patient and wait for them to speak instead of blurting out my questions. I sensed that Katya was feeling the same way.

"We have made some progress," Avraham said. He looked at Katya. "We believe your husband may be a hostage."

"Why?" she said.

"Where?" I said.

"We do not know why or where, yet" he said, "but we are taking the necessary steps to find out as soon as possible."

"Then what leads you to believe he's a hostage?" Katya asked. "What brought about that conclusion?"

"It is not a conclusion, but we have picked up some—" He turned to his assistant and spoke in Hebrew.

"Chatter," the assistant said.

Avraham turned back and addressed Katya again. "We have what is called 'chatter' from cafés, the Internet, and other sources that lead us to think we are dealing with a kidnapping."

"What kind of chatter?" I asked. "Who is saying this?"

He didn't even acknowledge me. I caught what may have been an apologetic glance from the assistant, but Avraham clearly wasn't concerned with my questions.

"Right now that is all the information we have. But we will need you to sign some forms."

"Forms?" Katya echoed.

"Yes." He produced some papers from the folder on the table and slid them across the surface, positioning them in front of Katya. The assistant placed a pen on the table near the papers.

THE QUEST

She picked up the papers. "What are these?"

"We are asking for your permission, um, should the opportunity arise, to plan and execute a rescue operation."

"Rescue operation?" She looked at me, as if for help.

"Where is he?" I asked, pressing my hands hard against the table top. "Why is this necessary? What do you think has happened to him?"

Avraham sighed and pressed his lips together into a hard, straight line. The assistant leaned forward and spread his hands out in front of him, almost in a pleading gesture. "Truly, we do not know. It is simply a case that, because it looks like it may be a kidnapping, it would be, um, wise to have your permission ahead of time. Then we do not have to hesitate if, in the future, more is discovered and an opportunity is presented."

Katya lifted her eyes from the pages and pinned her gaze on the assistant. "Mr. Yadin, is that right?"

I was amazed that she remembered his name. I sure didn't.

He smiled. "Yes, that is right."

"Why would anyone kidnap my husband?" Her tone was plaintive, pleading.

I thought I could see genuine compassion in his eyes, though Mr. Avraham only appeared impatient for this business to be completed. "Incidents of kidnapping are becoming more and more common, all around the world. Westerners—and Americans in particular—are popular targets, because many militant groups believe they have access to resources that others do not have."

"So," she said, slowly, "you think he was kidnapped because he is American."

"I do not know," Yadin said.

"If that is the case, do you think he is alive?"

"I do not know that either. But most hostages do survive, even hostages of the most extreme groups."

Katya's poise amazed me. I wanted to cry, scream, throw something. But she continued, speaking in a measured tone, her voice neither quivering nor cracking with emotion. "And what is the most likely way to gain his release—in your experience?"

"It depends on the country where the kidnapping occurs—"

"This country," she said. "I want to know about this country."

"It also depends on the country the hostage is from. Each government approaches the problem differently, and no one has yet designed any kind of coordinated response."

Avraham and I were no longer participants, but spectators. We observed Katya's determined interview of Mr. Yadin like spectators at a tennis match.

"Mr. Yadin," she said patiently. "If my husband is a hostage, we know the country in which he was taken—this one—and we know also the country the hostage is from—the United States. So, based on what we know, how is his release most likely to happen?"

Yadin glanced at Avraham, then at me, then back at Katya. "The American government does not negotiate with kidnappers, and they do not pay ransoms. So, in most cases, the hostage's family or company empty their bank accounts, sell their cars and homes, and leverage everything they possess in order to meet the kidnappers' demands." He glanced at Avraham. "However, we do not advocate such a course of action."

"Why not?" I asked.

"Every time a ransom is paid and a life is saved, it encourages the next kidnapping."

"I don't care about the next kidnapping," I said, standing up and leaning on the table. "I only care about this one."

"I understand. But if you plan to pay a ransom, there is not so much need for a security company."

"Not so much—"

THE QUEST

"Mr. Yadin," Katya said, placing a hand on one of mine and speaking calmly. "How do you get a hostage freed, if there's no ransom paid?"

The two men exchanged a short glance. Then the assistant spoke. "Snatch and grab," he said, before going on to explain that sometimes other exchanges are arranged, exchanges that don't involve money.

"What kind of exchange?" I asked, sitting again.

"Prisoners. Medical supplies. Vehicles. Those sorts of things."

"But we have no more access to those things than we do to money," Katya protested.

"But we do," Yadin said.

Suddenly the room fell silent. Katya looked at me. I was still working to control my anger.

She lifted the papers and looked over them. "If I sign these, would we be contacted before you do anything?"

"If it is possible," Yadin said. "We will of course keep you informed every step of the way. But there may come a moment when we cannot delay but must act when there is the best probability of success."

Katya looked at me. "What do you think?"

I bit my lip. "I don't know."

"I won't sign if you don't think I should."

I looked away, stared at a potted plant in the corner of the room. It wasn't fair. I wasn't yet used to the awful feeling of not knowing where my dad was or if he was okay. So just like that, I'm supposed to accept that he might be—*might be*—a hostage somewhere, but we don't know where. And if we find out where, we might launch some kind of half-baked military—*what did he call it?*—snatch-and-grab operation that could place him in more danger than he was to begin with? I'm just supposed to nod and say "Okey dokey"? That seemed to be the expectation.

Then again, if my dad *was* a hostage, I wanted the right people—skilled people—to do whatever they had to do to free him. I didn't want it to have to wait on a phone call, a signature, or anything like that. I would not want a second's delay—not a moment's hesitation.

"Can we take a day or two to think about it?" Katya asked.

Yadin answered. "Yes, of course."

I shook my head. "No, just sign the papers."

CHAPTER 39

We sat in Katya's car. Neither of us had spoken since leaving the CID offices. She made no move to start the car. We both just sat there, staring out the windshield.

The silence lasted several minutes, until I finally said, "How are you doing?"

She answered without turning to look at me. "I don't know. You?"

"I don't know either."

A few more silent moments followed. Finally, she reached for the ignition, started the car, and put it in gear. Before backing out, though, she turned to me. "I think I could use some strong coffee or tea. Does that sound good to you?"

I shrugged. "Sure."

She drove, and after only a few minutes, she swung the little car sharply and, bouncing off the curb, landed us in a tight parking space beside the stone walls of Jerusalem's Old City. "Let's go," she said.

I climbed out of the car and stared like a tourist. The large white stones of the city walls stretched in both directions. Katya pointed to the walls on our right.

"That's Migdal David. The Tower of David complex." She went on to say it was a fortress that dated back to the second century. "It was named the Tower of David by Crusaders, who thought it was the palace of King David."

"It's not?"

She shook her head. "No, but it's still full of history."

It was like nothing I'd ever seen. A massive wall enclosing a teeming city. As we walked along the walls, Katya pointed out pock marks in the surface, which became more numerous and noticeable as we approached the entrance.

"Those are bullet marks from the 1948 war for Israel's independence. The fighting in and around this area was especially fierce."

She guided me through a broad gate in the wall that she said was called the Jaffa Gate, because the road from there pointed toward the port city of Jaffa, or Joppa. "Close to where you landed in Tel Aviv," she explained.

Inside the gate, where a mishmash of people and cars, carts, and bicycles pointed every which way, we quickly sat down at a table outside a café. Immediately, a waiter was there to take our orders. We each ordered coffee, but Katya specified "American coffee," asking also for a pot of hot water.

"The coffee here is very strong," she said. "And even if you order 'American coffee,' which is watered down somewhat, it's still too strong for me. So I always order hot water with my coffee, and then I dilute it until it tastes less like tar."

We watched the activity in the area. It was all so fascinating, and so … foreign, to me, of course. Two soldiers with rifles slung over their shoulders. An Orthodox Jew dressed in black with a big boxy hat. Women in scarves and some in robes that covered them from head to toe. Students wearing backpacks. Tourists taking pictures. As we watched, a noisy procession following a black-robed priest holding a large gold cross came down one street and turned up another.

"Who are they?" I asked Katya just as the waiter arrived with our coffees and hot water.

She thanked him and then answered me. "Armenian Orthodox Christians. They do that a lot. I think they are on their way to the Church of the Holy Sepulchre."

"What's that?"

She sipped her coffee and made a face. "The Church of the Holy Sepulchre?"

I nodded.

"That's the church built over the site where Jesus was crucified and buried. It's ancient."

"Wow," I said. I stirred some of the water into my coffee cup and tasted it. It was still way too strong. More water.

"It takes a while sometimes, before it's drinkable."

We sat again in silence for awhile, each of us doctoring our coffee, until Katya said, "That was a hard meeting—at CID."

I didn't respond. I added a little more water and took a sip. That was more like it.

"I hated to sign those papers, but—"

"Can we talk about something else?" I said.

"Okay. Like what?"

"Anything," I said. "Anything but that."

We fell into silence for the next few moments. After a few minutes, she made a suggestion.

"I could pick up where we left off last night. If you're still interested."

"What do you mean?"

"Our conversation about why I read the Bible. Why I trust it."

"Oh, yeah, that …" A young boy—he couldn't have been more than twelve years old—pushed a huge cart filled with crates of tomatoes, leafy lettuce, cucumbers, and other vegetables past our table. It wouldn't hurt to be distracted for a while from the stress of that meeting. "I guess that'd be all right," I said, lifting the cup to my lips again.

"I don't want to bore you," she said.

"I don't mind."

"Oh," she said, stretching the word out dramatically. "So I did bore you last night."

"That's not what I meant."

She winked. I smiled. Then she stood up from her chair, fished some money out of her pocket and slid it under her cup and saucer.

"Tell you what. Finish your coffee and come with me," she said.

"Where to?" I asked. There wasn't much coffee in my cup anyway so I left it.

"You'll see."

She led me back to the car, where she unlocked the door and reached into the back seat. She pulled out a small stack of papers and handed half of the stack to me.

"We might as well start handing these out."

I looked at the page on top. Dad smiled at me from a large black-and-white photo. Above his picture, in large block letters, was the word "MISSING." Listed under the photo was his name, age, height, hair and eye color, and a phone number, with an appeal to call with any information regarding him. It promised a reward: 15,000 NIS.

"What does NIS mean?" I asked.

"New Israeli Shekel."

"Oh. How much is fifteen thousand?"

"About four thousand dollars."

"Are these the flyers you posted at bus stops?"

"Yes, bus stops, store windows, anywhere I could."

We walked back through the gate and into the Old City. "Think it'll work?"

"I have no idea. But it can't hurt."

"You still haven't told me where we're going," I said.

"I know. It's not far. And along the way, we'll hand out these flyers and hope for the best."

She led me past the café and down a narrow street. "This is King David Street. It runs all the way from the Jaffa Gate to the Kotel—the Western Wall and the Temple Mount."

We passed one tiny shop after another, all crammed together. Guitars, mandolins, mats, clothing, rugs, toys, bowls, pitchers, pipes, lamps, chess sets, checker boards, all manner of items hung from the ceilings and filled the shelves and store windows. As we walked side by side, we offered the flyers to shopkeepers and tourists and people just passing by. Most refused them, of course, but many took them. Several times, Katya stopped and talked to people, asking them to take several copies and help us spread the word. Once, she even saw someone she knew and called out to her by name. The woman listened politely and took a flyer with her when we parted.

At various times, the constant flow of traffic around us made it difficult to stay together, and we would wait until a handcart passed or an opening appeared. Slowly, however, we threaded our way through the constant current of people that jammed the street, handing out the flyers until they were all gone. A few sharp turns and a couple of minutes later and we apparently had arrived at our destination. Katya stopped at a railing and turned to me.

I gripped the railing and looked around. I didn't spot anything I thought warranted her excitement. "What did you want to show me?"

"This," she said, sweeping her arm to indicate a long pile of rocks we could look down on from where we stood.

"This?"

"This is part of my answer to your question last night."

"About how you can believe the Bible?"

"Yes. This is what is known as the 'Broad Wall.' It's the remains of a fortified part of the city wall, built in the eighth century BC."

"That's a wall?"

"Yes," she said. She moved around me. "Step over here. You can see it better from this angle."

I followed her and she was right. It was clearly part of a wall. Looking down on it, as we were, it was easy to see that the top of the wall would have been wide enough for one of the merchant's carts I'd seen in the Old City to roll along its length. "But it's in the middle of the city."

"Now it is, yes. But when it was built, this was as far as the walled city of Jerusalem went. And, as you can see, street level in those days was quite a bit lower than street level today. We're literally standing on top of several millennia of history."

"Okay, but I still don't get why it's a big deal to you."

She smiled. "It's the closest place I can think of to actually *show* you the third reason I trust the Bible so much. It's just one example I've seen where a new discovery of some kind supports the accuracy of the Bible, even though in many cases scholars and experts have long doubted it.

"The wall was built during the days of King Hezekiah, who is talked about in the Old Testament. It was intended to protect the city against the Assyrians, who besieged Jerusalem but failed to conquer it. The work it took to build it is mentioned in the book of Isaiah, and the wall itself, by its name, the 'Broad Wall,' is mentioned in the book of Nehemiah."

I shook my head. "Okay, sure, but I'm still not getting it."

"There's not that much to get. My point is simply that the words recorded in the Bible, about Hezekiah's building project and Nehemiah's mention of the Broad Wall, were confirmed—after two thousand years underground—by an archaeological discovery that was made right here in 1970. And you're looking at it."

"Oh, okay, then. I get it. I guess that's kind of cool."

"It is—at least to me. What you're seeing with your very own eyes is a physical, visual confirmation of the trustworthiness of the biblical record. I brought you here, to the Broad Wall, simply because it's convenient. It was—what—maybe a twenty minute walk from our café, even with us passing out the flyers along the way. But I would love to show you other examples sometime."

"Yeah, okay. Sure," I said. I wasn't particularly interested in seeing more, at least not until I knew my dad was okay, but Katya was on a roll.

"For example, there's Hezekiah's tunnel, which isn't far from here, but completely underground. The Bible tells how, seven hundred years before Jesus was born, an Assyrian army was invading the area around here. The Assyrians had already totally conquered everything north of here. The king in Jerusalem at that time was a man named Hezekiah, and he knew that once the Assyrians got to Jerusalem, they would lay siege to the city, choke off their water and food supply, and basically starve them until they surrendered. To make matters worse, the main water supply for the city at that time was the Gihon Spring, which was *outside* the city walls.

"So King Hezekiah had workers start at two different points, digging underground, one outside the walls at the Gihon Spring and the other inside the walls at the Pool of Siloam, about a third of a mile apart. They dug through solid rock and, amazingly, met in the middle, completing the tunnel. Once that was done, they covered and disguised the original entrance to the Gihon Spring, so the Assyrian army wouldn't even know it was there. So not only did the people of Jerusalem survive the siege, but the Bible says God answered their prayers by sending disaster on the enemy camp, causing the Assyrian king and his army to go home with their tails between their legs, basically.

"But the best part is this: While scholars never doubted the existence of the tunnel, some believed the Bible was wrong when it described it as being dug in Hezekiah's day. They thought it was completed much closer to Jesus' time. But about fifty years after the tunnel itself was discovered, in eighteen-hundred-something, an inscription was found at the point where the two teams met in the middle. And the writing in the inscription was conclusively dated to the time of King Hezekiah. Once again, the Bible account was vindicated. And today, you can actually walk through the tunnel. You can navigate the turn in the walls where the two teams met in the middle. And you can see the spot on the wall where the workers chiseled that inscription about their accomplishment."

"Huh. You're right, that'd be great to see sometime," I said, hoping she'd take the hint that I was ready to start back, but she didn't.

"This country is full of things like that. Like, in Caesarea, on the Mediterranean coast, a limestone block with an inscription on it that ended centuries of scholarly debate about Pontius Pilate, the Roman governor who presided over the civil trial of Jesus. At one time scholars doubted that Pilate ever really existed, because there had been no archaeological evidence of his existence."

"Until that limestone block."

"Exactly right. And I've seen that happen over and over. There used to be scholars who thought that King David, the shepherd king of Israel, was a mythical figure, like King Arthur of England. But then, in 1993, an archeologist discovered a fragment of a stone monument that had inscriptions that referred to King David and his dynasty. In fact, you can hardly take a step here in Israel without running into something that corresponds to places, events, and people the Bible describes."

"So, the people who say the Bible is all a bunch of myths ..."

"I can't believe they've ever been to Israel," she said with a smile.

CHAPTER 40

I took one last glance at the Broad Wall as we started our walk back to where we had parked the car. I tried to wrap my brain around the fact that I was looking at something that had been built almost three thousand years ago and had been hidden under dirt and rubble until recently. It was there all the time, waiting to be discovered.

I was glad to be moving again. "I thought you said there were four reasons."

"About what?"

"You know, last night, when I asked you how you could believe all that stuff in the Bible. Didn't you say there were four reasons?"

"Oh, yes, I did," she said.

"So what's number four?"

She didn't answer immediately, and I was momentarily distracted by the sight of a man carrying two live chickens, upside down, holding them by their feet. For a moment, I wasn't sure she had heard my question in the cacophony of the crowded street.

"I'm not sure I can adequately express it," she said, finally. "But I'll try." She inhaled deeply, and we started walking more slowly past the shops and businesses that seemed to spill right into each other. "It's like the notebook I gave you about your father's disappearance. How much of that did you read?"

"All of it," I said, a little surprised by the question.

"Right. I thought so. Why?"

"Why?" I was even more surprised by that question. "Well, because, I want to find my dad."

"And when you were reading it, turning pages and so on … what kind of thoughts or emotions did you experience?"

"Wow, just a whole lot of different things. I felt closer to him just by reading. I guess it made me miss him even more—a lot of things."

She was nodding as I spoke. "Exactly. That is much like what happens to me when I read the Bible." She stopped walking. I did, too. I watched her, and her brow furrowed. "See, I believe the Bible was written for one main reason, to help us have a relationship with God. It's not a history book or a science manual. It's like that notebook; it's intended to draw me closer to God and help me to learn about him and his ways. And the more I read it, the more it does that.

"The words in the Bible are not just words on a page to me. They're part of the conversation between my Father and me. My heart responds to them, and honestly, it seems like much of the time those words—and the God who speaks them to me—know exactly what I need, when I need it.

"So, while the other things I've talked about—the internal evidences, the documentary evidence, and the external evidences like archaeology—those have played a part in building my confidence, in showing me just how amazing the Bible is. But the biggest reason I trust it, the main reason, is because of what it does to me and for me. No other book—and I've read a lot—conveys my Father's words to me. But that book does."

Her eyes were actually misty as she finished speaking. She smiled self-consciously and said, "Thanks for asking."

We started to walk again, slowly. Neither of us spoke for a few moments, until I said, "It took you long enough to answer."

She glanced at me, threw her head back, and laughed out loud.

American Missionary Found Slain

 EMAIL   PRINT   + SHARE

A 23-year-old American woman visiting Israel was found slain in the Amud Stream Nature Reserve in Galilee yesterday.

Marian Wilkinson had been stabbed to death less than 24 hours prior to the discovery of her body, according to Israel Police. She had been reported missing on Monday by a friend and colleague at Christian Mission to Israel (CMI), an organization she had been working for since arriving in Israel last December.

According to the CMI website, Wilkinson had planned to move to Israel since visiting Jerusalem on a 2009 study tour. Israel Police believe that Wilkinson was hiking when she was attacked by more than one assailant. Police spokesman Albert Basevi said authorities are treating the attack as politically motivated, though the motivation has not been confirmed. No suspects have been identified, and there has been no claim of responsibility, leading Basevi to conjecture that the attack was a crime of opportunity rather than the work of a militant group.

Anyone with information about this crime is requested to contact Albert Basevi at the Israel Police office of Public Information, 02-5439615.

CHAPTER 41

As we continued our walk back to the Jaffa Gate and the car, we went at a more leisurely pace than our dash to the Broad Wall. Much of the time, I walked behind Katya, as there was frequently no room to walk side by side because of the crowds threading their way along the narrow lane between the shops. The street was paved with stone, and overhead was an arched roof, so that although our surroundings felt like an outdoor street, we could not tell—except with an occasional glance down a side street—whether the sky was clear or cloudy.

Suddenly, Katya pulled her cell phone from her pocket. It was ringing. She looked at it and stopped.

"It's one of our friends from church." She put the phone to her ear and greeted someone named Sylvia. We kept walking as she talked. From time to time I heard her thank Sylvia for her concern and tell her that we still didn't know anything. Walking in single file, there was no practical way for us to maintain eye contact with each other, so Katya would occasionally glance back to make sure I still followed. We were seldom more than a few yards apart, but once in a while a tourist or shopper would come between us, and Katya would step aside and wait for that person to pass so I could catch up again. This went on for some time. But just after she had faced forward again after checking on me, I felt a hand grab my arm and pull me into one of the shops.

The man who held my forearm smiled broadly from under a mustache. "Hello," he said. "You are American, yes? Come see my shop. I show you very good deals."

THE QUEST

I tried to pull away, but his grip was too tight. "No, thank you," I said.

He gripped my arm even tighter, and I found myself in a narrow aisle, shelves on each side stretching from the floor to the ceiling, stuffed with what looked like scarves and skirts and other articles of clothing.

"I have beautiful things for you. You like beautiful things?"

I looked back toward the arched doorway to the shop, and he had pulled me far enough down the aisle that I could no longer see the street. I looked in the opposite direction and saw that we seemed to be heading toward a doorway at the back, separated from the store by a curtain.

"No!" I said, emphatically. "I'm with someone."

"You are very beautiful; you should have beautiful things," he said. A sharp edge had crept into his voice, and he moved his hand farther up my arm for a tighter grip. He was hurting me. It felt as if he could have broken my arm if he had twisted his hand ever so slightly.

Suddenly, Israel didn't seem so safe.

I looked around desperately for Katya, hoping she had seen me disappear into the shop. I was convinced this was not just a hard-sell tactic, but that I was in real danger.

A man stepped into view at the front of the shop. He looked like he could be American or perhaps European. His back was to us, and he seemed to be examining a piece of cloth.

"Sweetheart!" I yelled. "There you are!" I waved in his direction.

The man turned, and I felt the shopkeeper's grip loosen. I quickly ripped my arm out of his grasp and hurried up the aisle without looking back to see if the shopkeeper followed. I kept talking.

"I can't take my eyes off you for a second, can I?" I said, loudly.

The man stared at me without moving. As I approached, he said, "Are you talking to me?"

I dashed past him and out into the street. "Katya!" I called. "Katya!"

Without looking behind me, I headed in the direction I had last seen her, and then I heard a voice behind me.

"Emma!"

I turned around.

"Where were you?" she said.

"Where were *you*?" I sobbed, before feeling myself crumple into her arms.

She threw her arm around my shoulder and kept it there all the way back through the Jaffa Gate and to our parking spot. Neither of us spoke another word until we were seated inside and the doors were locked.

She turned to me without starting the car. "What happened back there?"

I was still crying and shaking all over. I did my best to tell her.

"Emma, I'm so, so sorry. I should never have let you out of my sight, not even for a minute. The merchants can be really aggressive, especially here in the souk. And I should've warned you, when they see red hair and fair skin like yours, they know you're not from around here."

I couldn't stop crying.

"I know how forward those men can be."

"He wasn't being forward!" I shouted. "He was—he was—" I didn't know exactly how to finish that sentence, but I knew she would never understand how threatened, how terrified I had felt.

"What, Emma? Tell me. What did he do to you?"

I shook my head. "Nothing. He didn't do anything. He just wouldn't let go of me. He kept pulling me back, farther and farther into his shop, and there was a room at the back, and—" I put my face in my hands.

"I'm so sorry."

"I just—I wish my dad was here."

THE QUEST

"I know. I do, too."

"You don't know," I said. I cursed her, loudly. "You don't know what it's like. You have no idea. You haven't lost a father, have you? The only man in your life, really? The only man you ever trusted? The only one you could ever count on for protection? You haven't watched him marry some stranger and move far away with her, as if you never existed. And then to have him disappear? To not know anything about where he is, and if he's even—even alive? So that you have to go to some stupid country thinking you're going to do something, you're going to find him, but you can't, you can't do anything! You can't do anything." The sobs threatened to choke me. I struggled to breathe.

We sat. I don't know how long we sat, until I said, "Just take me back to the apartment."

Katya started the car, and moments later we were behind locked doors again. But I still didn't feel safe.

CHAPTER 42

While Katya fixed a simple, cold lunch, I lay down on the bed. I knew I was feeling sorry for myself, but I didn't care. My dad was missing. No one knew where he was or even if he was alive. I was half a world away from home, where the only person I knew was my dad's wife, and I'd never been crazy about her. And I'd just been assaulted and felt like I'd narrowly escaped something much worse. My life had turned upside down, and I just wanted it all to go away. I wanted my life back. I wanted my dad back. I wanted to close my eyes and open them again onto a world I knew, a world I could handle.

Katya soon called me and we ate a light lunch together—mostly tomatoes and cucumbers—mostly in silence. Then Katya asked me a question.

"What do you think about CID?"

"CID? What about them?"

"I know I signed the papers, but I want to know if you think we're doing the right thing."

"I don't know."

"I don't mean just with the rescue papers, I mean the whole thing. Do you think we should keep moving forward with CID?"

I rolled my eyes. "I don't know. I don't really know what choice we have. What are the alternatives?"

"That's just it. I don't know of any. Not one. And they did come with Tom and Stella's recommendation."

THE QUEST

"Maybe we're just freaked out because they said Dad's a hostage."

"And because Mr. Avraham has absolutely *no* social skills."

I smiled. "At least his sidekick got onto your wavelength after a while."

"Only after you nearly climbed onto the table to get at him."

I laughed then. Actually laughed. It felt ... good. "I did, didn't I?"

"I was proud of you," she said.

I looked away. I knew I'd been really unkind to her just a little while ago. I felt bad about that, but I knew she couldn't understand what I'd been going through—what I was still going through. How could she? Her life, at least until Dad disappeared, had seemed perfect to me. A sweet wedding. A caring husband. A naïve kind of faith. I knew it wasn't her fault, but I resented her for not having suffered like I had. "Thanks," I said. "You did okay, too—the way you kept your cool."

She arched her eyebrows. "Maybe we make a pretty good team."

I smiled. "Maybe we do," I said.

An awkward moment passed between us. Finally, I said, "So what happens now?"

"We have a lot of work to do," Katya said.

"Like what?"

We carried the lunch dishes into the kitchen, and she started filling the sink with water.

"You wash by hand?" I asked.

"The old-fashioned way," she said.

"Wow. I've never done that."

"You're kidding."

"No. We've always had a dishwasher, I guess."

She set a drainer and rack on the counter, and handed me a towel. "I'll wash, you dry?"

I shrugged. "Sure. So what do you think happens next?"

"I think we're back to my earlier plan, only on a slightly different schedule. We can get started today with whatever fundraising efforts we can muster, and then maybe when those are well under way, we start talking to people, conducting our own research in the area, distributing flyers like we did this morning. Unless you have a better idea."

I had no ideas at all, so we agreed to follow her plan, at least until something better occurred to us or more news came from CID. While she washed and I dried, we brainstormed initial ideas for raising funds, until I darted into the next room to grab a pencil and notebook from her little command center. Between drying the dishes and, later, putting them away, we compiled a decent little list. Before long, she was seated again at the table, and I folded my legs beneath me on the couch. Each of us had a note pad and pen in one hand and a cell phone in the other. She started by calling her friends at the institute, and I began by calling Artie back in Ohio.

He sounded so glad to hear my voice, and I was unspeakably glad to hear his. He sounded to my ears like an oasis in the desert must look to a weary traveler. I tried to fill him in on everything that had happened as quickly as possible. While I had only been in Israel a few days, it felt like weeks. And it seemed so very long ago since I had spoken to such a friendly voice. Eventually, though, I knew I needed to get down to business.

"I need your help, Artie," I said.

"Anything. You know that."

"I need to raise money."

"How much?"

"Not from you. I need as much as I can possibly raise." I told him about CID but not about the financial aspect of it all.

"Are we talking thousands, or tens of thousands, or—what?"

"Tens, at least. It's impossible to tell right now, because there is so much we don't know. And we don't know how long it'll be before Dad is found—or even … even if he will be found."

"He will be found, Red, I'm sure of it," Artie said. It was so good to hear him call me that.

"I really hope so," I said, trying not to get emotional.

"So, we're talking tens of thousands. I guess that kind of messes up my bake sale idea."

"You're a rotten baker, anyway," I said.

"You got a better idea?"

"Lots of them. First, I'm going to compile a list of every family member I can think of. I don't have many—"

"I have a lot. I'll add my family to your list."

"Okay. And then I'm going to have to get you a letter to send out to everyone on the list, asking them to give to the cause."

"Who are they going to write checks to?" he asked.

"Katya's working on that. She thinks we can somehow receive the funds through her agency, Sar Shalom Institute. They're nonprofit and everything."

"Okay. What about the university?"

"What about it?"

"You have a lot of friends there—classmates and professors. You're still officially a student, aren't you?"

"Yeah, as far as I know."

"I would think the school could really get behind this thing. Maybe we can get it into the newspapers and really get some wind behind it, you know?"

"Wait a minute, Artie," I said. "CID—the security company—says that publicity is a bad idea. They had us sign a form promising to avoid publicity, because if Dad is a hostage, any publicity will just make his captors think he's worth more money, and it could prolong his captivity."

"Wow. That makes it seem so real."

"It *is* real, Artie."

"I know, Red. I'm sorry. I'm just so sorry this is happening—"

"Don't go there," I said firmly. "If you get me started crying, I swear, I will fly back home and hunt you down—" My voice quivered at the mention of home, and I started to cry without Artie's help.

"Okay, but there still have to be a lot of ways to get the university involved. I'll look into that," he said.

"Thanks," I said. Not only for his idea but also for changing the subject as quickly as he had.

"What else can I do?" he asked.

I think my answer shocked both of us. "Pray," I said.

After I hung up from Artie, Katya signaled to me. She stood from her chair at the table, and I could tell she was wrapping up her conversation as quickly as possible. When she hung up, she set the phone on the table and took a few steps in my direction.

"Sar Shalom said our insurance policy is no help, and they didn't think their financial person would like the idea of having people give to us through them. But they have already pledged to pay our first five thousand dollars of expenses. So that's something!"

"That's great," I said.

"And I was just talking to my sister in the States, and she's going to start contacting people."

"Do you have just the one sister?"

She nodded.

"What about your parents?"

She flashed a sad smile. "They're both gone."

"Gone?"

A tiny nod. "They died. When I was in college."

"Oh," I said. "I'm sorry."

The next words were out of my mouth before I knew what I was even saying. I could have kicked myself for asking the question, before I even finished asking it.

THE QUEST

"How did they die?"

She lowered her head. I thought she was looking at the floor. She lifted her head, and I saw tears in her eyes.

I felt trapped by my own stupidity—and curiosity. I had obviously stepped in it. But I didn't know how to ... *un*-step in it, so I just waited.

She looked at me. For a moment, she didn't even look like herself. She seemed like another person. "They were the victims of a home invasion. They were both tied up and beaten. My mother was raped and killed. My father had to watch. He killed himself less than a month later."

I felt my mouth hanging open, but I couldn't close it. I couldn't move. I could barely breathe.

"My sister and I are all the family we have left. And now, you and your father, of course."

I suddenly remembered her and Dad's wedding. Her sister—who didn't look anything like her—was in the ceremony, but Katya walked down the aisle alone. No one gave her away. I had never thought much of it, I guess, because—well, because she was older than the typical bride. But I realized only now that my assumptions had been wrong. Wrong in a lot of ways. I cringed at the thought of the accusatory things I had said to her since I arrived in Israel, all because I thought I had it so much worse than she did.

I had been holding my breath, but suddenly I inhaled sharply. "I—I'm sorry," I said. "I shouldn't have—"

"It's okay. There's never a good time to share information like that."

I nodded. That sure sounded like absolute truth.

Georgetown Couple Victims of Fatal Home Invasion

✉ EMAIL   🖨 PRINT   + SHARE

GEORGETOWN, SC—Georgetown police are requesting help from citizens in solving a brutal home invasion, beating, rape, and murder in the area.

Police were summoned to the 1800 block of Eastman Pines on Monday. Investigators say the couple, Clifford Hopkins, 49, and his wife, Darya, 47, were found bound and severely beaten. Mr. Hopkins was unconscious and tied to a chair. He later told police that two armed, masked men had broken into the home, subdued the couple, robbed them, and then brutalized them. According to investigators, Mrs. Hopkins had been raped and stabbed repeatedly, resulting in her death.

There has been no arrest to date, and police have not yet identified any suspects. Georgetown police spokesperson Angela McDermott said the homicide department is in charge of the investigation. She asked that anyone with knowledge of the attack call Crime Stoppers at 843-567-CASH. Callers will be issued an ID number and they will remain anonymous. In addition, a secure website, http://www.crimestopper-sc.org, allows visitors to the site to anonymously provide information on this crime and any others.

CHAPTER 43

We fell silent. Katya stood just a few feet from me, and I remained in my position on the couch. There was nothing I could say or do to force a rewind to get back to the moment before I asked her that horrible question. I'd felt disoriented since arriving in Israel, and now my sense of confusion had increased. I'd come to this place feeling resentful toward Katya. And I'd been holding onto that feeling, assuming things about her that simply weren't true.

I'd thought she was this sheltered beauty who had never experienced the depths of hurt that I was suffering—partly *because* of her, I told myself. To top it off, I felt like I was falling apart while she seemed so steady in the face of all that was happening. Several times I had retreated to the bedroom to cry, while she had lounged in a chair, reading her Bible. I had translated that into … I don't know what. An assumption that she wasn't suffering because I couldn't see it? But it was more than that. It was the idea that she had never really suffered. Because, if she had, how could she sit there and read her Bible? How could she believe in a God of love?

That was it. I had a mental impression of her based on the fact that she believed in God. I couldn't see how anyone could believe in God, with all the suffering that goes on in the world. But to believe in God after what had happened to her parents? After going through something like that? It made no sense. And how could she believe in him *now*, with Dad—her husband—missing, dead, or enduring God knows what?

THE QUEST

She still stood a few feet away, watching me. I didn't want to open the subject of her parents again ... but I did. It suddenly felt as if we could never really be close, never really understand each other if I didn't get an answer to my question. So I asked it.

"How can you still believe in God," I said, shaking my head slowly back and forth, "after all that?"

She didn't answer quickly, for which I was grateful. She moved to the couch and sat next to me. "That's not quite the way it happened for me," she said.

"What do you mean?"

"I believed in God even before my parents died, though I didn't have a relationship with Jesus. So when ... they ... died, I didn't struggle with the question of God's existence. I struggled with the question of his goodness."

"Isn't that the same thing?" I asked.

She shook her head. "No, definitely not."

"I don't understand," I said.

"Like I said, I believed in God. Partly because earlier I had figured out that the person who *doesn't* believe in God has just as big a problem when it comes to issues of good and evil as the person who *does* believe in God."

"I'm not following you."

She pursed her lips for a few seconds. "Okay, bear with me. I don't know if I can say this in a way that makes sense, but I'll give it a whirl."

"All right."

"There is both good and evil in the world we live in. Right?"

"Right."

"One person may say, 'I can't believe in God because there is so much evil and suffering in the world.'"

I agreed.

"But the same evidence that could be used to refute the existence of God could also be used to support his existence."

"How?" She was making no sense to me.

"The presence of evil in the world can argue just as much—maybe more—for the existence of God than against it. And it is not just the existence of evil and suffering that presents a philosophical problem; the existence of good does, too. It just presents the opposite problem."

"I don't get that at all," I said.

"Stick with me. I may not be doing a very good job, but I'll keep trying." She smiled broadly. "I may not be smart, but I'm persistent."

"Yeah, okay," I said sarcastically. I was starting to think she was plenty smart.

"If there is no God, then we live in a world of evolutionary cause and effect. Every creature, every species, has one job: to survive."

"Sure," I said, shrugging.

"In that world, there is no right and wrong attached to an animal that kills or brutalizes another animal. The strong survive. The weak suffer. End of story. It's not wrong for a lion to kill and eat a giraffe. It's just the way things are, right?"

"I guess," I said.

"You guess? How else can it be?"

"I don't know. I guess it can't."

"Right, it can't be otherwise. That's what natural selection is all about. The survival of the fittest. Every many for himself."

She looked at me. I said nothing.

"In that world," she continued, "the man who did such terrible things to my parents did nothing wrong."

"Wait a minute. That can't be right."

"Why not?"

"Because," I said, not knowing what I would say next. "Because it's just not."

THE QUEST

"Why … not?" she insisted.

"Because there is no way what happened to your mom and dad could be right. *No way.*"

"I agree." She said that as if it was the end of our discussion, as if something had been settled.

"But—"

"But what?"

"But that's not what you were just saying!" I protested.

"You mean when I was describing a world of pure evolutionary cause and effect?"

"Yes! You said in that kind of world the man who killed your mom did nothing wrong."

"In that kind of world, yes. But that's not what you were arguing. You argued that there was no way what he did could be called right."

"I know!"

"And I agreed with that."

She was starting to make me mad. "You're talking in circles!"

"No," she said, shaking her head. "I don't think I am. I'm simply saying that I find it impossible to view that man's actions from a purely naturalistic, evolutionary viewpoint. If I come to the conclusion that there is no God, then that man was no more or less than a fulfillment of Darwinian ethics: The strong survive, and the weak suffer. In that worldview, he was not wrong for being strong, any more than my parents were wrong for having suffered."

Her voice quivered just a little as she spoke that last phrase. But she continued: "My point is, I am not willing to come to that conclusion. That is much too much for me to believe."

I was stunned. All at once, I saw her point. I jumped up from the couch and took a minute to pace around the room, thinking. "So you're saying," I said, processing, "that you think the evil that happened to your parents … actually helps you to believe in God?"

"In his existence, at least, yes."

"Because otherwise, then what happened to them is neither good nor evil."

She smiled. "Exactly. And I *know* that what happened to them … is evil."

From the Georgetown Herald website

Victim of Recent Home Invasion Takes His Own Life

✉ EMAIL   🖨 PRINT   + SHARE

GEORGETOWN, SC—Clifford Hopkins, 49, the victim of a brutal home invasion last month that claimed the life of his wife of 23 years, took his own life last night.

Hopkins and his wife, Darya, 47, were robbed and beaten in their Eastman Pines home by two armed intruders on March 27. Darya Hopkins was reportedly raped and murdered while her husband was forced to watch. Funeral services for her were held March 30 at Franklin Funeral Home in Westover. Funeral arrangements for Clifford Hopkins have not been announced.

Hopkins is survived by two daughters, Elena and Katya. Both women attend Wesleyan College in Tennessee.

Georgetown Police ask that anyone with knowledge of the home invasion call Crime Stoppers at 843-567-CASH. Callers will be issued an ID number and will remain anonymous. In addition, a secure website, http://www.crimestopper-sc.org, allows visitors to the site to anonymously provide information on this crime and any others.

CHAPTER 44

My head was spinning. I felt like my world had just turned upside down. As if the sky had become green and the grass blue. "Wow," I said, still pacing. "I think I get it. I see what you're saying."

"Good. But I'm not done."

I stopped pacing and looked at her.

"It's not just that I can't look at what happened to my parents and say, 'Oh, well, you know, he was strong, they were weak, that's just the way things are.' It works the other way around, too."

"What do you mean?"

"Like I said, the existence of good would be a problem for me if God didn't exist."

I sat on the couch again. "Ohhhkay," I said. "Walk me through it."

She chuckled. "It's basically the other side of the same coin. In a world of pure evolutionary cause and effect, there's no sensible way to understand a person who, say, doesn't cheat on an exam. Or doesn't cheat on his wife."

"Sure there is. He's afraid of getting caught."

"Well, okay, I'll give you that. But what about the man who gives his life to save another? Or even on a smaller scale, someone who donates money—or blood? With nothing in it for them, they give away what they have for the good of others?"

"They get something out of it. They get the satisfaction of having helped someone else."

"But why should that be satisfying? In a world of simple evolutionary cause and effect, that's not satisfying, that's stupid! It doesn't increase their chances of survival."

"It gives them pleasure!"

"But why should it give them pleasure?"

"Because it's a good thing to do!"

She smiled like she'd just won a prize. "That's what I'm saying. In the world I'm describing, there is no solid reason for 'good' to exist. Or, to put it another way, in a world of pure evolutionary cause and effect, there is no good; there is only that which makes me strong and helps me survive and that which doesn't. That's why, for me, believing in God is actually easier than not believing in God. Because I'm not willing to say that someone who gives away his money or blood—or his life—is a weak, stupid fool."

"They could just be someone who believes in God."

"They often are, but sometimes they aren't."

"Yeah, I guess that's right."

"And think about it, Emma. When someone does something selfless or sacrificial, most of us recognize that as good. We name buildings after people who save lives and erect statues of people who die for a cause because we believe that we live in a world where good exists, not in a world where the only good is surviving and propagating the species."

"I guess you're right. I can see that."

"So that's what I mean when I say the existence of good and evil may present a problem for the person who believes in God, but it may present an even bigger problem for the person who doesn't."

"I've honestly never looked at it that way."

"Most people don't. Most of us get so offended when bad things happen that we don't really think of what our appreciation of good and our revulsion in the face of evil says about us and about the kind of world we live in."

I shook my head in amazement. It was so much to process. And too much to believe. "I just can't," I said.

"Can't … what?"

I sighed. "I just can't believe, after what happened to your parents, that you could just go on believing in God."

She smiled. A sad smile, I thought. "Like I said, I didn't find it that hard to believe in his existence. But for a long time, I stopped believing in his goodness."

"How does that work?" I said. "How can you go on believing in God without believing in his goodness?"

"Oh, easy," she said, half smiling. "At least, at the time, it was easy."

I wanted her to go on, but our conversation was interrupted by the sound of someone knocking on the door. We exchanged a glance. Katya shrugged, went to the door, and opened it a crack.

"Sarah!" she said. She swung the door open and stepped back. "Come in."

Sarah—whoever she was—carried a large dish of some kind, covered with a towel.

"It's so nice to see you," Katya said, guiding Sarah in until they both stood beside the table. "Please excuse the mess."

She introduced me and Sarah to each other, explaining that Sarah and her husband were close neighbors. For a moment after the introductions, the three of us stood around awkwardly.

"What brings you here?" Katya finally asked.

Sarah extended the covered dish in Katya's direction. She seemed embarrassed, uncomfortable. "I heard that your husband has disappeared, no?"

Katya took the dish in both hands. "Yes. That's true."

"I am sorry to know that," Sarah said. "Reuben is sorry, too."

THE QUEST

"Thank you."

"You have been so very kind to us, especially when Reuben's mother died. We wanted to tell you that we hope … we hope the best."

"Thank you, Sarah. Would you—would you like to sit?"

Sarah seemed to hesitate before nodding. "Yes," she said.

The three of us sat at the table. Katya patted the top of the covered dish. "Is this what I think it is?"

Sarah blushed. I mean, visibly blushed. "It is my kugel."

Katya pretended to swoon as she explained to me, "Sarah makes the absolute best sweet noodle kugel with raisins."

"It is nothing," Sarah said.

"Emma, you're going to love this," Katya said. "We'll have it tonight." Another awkward silence descended on us, until Sarah spoke again.

"We pray for your Daniel."

"Thank you." Katya's eyes teared up. "Thank you so much."

"You have heard nothing?"

Katya shook her head.

"Nothing from police?"

"No," Katya said. She explained that she had hired a private security company but that so far there was no information. Sarah dropped her gaze and bit her lip.

"Sarah," Katya said quietly, slowly. "Is there something you want to tell us?"

She nodded without lifting her head.

"What? What is it? Whatever it is, please tell us."

She looked from Katya to me, then back to Katya. "I have … information," she said.

Chapter 45

Katya took a deep breath. "What kind of information?" she asked.

"It is probably nothing," Sarah said.

"It's more than we have right now," Katya countered.

"Reuben sometimes goes to Bethlehem." She pronounced it with a hard "t" instead of the "th" sound, like I'd always heard it.

"For his business?" Katya prodded.

"Yes," she said. She hesitated, as though she was about to say more and then reconsidered. "For his business."

"I didn't know that," Katya said.

"Daniel your husband has an automobile."

"Yes, a Hyundai," Katya said.

"A white automobile."

"Yes!"

"It has four doors."

"Yes, Sarah, a white Hyundai Getz with four doors."

Sarah nodded. "It is sometimes parked on Manger Square."

"What? Are you sure? Are you sure it's Daniel's car?"

She raised her shoulders, her gesture suggesting some uncertainty.

"How does he know it's Daniel's car?" Katya asked.

"There is a sticker on the windshield."

THE QUEST

"A sticker on the windshield?" It took Katya a moment, then she seemed to come to a realization and turned to me. "There *is* a sticker on the windshield! A Sar Shalom Institute sticker! A parking permit." She turned back to Sarah. "The car has a Sar Shalom sticker?"

Sarah nodded.

"Has he seen who's driving it?"

She shook her head. "No. He has tried. He waited but never saw anyone in the auto."

Katya reached out and tenderly touched Sarah's forearm. "Thank you, Sarah, thank you so much. This is the first news we've had since Daniel disappeared."

Sarah nodded without smiling and stood up. "I will tell you if I learn more," she said. "I hope you like the kugel."

Katya and I stood, too, and Katya followed Sarah to the door. She kissed her on both cheeks and shut the door behind her.

A moment later, we both sat again at the table.

"What happens now?" I asked.

"I don't know. I suppose I should call CID."

"What will they do?"

"I don't know."

"Why don't we go?"

"Go … where?"

"To Bethlehem! We could go right now."

"Uh, no, we couldn't."

"Why not?"

"It's the West Bank, Emma. It can be complicated to cross the border … in either direction."

"What do you mean? They won't let us in?"

"Not without the proper papers. I can do it, because I work for Sar Shalom Institute, and they are recognized by the Israeli government as a humanitarian organization. But getting you in is a different matter. We would have to get a West Bank visitor visa for you, and that could take weeks. Months, maybe."

"You're kidding."

She shook her head. "I'm not kidding at all."

"Don't American tourists go to Bethlehem?"

"All the time. But that's different."

"Well, call me a tourist, then."

"It's not that easy."

"I don't care if it's easy. This is my dad! I don't care if I have to climb a fence or hide in the trunk. We've got to do something, and I don't mean tomorrow."

"You don't understand," she started, but I interrupted.

"No, *you* don't understand. I came all this way to find my dad, and you expect me to be patient because it's complicated? No way!" I tacked on a spicier phrase that indicated my level of frustration, but Katya didn't flinch.

"Emma, getting in is not the main obstacle. Getting out is."

After I calmed down, Katya explained that entering the Palestinian territories from Israel was relatively easy, but the border crossings coming back into Israel often involved more difficulties. She said that Israeli officials were constantly concerned with the possibility of terrorists, such as suicide bombers, entering into Israel, whereas there was basically no threat of terrorist acts in the Palestinian territories. The main concern of Palestinians, she said, was getting back and forth to jobs in the more prosperous Israeli areas, which occasionally wasn't possible because the Israeli authorities sometimes closed border crossings without notice.

We eventually agreed to a compromise. Katya would call CID and relay Sarah's information about Dad's car, but then she and I would also go to Bethlehem. But then Katya threw another wrench into the works.

THE QUEST

"Emma, if we go now, night will fall very soon."

"So?"

"I'm just thinking, if we don't see Daniel's car right away, we won't have much time to wait around. We might have to turn around and come home as soon as we get there."

"So what do you suggest?" I felt like she was just putting up one roadblock after another, and I didn't understand why.

"Bear with me. We go first thing in the morning. We stay all day, if we have to. That way, there's a much greater chance we'll see it than if we go now and have only an hour or two before sunset."

I shook my head. I didn't like it. But I had to admit she had a point. "First thing tomorrow morning?"

"First thing."

We ate Sarah's kugel with our dinner that evening, and Katya was right: It was amazing. Noodles, cinnamon, raisins, and I don't know what else, but it was delicious. Katya said it was a popular Israeli dish, particularly around the season of Purim. I asked what that was, and she described it as one of the big holidays among Jews, celebrating their deliverance from an ancient holocaust during the days of Queen Esther and King "Somebody."

Our conversation meandered a little, but eventually I returned to what we had been discussing before Sarah appeared at the door.

"How can you say you believed in God, after your parents … died … but without believing—what did you say?"

She smiled. "I believed in God's existence but not in his goodness."

"Yeah, I don't get that."

She leaned back in her chair. "I don't think it's all that uncommon," she said. "I think many people, when something bad happens to them, say they stop believing in God, when really they still believe in him, but they just don't believe in his goodness."

"How do *you* know they still believe in him?"

She shrugged slightly. "I suppose it is too much of a generalization. I've known a lot of people—my sister included—who've told me they stopped believing in God because of something bad that happened to them, but they're as angry as can be at God!"

"You can't understand that?" I asked. "I can totally understand that."

"Really? It makes no sense to me."

"What do you mean? How could anyone not be mad after God let something like that happen to your parents?"

"I understand being angry with God, but you can't have it both ways."

"Both ways?"

"Emma," she said, leaning her elbows on the table and lowering her voice. "How can you be angry at someone who doesn't exist?"

I stared at her. No one had ever asked me that question before.

She didn't wait for me to answer. "That's what I'm talking about. I'm not saying there aren't sincere atheists in the world; there are. I'm just saying that many of the people I've talked to who deny the existence of God do so because they think they're getting back at him for what he did to them … or what he *allowed* to happen.

"And I've seen their anger eat them up, Emma. I've seen it eat them up. Because it's harmful enough to have such deep anger, but it's even more harmful when you can't really be angry at the person you're angry with … because you've told yourself he doesn't exist. And so, what happens—at least what I watched happen with my sister, for a long time—is that we just get more and more angry, and yet we become entrenched in our position that there is no God because we think we're getting our revenge on him by denying his existence. And the whole time, that anger just burrows deeper and deeper and turns into depression. It can end up threatening our very life."

"Wow. I guess I can see what you mean. But you said you didn't do that."

"No," she answered. "I didn't take that route. Like I said, my sister did, for years."

THE QUEST

"But you just stopped believing in God's goodness?"

"After what happened to my parents, I really struggled, as you can imagine. It was horrible. But like I said, I knew pretty early on that denying God's existence wouldn't bring me any peace because then I'd be living in a purely naturalistic world—a world where you can't blame an animal for being an animal."

"You wanted to blame your mom's killer."

"I did, but it was more than that. I had to. I couldn't conceive, under any circumstances, that what he did—what they did—could ever be considered anything but absolutely evil, utterly and incontrovertibly immoral."

"Were they ever caught?" I asked.

She stopped looking at me and lowered her eyes. "No," she said.

"I'm sorry," I said.

"I don't know if that made it harder or easier to deal with. Harder, I guess."

"I'm so sorry," I said. It was all I could think of to say.

"As time went on, I figured I had one of four pretty clear choices. *One*, God doesn't exist, in which case, everything I said earlier was true. Mom and Dad's deaths were just evolution in action, the strong eliminating the weak. No right, no wrong. Just time marching along and the human species advancing little by little into something stronger and better."

"Better? How could something like that be better?"

She lifted her gaze and looked at me again. "In terms of evolution, 'better' means just more fit to survive."

"Yeah, well, I would have rejected that choice, too." I blinked. It suddenly occurred to me that the choice she had just described was pretty much the one I had been making all my life, in terms of not believing in God. But when she put it the way she did, it didn't seem at all like the smart position I'd always thought it was.

She smiled. "The second choice really wasn't any better, though."

"What's that?"

"Someone—at my father's funeral, no less—tried to comfort me by saying something like, 'Some things just happen. God can't watch everybody,' or something inane like that. You know, it's the idea that God would have prevented this abomination if he could have—but he couldn't, so he didn't."

I wrinkled my nose. "That doesn't sound right at all."

"Well, no, it doesn't, and I knew that instinctively. It messes with the whole definition of the word 'god.' I could not imagine a God who is powerful enough to create this stunning universe, down to the amazing detail of, say, the design on a butterfly's wing, and yet who isn't powerful enough to keep a couple of sick men away from my parents' doorstep. It made no sense to me. Which is easier, to make a solar system … or stop someone from committing rape and murder?"

I nodded but didn't say anything.

"Even looking through my grief, through my endless supply of tears at that time in my life, I could see that a God who didn't know or couldn't stop what was happening to my parents wouldn't be a god at all, at least in my lexicon."

She smiled. "*Third* choice was that God exists, and he's omniscient and omnipotent, but he's not good, he's not loving, he's not going to keep awful things from happening to good people."

"That's the choice you made."

"Not at first. I spent a lot of time ranting and raving at God, asking him, *Where were you?* and *How could you let this happen?* and things like that."

"I don't blame you," I said.

"Yeah, well. It was a pretty one-sided conversation. This went on for months and months. I was hurting, I was depressed, I was angry. Basically, you can name any negative emotion and I was feeling it. And, most of those emotions, I was feeling toward God. After a while, I just gave up."

"Gave up?"

THE QUEST

She rose from the table and kept talking as she went into the kitchen and put the tea kettle on the stove. "I gave up on God. On believing in his goodness. I decided he couldn't possibly be loving and kind, after what happened to my parents. I resigned myself to believing that he was a mean old man, basically, who didn't care if people were raped or murdered or driven to despair."

"Wow," I said.

She asked if I wanted a cup of tea with her, and when I agreed, she pulled down two cups from the kitchen cabinet next to the little stove. The room fell silent for a few minutes, while she got out the teabags, and cream, sugar, and honey, and set them out on the table in front of us. Moments later, a steaming cup was brewing peach tea right under my nose.

"But that's not what you believe today," I said eventually, picking up the conversation where we had left off.

"No," she answered. "Not by a long shot."

"Why?" I asked. "What changed your mind?"

I couldn't believe that once again I was asking her to continue all this God-talk.

Chapter 46

Katya stirred her tea for a few moments after I asked my question. Finally, she set down her spoon. "It wasn't just one thing. It was a series of things. Big things, little things—all kinds of things. Over a period of time."

I listened.

"I was so depressed. I'd never had a relationship with God, not really, not like I do now; that came later. But, once I stopped believing that God was good, that he didn't love me and never had … I missed him. I didn't know that's what it was at first, but over time, I became more and more overwhelmed with the emptiness, the void that had entered my life when all faith in a good, loving, caring God went out of it.

"From that point, I just spiraled deeper and deeper into depression. I tried to immerse myself in work, thinking that I just needed to crowd the grief and anger out of my mind, you know? But that only helped when I was at work; when I tried to go to sleep or tried to read, which I always loved to do, the tears and the rage would come roaring back, and it didn't show any signs of decreasing.

"So I went to my doctor, and he prescribed some anti-depressants and sleeping pills, and told me I should eat better, but nothing changed. The funny thing is, I think I knew all along that I wasn't helping myself, that choosing to believe in a God who didn't care just made matters worse. And I think I knew, too, that I hadn't really changed my belief. Not really. I knew, in my heart of hearts, that God *was* good, but I was so mad at him that I wanted to hurt him, and basically calling him a mean, uncaring, heartless something-or-other was the best way I knew to do that."

She picked up her cup. Neither of us had touched our tea yet, but now we sipped simultaneously. It was good. I braced my elbows on the table and kept the cup near my lips while she set hers down on the table again.

"After a long time of barely living, barely getting through the days and even less successfully getting through the nights, a friend recommended a professional counselor—even offered to pay, but I didn't let her—and so I started seeing Dr. Oldman."

She took another sip of tea. "Turns out she was a Christian. I didn't know it at the time, and I might not have gone to her if I had known it. But several months after I started seeing her, she had gotten to know me enough to prescribe something I would never have thought of on my own."

"What's that?" I asked.

"She knew my love for literature, and of course I had talked a lot about what happened to my parents and how a good God couldn't have allowed that, so I had decided that God wasn't good. We talked about other things, of course, but we kept coming back to that. So, after a while, she asked me if I'd be willing to read a book. I said, sure, that I used to read constantly, before I'd gotten so depressed. And then she told me what book she wanted me to read."

"What was it?"

"It was a book in the Bible. The book of Job."

"I've heard of it."

"So had I," she said. "But I had never read it. And I wasn't prepared for it."

"What do you mean?"

"I mean that book rocked my world. It made me mad. It made me think. And it changed my life." She scooted her chair back from the table and turned slightly to face me a little more squarely. "I bet I read that book four or five times, all the way through."

"How long is it?" I asked.

"Not that long. Not like a Stephen King novel or anything like that. It's forty-two chapters long, which is pretty long for a Bible book."

"Is it, like, a story?"

"It starts out that way, and then it becomes more of a conversation. The first couple of chapters tell about Job, who was a righteous man, a good man who did all the right things, and God was pretty pleased with him. Then it shows Satan, the devil, appearing before God's throne."

"The devil. Really?"

She smiled. "Yes. The Bible doesn't depict him wearing red tights and carting a pitchfork but it does depict him as a fallen angel who proposes a sort of cosmic test to see if Job serves God only because he's had an easy life. So God gives Satan permission to afflict Job. He sets some limits to what the devil can do, but he gives him the go-ahead to make Job suffer."

"No way," I said.

She smiled wanly, nodding. "That's one of the things that made me mad. The idea of God letting bad things happen to good people was kind of the crux of my whole struggle, the source of my depression. It just made me madder at God to think he would do something like that."

"But it's just a story, right? I mean, it didn't actually happen."

She smiled and shrugged. "As the story goes on, a series of horrible things happen to Job, and he ends up losing his children, his wealth— even his health. The only thing he has left in this world is his wife, and she nags him to 'Curse God, and die!' But he refuses. He says, 'Shall we accept good from God, and not trouble?'"

"Wow. That's in the Bible?"

She said it was. "After that, some of Job's friends come by, and after awhile, they start offering their theories as to why these awful things happened to him. That's when the story turns into a long poem, with

Job speaking a soliloquy, and then one of his friends, and then Job, and then another of his friends, and so on, back and forth."

"Okay, that sounds kind of boring."

"To some, I guess it would be. But to me, it was intensely interesting, because it related exactly to what I was going through. It still does."

"How?"

"I'll get to that in a minute, but first let me tell you how the book ends." She paused, as if to find her place again. "The climax of the story is that after all of Job's friends have spouted their opinions—most of which are garbage—God shows up."

"How?"

"He speaks—and not in a soft voice. He doesn't say anything you'd expect him to say. The Bible says God spoke to Job out of a whirlwind."

"What did he say?"

She virtually leaped up from her chair. "Give me a minute." She moved quickly to her favorite chair and brought her Bible back to the table. She held it in one hand while she flipped pages with the other. "Here it is. Chapter 38. It says things like, 'Who is this who questions my wisdom with silly words? Man up! I will ask the questions, and you will answer.'"

"It really says that?"

"It goes on, 'Where were you when I was busy creating the world? Tell me, if you're so smart. Who drew up the plans and cleared the site? You must remember, since you know so much.'

"It says, 'Have you ever summoned the morning or told the dawn when to appear? Have you stretched out daylight across the face of the earth and made the darkness flee from it? Do you know the depths of the sea? Have you seen the gates of death? Have you explored the ends of the earth? If you have, feel free to instruct me!'"

She looked up from the page. "And it goes on like that for page after page!"

"I don't get it," I said.

"I know, neither did I. I didn't understand why God was being so—what's the word—confrontational, maybe."

"Does he ever get to the point? Does God ever explain himself?"

She smiled. "That's exactly what I found so frustrating! He never does. I read those chapters over and over again, trying to understand God's response to Job, because he never gives Job one word of explanation. And then finally, one day it hit me. And it made all the difference, not only in my understanding of Job, but in my own personal struggle with God."

I was all ears. She laid both hands on the open pages of the Bible, and leaned forward. "God's response to Job helped me see the wrongness of what I had been doing."

"What? What are you talking about? The wrongness of—you hadn't done anything wrong."

"Yes, I had. The same thing Job and his friends had done. I had set myself up as God's judge. Which is absurd on its face, of course, because, if I'm capable of judging God, then *he's* not God—I am!"

I said nothing, but I'm sure my confusion showed on my face.

"Once that realization dawned on me," she continued, "the whole book of Job made sense."

"I'm glad it did for you, because it still doesn't for me."

"Stick with me here. After reading it over and over, I realized that this ancient book—some say it predates the books of Moses—taught me three very contemporary things about evil and suffering in this world."

"I'm listening," I said, in a tone that said "Get to it."

"From the beginning, the story tells me that evil has a source, but it's not God. The perpetrator is the same Evil One who introduced sin and suffering into this world way back in the Garden of Eden. So, although I blamed God for my parents' suffering—and mine—Job's story showed me that it didn't come from him."

"Yeah, but you said God allowed it."

"Yes, that's the second thing Job's story taught me. Though God does not cause evil, he doesn't always prevent it from happening. It's a consequence of the Fall, when sin entered the world. It results from humanity's sinfulness, and there's not a person in the world who doesn't participate in it. I don't get indignant when God allows me to assert my own will instead of following his, yet I tend to blame him that he doesn't prevent others from sinning. He has not yet put a stop to evil—in me or in others."

"What difference does it make? Whether he makes it happen or allows it to happen, it has the same results!"

"You're right," she said.

"Bu—" I had expected her to argue the point, and I was already launching my counter argument when she admitted it. "But ... doesn't that leave you right back where you started?"

"It would, if Job's story had ended after the second chapter. Or maybe even if it had ended after chapter 37. But it didn't, and I'm so glad it didn't. Because when Job and his friends sought an answer to why God allowed Job to suffer so much, God didn't really answer, except to say, basically, 'Who do you think you are?'"

"What kind of answer is that?"

"I think it may be the only answer we get in this life."

I didn't like where this was going at all. I shook my head. "I just don't—"

"God answered Job's questions with questions. He asked, 'Where were you when I laid the foundation of the earth?' and 'Are you the one who summons the sun every morning?' and 'Do you know where the dark goes when light chases it away?' His point is, 'Job, you can't enter into my mind. You don't comprehend the wonders of the world around you, so how can you possibly hope to understand my reasons, my plans, my explanations?

"He's not only saying, 'I don't have to explain myself to you, because I'm your Judge, not the other way around,' he's also saying, 'If I explained these things to you, your poor little human brain would crash, like an old computer running new software.'"

I felt a sour expression form on my face. "I don't know. I don't see how that could have been at all helpful or—satisfying to you."

She shrugged and smiled. "Maybe it wouldn't be to most other people."

"It's like saying, 'God has his reasons; you'll never understand; just get used to it.'"

She chuckled. "I guess it is. But it made sense to me. And, when I stopped to think about it, no reason on earth could ever have made me feel better about my mom and dad's deaths."

"So you feel better not having a reason?"

"I think I feel better not expecting to understand, at least not while I'm on this earth."

"But you think someday you will. Like, in heaven." I heard the sarcastic note enter my voice. I figured she probably heard it, too. But she didn't get offended.

"The Bible says that now, it's like we're looking through a dirty window. But then—after this life—we will see all things clearly, as clearly as God sees into our hearts right now."

"And that's good enough for you?"

She tilted her head, thinking. "Good enough? I don't know. I might not go that far, but it's definitely better than before. It helped me get through my grief and depression. And it eventually turned into something good, because I may be the only person on earth who can say the book of Job played a role in them turning to God and coming to faith in Jesus Christ, which it did."

I sensed another long story coming on. It felt like we'd been talking about this stuff all day—because we pretty much had, at least half the day. We'd been talking long enough that the sun had gone down, and the dinner dishes still needed to be washed.

I went to bed not long after that, after helping Katya with the dinner dishes and turning the final bites of Sarah's kugel into an after-dinner, after-tea snack. I realized soon after I closed the bedroom door behind me that I'd been shaking my head as I walked from the kitchen to the bedroom.

Katya was a mystery to me. It was like she had an answer for everything, every objection or obstacle I had to believing in God. But she was just telling her story. And I had to admit it was a pretty amazing story.

I had assumed she had led a perfect, tidy life before she met my dad. She always seemed so poised and calm. At peace, I guess. Like now, I was sure she had finished in the kitchen and made her way to her chair, where she was probably reading the Bible again.

It took just a few minutes to undress for bed, after which I stepped across the hall to wash and brush my teeth. The light in the living room was still on when I came out and returned to the bedroom. As I slipped between the covers, I noticed what looked like a Bible on the bookcase in the corner. Upon closer inspection, I found several Bibles.

I pulled one off the shelf and opened it, fanning the pages.

It looked strange to me, unlike any book I'd ever read. I checked in the front for a table of contents and found Job on page 518. I crawled back in bed and started to read.

CHAPTER 47

Oh, Lord, thank you for this day. Thank you for Emma. Thank you for the progress she seems to be making toward you. At least, I pray that it is progress toward you.

Please continue to draw her to yourself. Draw her into your Word. Draw her into your presence.

I pray that she may come to know you. Open her eyes. Open her heart. Shine your light into her spirit, and let her hear you calling her into hope, into new life. Let the things we've been talking about find a soft place in her soul, a place where even the tiniest seeds of faith can start to take root and grow. Help me not to push, but to be sensitive and responsive to plant the right seeds and nurture them, until they break forth into the light of day.

Exert that power tonight on Daniel's behalf, Lord God. Please comfort and sustain him. Protect and preserve him. Hold him. Help him. And help Emma and me, as we await his deliverance. Help us as we enter Bethlehem tomorrow. Make our trip productive. Use it to bring us closer to Daniel, closer to his release. Use it to bring Emma closer to you.

Is that what you're doing, Lord? Is that part of your purpose in all this? Is it to swing open the door of your kingdom to Emma? Is that why she is here—to find not only her father, but her Father?

I pray for that. I pray for both. Make it so, Lord, in Jesus' name, amen.

CHAPTER 48

I awakened while it was still dark and reached into my duffle bag for a new change of clothes; I was running low and would soon have to do laundry. But as I fished around in the duffle bag, my hand found the book Travis had given me at the airport. I dressed quickly and went out into the living room, expecting to find Katya still asleep, but she was in the kitchen, brewing coffee and chopping vegetables.

"I should get in touch with Travis," I said to Katya.

"Travis?" she asked.

"The guy I met on the plane."

"Oh, I thought you didn't have his number."

"I don't. When we landed, neither one of us had cell phones, remember?"

"That's right. He wrote down my number."

"But he hasn't called you, has he?"

"No," she said. A pause. "But it's only been a few days, Emma."

"Yeah, I know." Still, it was disappointing. I mean, sure, my life had been a whirlwind, but he should've had lots of opportunities to call.

"Do you know where he is?"

I shook my head. "I think he said where he was going, but I can't remember. Some archaeological dig."

"That's right," she said. "It was in Galilee. He mentioned it there in the terminal, right after I'd met him."

THE QUEST

"You're right. Right before you gave him your cell number. He wrote it on the back of his hand."

"I should remember. Give me a minute." She turned and seemed to be staring at the wall, mentally recalling that scene in the airport. Finally, she looked at me and smiled. "I've got it: Tel Hazor." She pronounced it "hot sore."

"Tel Hazor," I echoed. "Where's that?"

"In Galilee, north of the lake—the Sea of Galilee. It's probably the most famous archaeological excavation ever—except for Megiddo, maybe. It's been going on for years."

"So, if he's there, how do I get a hold of him?"

"Good question. Give me some time. It shouldn't take me too long online to find out who's in charge of the dig, and from there I should be able to get some contact information."

"Okay, great. That's awesome."

"I'm probably going to need his last name. Do you know it?"

If he'd told me, I couldn't remember. I searched my brain, but finally had to admit I didn't have an answer.

"Well, it's not that common a name. I'll just give it a shot and hope for the best."

She went to the table, sat down, and positioned her laptop in front of her. I watched her anxiously for a few minutes, until a thought suddenly occurred to me. I dashed into the bedroom and picked up the book from the bed, where I'd left it. I opened the cover.

There on the upper right corner of the title page was the name: Travis Richmond.

Jewish Family Murdered in Their Sleep

⤢ EMAIL   🖶 PRINT   + SHARE

MA'ALE ASHER, WEST BANK—An extended period of relative calm in the West Bank was shattered Wednesday night when a Jewish family of four were executed in their West Bank home by unknown assailants. A fifth member of the family, a 10-year-old daughter who had spent the night at a friend's house, discovered the bodies on Thursday morning.

Binyamin Blumenthal, 37, and his wife, Dena, 36, and their children Levi, 4, and Rachel, 7, all residents of the Ma'ale Asher settlement, were fatally stabbed. According to police, two armed men broke into the house while the family slept, slitting the throats of the parents first and then killing the children. A paramedic who arrived at the home Thursday morning described the scene as "horrific."

"They were all murdered in their sleep," said Bernard Fiedler. "There was nothing we could do for them. They bled out in minutes." He described the sight of one of the children clutching a stuffed animal that was bathed in the child's blood.

Authorities believe the crime was the work of more than one individual. A police spokesman said that it appeared at least two suspects had cut the fence surrounding the settlement compound and entered the Blumenthal home through a window. IDF troops immediately sealed all entrances to the settlement, but it is believed the attackers had already escaped. No other homes in the settlement were disturbed.

Prime Minister Yoel Nachmann was immediately informed of the killings and directed the IDF and Israel security services to take all necessary measures to identify and

THE QUEST

capture the killers. The prime minister issued the following statement: "The perpetrators of this unconscionable attack on innocents—parents and children, asleep in their home—will be found and will be punished. This heinous act is not a crime against one family; it is an attack on all, an attack on peace itself." Nachmann also called on the Palestinian Authority to help find the murderers.

Ma'ale Asher is a religious Jewish settlement of approximately 32,000 near Jerusalem in the West Bank. Like all settlements, it is often involved in controversy. The attack on the Blumenthal family is the first attack against settlers in more than six months.

CHAPTER 49

I gave Katya Travis's full name, and she quickly found out online that the excavations at Tel Hazor, north of the Sea of Galilee, which had been started by the legendary Israeli archaeologist Yigal Yadin, were being conducted by the Hebrew University and led by the famous Binyamin Goodman. She then called the Hebrew University information line in Jerusalem and asked for contact information at the excavation site. That's when things slowed.

Actually, they stopped.

After being repeatedly put on hold or transferred from one department to another, she hung up and set the phone on the table. "This is ridiculous," she said.

"What?" I asked.

"The Israelis are very security conscious, so it can be really hard to get information out of someone. No one wants to take the risk that they might be giving information that could get them reprimanded or fired … or mentioned on the evening news."

"Even for something like this?"

"Even for the number or address of a grocery store," she said. She sighed loudly, then bent over her computer again. In what seemed like less than a minute, she leaned back. "I don't believe it."

"What?" I asked.

"I just put in the search phrase 'telephone tel hazor excavation site,' and the first link I clicked lists every current excavation in Israel, the director, the dates, how to volunteer, the workdays—and the telephone number for that location."

"So call it!"

"I'll probably have to leave a message," she said.

"That's okay. We have to leave soon for Bethlehem, right?"

She nodded and punched in the numbers. A few seconds passed. "I was right—voicemail." She left a message, requesting a callback from Travis Richmond to Emma Seeger, and carefully dictated her cell number.

Moments later, we were in the car, heading for Bethlehem. On the way, Katya called CID, though neither of us expected them to answer, as it was still early in the morning. As we drove past the ancient walls, the Old City seemed to be just shaking itself awake, as taxis started gathering and merchants had begun setting out their wares.

We were right; CID was not yet answering the phone.

"Help me remember, and I'll try in a little while."

It seemed only minutes later that she whipped the little car into a parking lot. We got out at the same time.

"You have your passport, right?" she asked.

"Yes," I answered. "You told me to bring it back at the apartment, remember?"

"Right," she said. "Sorry."

We started walking toward the massive concrete wall slightly uphill from the parking lot. She explained that it was part of the controversial security barrier Israel had started constructing a dozen years earlier. She said parts of it were fence, but around here it was a solid concrete wall.

She led the way, of course, and we joined a line of people waiting to pass through a checkpoint. A few buses, taxis, and other vehicles were lining up, too, but I could already see that the traffic coming the other direction—from Bethlehem into Israel—was several times longer.

We both fell silent while we waited. I listened to the rapid syllables of conversation around us, which I assumed were either Hebrew or Arabic—or both. Within ten or twelve minutes, a man in uniform, my age or younger, glanced at each of our passports and then at our faces, and waved us through without a word.

"That was easy," I said, as we started walking down a sidewalk lined with taxis parked at the curb.

"Fifty shekel," one of the cab drivers said, repeatedly, to us as we passed. He left his car behind and started walking alongside us. Katya ignored him, and I followed suit, but he persisted. His price dropped to forty-five, then forty shekels. Then thirty-five, thirty, twenty-five. He gave up and turned back up the hill after we declined a ride for fifteen shekels.

Once he had gone, I asked Katya, "How far do we have to walk?"

"A couple of miles," she said.

"A couple of *miles?*" I echoed. "Then why didn't we take a cab?"

She shrugged. "It's a nice day for a walk."

Katya was right—it was a nice day, but I was anxious to complete our mission. I thought maybe she was just being super-careful. Maybe she didn't trust the taxi drivers or something like that.

We walked downhill for fifteen or twenty minutes, past what looked like ramshackle homes and businesses, though most seemed empty. Chickens and dogs roamed freely, and on the opposite hillside I could actually see a shepherd standing amid a flock of sheep. It made me think of the Christmas song, "O Little Town of Bethlehem."

But the town we were walking through bore no resemblance to the little town of my Christmas imagination. Big potholes dotted the street. The path on which we walked turned from sidewalk to dirt path several times. Signs and other parts of buildings seemed to be falling off. At one point we had to walk around an abandoned desk, just sitting on the walkway.

Soon, however, our course changed, and we began walking uphill. I saw increasing activity and even sensed a little prosperity. Instead of being boarded up, homes were occupied and businesses were open, though they were still nothing like the shops and grocery stores I was accustomed to at home. We even passed a coffee shop with a green sign that proudly identified it as the "Stars and Bucks Café," along with a round symbol that looked a lot like the Starbucks logo.

I was just becoming aware of the fact that I was panting slightly— Katya seemed to be having no trouble breathing—when she announced, "Here we are."

"Here?" I said. An expansive stone-paved plaza stood before us, surrounded by buildings made of stone.

"Yes," she said, standing still and looking around. "Manger Square."

I turned my head and looked all around. On one end of the open area was a massive stone church; on the other end was a tall tower with a crescent moon on top. One large building to our right was identified in English, with Arabic letters above, as the "Bethlehem Peace Center." Twisting olive trees and cedars and a few palms seemed to rise out of the stone pavement. Traffic barricades, some made of metal and some of stone, prevented any vehicles from entering the main part of the plaza. "This is Manger Square."

"Yes," she answered. "What did you expect?"

"I don't know, but it wasn't this. This is just a big empty space."

"At Christmas time," she said, "it's packed from one end to the other with people. You wouldn't recognize it as the same place."

"Okay," I said. "I'll take your word for it."

We stood for a few moments, neither of us speaking. Finally, I asked, "What do we do now?"

"I'm thinking," she said.

"We're looking for Dad's Hyundai, right?"

She nodded. "It would have been smart to bring some binoculars." Many cars were parked or driving along the perimeter of the square, but the space was so vast, it would be hard to scan the area for one car among many.

I spun around until I thought I might get dizzy. We weren't quite in the middle of the square, but we also weren't particularly close to any of the buildings surrounding it. "It's hopeless. We can't possibly see all we need to see."

Katya gripped my arm. "I have an idea." She pulled me after her and we headed for the Bethlehem Peace Center.

On entering the building, we saw a tourist information center. We walked together to the counter, where a woman wearing a dark blue scarf watched us approach. Katya asked, in English, if there was any place to rent bicycles in the area.

"Bicycles?" I asked.

She nodded at me, and then turned her attention back to the woman, who looked at her quizzically. Katya rephrased her question, and the woman shook her head gloomily.

Katya thanked her, and we turned from the counter and walked back out into the square. We paused in front of the center. "I was thinking," Katya said, "if we could each ride a bike, we could at least kind of patrol the perimeter of the square. And if we saw anything from a distance, we could get there quickly."

"Oh," I said. I guess I could see the logic in her idea. But it was a moot point now.

We turned right and by some silent agreement started to walk around the perimeter of the square, scanning the area for white cars. We hadn't gone more than a few dozen steps when a man came up behind us, wheeling a bicycle on each side.

"You wish for bicycles?" he said, in a heavy accent.

"Yes," we both answered simultaneously, though I admit I stammered my reply. How did this guy know we needed bikes? Had he heard us ask the woman at the counter?

"How much to rent?" Katya said.

"I sell you," he said.

"No, no," she answered. "We only want to rent. How much to rent?"

"I sell you," he repeated.

"How much to buy?" I asked.

She turned to me. "We don't want to buy," she insisted.

"How much?" I said.

"Fifty shekel," he said, indicating one bike. Then, patting the other bike, he added, "Fifty shekel."

"A hundred shekels," I said, turning to Katya. "How much is that?"

She looked at him, then at me. "Um, twenty-seven, twenty-eight dollars."

"Isn't that worth it?" I asked.

"Yes, but we don't want to buy them!"

I rolled my eyes. "Katya, just buy the bikes! We can find a kid and donate them to him when we're done. Just buy the bikes."

She looked stunned for a moment, and the man looked back and forth between us. Finally, a smile spread across her lips. "What was I thinking? You're right." She pulled a wad of one-dollar bills from her pocket and counted them.

"I have twenty-five American dollars," she told the man, returning what looked like a few fives and tens to her pocket.

"Yes, yes," the man answered. "Good, good."

She gave him the money. He flashed a broad and largely toothless smile.

We thanked him and straddled our newly purchased bikes.

Gaza Town Celebrates Blumenthal Murders

EMAIL   PRINT   + SHARE

BAYT TAMA, GAZA—Residents of the Gaza town of Bayt Tama, thirteen miles from the Israeli border, handed out candy on Saturday to celebrate the murder of a Jewish family in a West Bank settlement.

Residents flooded the streets and passed out sweets to neighbors and children, rejoicing in the deaths of Binyamin and Dena Blumenthal and two of their children, who were murdered in their sleep last Wednesday. One resident explained his jubilation over the murders as "a proper response to the damage settlers inflict on the Palestinian homeland."

Palestinian Prime Minister Salam Nabulsi condemned the attacks. "We denounce all violence. We are against all violence. We call for an end to such attacks, whether the perpetrators are Jewish or Palestinian."

IDF and Israel security forces have been scouring the West Bank since the murders in the hope of bringing the killers to justice. To date, no suspects have been identified.

CHAPTER 50

We agreed to stick together and ride around Manger Square in a circle, keeping an eagle eye on all white cars, and especially anything resembling a white Hyundai Getz. Our first circuit took no more than five or six minutes, I guessed.

We saw quite a few white cars but nothing close enough to Dad's car to warrant even a moment's hesitation, so we kept circling. An hour passed, then a second hour. The day warmed considerably, and though the breeze we generated with our forward motion kept us cool, I began to sweat, and my legs started to tire. Then I saw it.

"Katya, look," I said. I gestured toward a car pulling up in front of a small café, wedged into a narrow storefront close to the mosque with the tall tower.

She followed my gaze, and we pulled to a stop a short distance away. A single driver exited the car.

"Is that it?" I asked.

"It looks like it," she said.

We watched as he dropped the car key into his pants pocket and strode into the café. "Let's go," she said. She led the way, and we pedaled slowly past the car, stopping again a few doors down.

"Well?" I said.

She nodded slowly, somberly. "The plates are different. But it has the Institute parking sticker in the window."

"That's it, then," I said, trying to control my excitement. We had actually found my dad's car. I almost couldn't believe it.

Katya pulled her cell phone out of a pocket and began punching in numbers.

"What are you doing?" I said.

"Calling CID."

"What? Why?"

"Because that man could be dangerous, and—Hello?" She paused. "Yes, I'd like to speak to Mr. Avraham or Mr. Yadin. I left a message this morning."

"What can they do?" I asked, holding out my hands in a pleading gesture. "They're not here. We are!"

She rotated the phone, moving the mouthpiece against her cheek. "I understand that, but we're in the West Bank here, and we have no idea who we're dealing with."

"What's he going to do?" I said, my voice rising. "We're in a freaking public square!"

"You'd be surprised," she answered. Suddenly she swung the cell phone into its former position. "Yes?" Her expression changed. "I see. Would you please tell them I called? Again? It's most urgent."

A moment later she had returned the phone to her pocket. She wore a grim expression. We both stared at the car, and it was clear that neither of us had any idea what to do.

Until the driver came out of the café and headed for the car.

I turned to Katya. "He's leaving!"

If he got in the car and drove away, we would be no better off than we were when we had left the apartment that morning, except to confirm that Dad's car had been seen in Manger Square. To be this close and to find out nothing was unthinkable to me.

I glanced back and forth from the man to Katya and saw that she felt as helpless as I did. I knew I had to do something—so I did.

I laid the bike down on the pavement and started toward the car.

"Emma! What are you doing?"

I shrugged and threw my hands up. I had no idea. But I was going to do something. I walked toward the car, reaching it just a few steps before the man did.

"Is this your car?" I asked.

He froze. The key was in his hand, and he stood by the rear fender. I was afraid for a moment that he might turn and run. Then his expression changed, and I was afraid that he might not turn and run.

"Yes," he said.

Katya arrived beside me. I patted the hood. "Because I've been looking for a car just like this."

"Emma, what are you doing?"

"Chill, Mom," I said. The man still had not gotten into the car. I turned to her and tried with my eyes to urge her to play along. "This is exactly the car I've been wanting." I turned back to the man. "It's a Hyundai Getz, right?"

He frowned darkly. "Yes," he said. He reached for the door handle.

I stepped closer to him and partially blocked him from opening the car door. "I've been telling her this is the car, a Hyundai Getz. It's perfect. Is it new?"

"No," he said.

"It's in great shape," I countered. "Would you be willing to sell it?"

"Emma," Katya said, even more sternly this time.

"Seriously, Mom, it might be better to buy it used."

His eyes narrowed. "It is not for sale."

"Why not?" I asked. "What if we offered you a good price?"

"I bought it recently."

"Oh," I said. "I see. Where did you buy it? Was it from a dealer? Do you think they might have more like this?"

He opened the door, pushing it open—and moving me with it—little by little.

I wasn't finished, though. "Can you at least tell me where you got it?" I held out a hand to Katya. "Mom, give me a pen, will you? I'll write the name on my hand."

"I must go," he insisted.

"Come on," I urged. "Help me out, will you? I've been looking all over for a car like this."

He glowered at me. "I bought it from a man."

"Great," I said, taking the pen Katya offered me. I positioned the pen over my palm. "What's his name?"

He looked around him, as if to make sure no one else was listening. "I don't know his name," he said with an air of finality. "He is a settler."

"A settler?" Katya burst out.

He sat in the driver's seat. He held open the door just long enough to say, "From Ma'ale Asher. That's all I know."

Then he closed the door, started the car, and drove away. I still held the pen poised above my palm. Katya and I watched the car—Dad's car—disappear down the narrow street.

As soon as it was out of sight, Katya placed her face just a few inches from mine. "Don't *ever* do anything like that again!"

Her anger shocked me. I stood speechless for a moment, then answered her. "Did you come up with anything better? Because I didn't see any ingenious plan coming out of *your* mouth!"

"You're right," she said, her tone still vehement. "But you didn't know who he was, you didn't know what he could do. For all you knew he could have been dangerous. For all you know, he still is!"

I put a hand on each of her arms. "I know. I'm sorry. I just didn't know what else to do." I saw actual tears in her eyes.

"What if something had happened to you, Emma?"

"Like what?"

"I don't know. But I don't know what I would do if I let that happen."

"You don't have to protect me, Katya. You can't. You shouldn't have to."

We stood there for a few moments, both of us silent in the middle of that great stone-paved square. I kept my hands on her arms until she broke my grip, threw her arms around me, and hugged me tight.

"Please don't take any more risks like that," she pleaded in my ear.

"I'll try, but I'll do anything to find my dad."

"I know," she answered. "Me too."

A few minutes later we picked up our bikes. We didn't need them anymore.

"What do we do with these?" I asked.

"We could ride them back to the checkpoint," Katya said.

I scanned our surroundings. "I've got a better idea," I said.

"Emma," she said, her tone mildly threatening. "What are you doing?"

"Don't worry. There's no danger involved."

I led the way, and we started riding slowly across Manger Square toward the massive Church of the Nativity.

As we pedaled side by side, I asked, "What did he mean when he said he bought the car from a settler?"

"That was a shock. He apparently bought it from someone in one of the Jewish settlements in the West Bank."

"What's that?"

"Zealous Jews—who don't believe Israel should ever give up the West Bank—band together and build communities here, so it will be harder for the land to ever be totally given away."

"Isn't that dangerous?"

"Very. They're like military bases—armed guards, razor wire, and so on."

"What was the name he used?"

THE QUEST

"Ma'ale Asher," she said, pronouncing it just like the man had.

"What's that mean?"

"I don't know. It's the name of a settlement."

"Where is it?"

"I don't know that either."

By that time, we arrived on the other side of the square. A group of boys were selling postcards to tourists near the entrance to the church. Two girls sat watching.

"I'll take the one on the left," I said.

We rode to within a few feet of the girls, sitting on a curb. Almost simultaneously, we dismounted from the bikes. I approached the girl on the left, while Katya watched.

"Here," I said. "I would like to give you this."

The girl looked at me, wide-eyed. Katya, smiling broadly, followed my lead and said the same thing to the other girl, who stood, reached out, and grabbed the handlebars.

"I give you this," I repeated. "Give."

"My" girl then stood and took the bike from me. "Give?" she said.

"Yes," I said, smiling and nodding. I pantomimed a giving motion to her, and her face brightened into a beautiful smile.

"Shukran, shukran," she said.

Katya explained, "That's Arabic for 'thank you.'"

"What's Arabic for 'you're welcome?'" I asked.

"I don't know, but I think it's okay."

Israel Closes Bethlehem Checkpoint

◻ EMAIL 🖨 PRINT + SHARE

BETHLEHEM—Israeli border police closed the 300 checkpoint at Rachel's Tomb in Bethlehem this morning. Border police representatives gave no explanation for the closure, though one source who chose not to be identified suggested that it was related to the ongoing investigation of the Blumenthal murders in Ma'ale Asher. Witnesses reported seeing IDF forces staging door-to-door maneuvers in the area.

Police said the 300 checkpoint could re-open this evening or tomorrow morning. Today marked the fourth time in three weeks that the 300 checkpoint has been closed, creating difficulty and disruption for many West Bank permit holders and foreign nationals attempting to enter and exit the city.

The Beit Jala checkpoint reportedly remains open, though an IDF spokesman declined to comment as to whether ID and passport holders would be able to use the alternative crossing into Israeli-controlled areas.

Chapter 51

"That was fun," Katya said, as we watched the girls pedal off, proud and giddy.

"It was, wasn't it?" I said.

We continued watching them for a few moments, until they turned a corner and were lost from our sight. We both let out a satisfied sigh at the same time, and faced each other with questioning expressions, as if to say, *What now?*

"We should probably start heading back soon," Katya said.

I agreed. "I guess so. It's a long walk."

"Before we go, would you mind doing something with me?"

"What?" I said.

"Don't worry," she answered, a teasing note in her voice. "There's no danger involved."

She took my hand and led the way toward the church entrance, a half-height opening at the intersection of two stone walls.

"Is this really the entrance?" I asked. We waited for two older women to go in first. They stooped and shuffled slowly through the aperture.

Katya pointed to the wall above. "It's called the Door of Humility, because you really can't enter without bowing. You can see where the arched doorway used to be. It was bricked up and made smaller during Crusader times as a security measure, really—to prevent men on horseback from entering the church."

THE QUEST

I followed her through the doorway, and once inside we paused to let our eyes adjust to the relative darkness of the interior. Even in midday, the inside of the church was very dimly lit. Pillars lined each side of the room we were in, which Katya said was called the "nave," and there was a row of windows above each row of pillars, near the wood beams of the roof. But the light streaming in the windows barely seemed to reach us.

Still holding my hand, Katya pulled me to what looked like a large hole in the floor. Turns out, that's what it was.

Katya pointed. I could see a mosaic design on the floor below the level on which we stood. "That is part of the floor of the fourth-century church that stood on this spot. The mosaic is almost seventeen-hundred years old."

"Wow," I said.

She turned and led me farther into the church. We joined a line of people waiting to go somewhere. I looked around Katya and saw that the people at the front of the line were descending a semi-circular set of steps.

"We're going to the basement?" I asked.

She smiled. "You could say that."

"Are you going to tell me what this is all about?"

"I'm taking you to the birthplace of Jesus Christ."

"The—what?"

"The place Jesus was born."

"You can't be serious."

She chuckled. "I sure can."

We were moving closer to the steps, and I had a suspicion that the old woman in line in front of Katya was listening to our conversation. "The place where Jesus was born. You mean, Bethlehem."

"No. We are already in Bethlehem. We're going to the spot where Jesus was born."

She had to be pulling my leg. "I don't understand. How can you say that?"

"Well, I'm not the only one saying it. History says it."

"History."

"Yes, history. I showed you that mosaic on the way in. That mosaic floor was part of the church that was built on this site by the Emperor Constantine and his mother, Helena, in the early fourth century."

"Okay. So that was hundreds of year after Jesus was born."

"True. But before that, there was a Roman shrine here."

"What's that got to do with anything?"

"The Romans put the shrine where they did to obliterate the spot where Christians had visited and worshiped, and venerated the place as the birthplace of Jesus, from as far back as the first century."

We started heading down the narrow stone staircase. She continued in a hushed voice. "Of course, the Romans didn't realize that they were simply marking the spot for later generations to know where Jesus' parents huddled in a cave, that served as a stable, where he was born more than two thousand years ago."

CHAPTER 52

I heard sounds of weeping.

A moment later we were in a cave crammed with seven or eight people. We maneuvered around, and I located the source of the weeping sound. A gray-haired woman in a scarf knelt on what looked like a marble hearth in front of a fireplace. When the person in front of me shifted, however, I could see that it wasn't a fireplace at all but a niche in the wall of the cave, framed by elaborate screens and curtains and hung with maybe a dozen silver lamps. The woman continued to sob and spoke in a low voice in a foreign language as she bowed repeatedly to kiss a silver star in the middle of the niche.

"What's going on?" I whispered to Katya.

She laid a hand on my arm and guided me away from the niche into the long narrow space at the back of the cave, which was empty except for a single man in black robes who sat on the marble floor in the farthest corner, either sleeping or praying. I couldn't tell which.

Katya pointed back to the niche. "That is the spot where Jesus was born."

"No way," I said, with a mixture of wonder and skepticism coloring the phrase.

"Believe it or not. And that," she continued, indicating another tiny area to our right, "is where the manger stood."

I watched, intrigued, as the weeping woman stood and backed away from the niche with the silver star. Two others took her place, both women, kissing and stroking the silver star. By the time they finished, a group of maybe ten or twelve people had come down the stairs and crowded into the space around the star.

Katya seemed in no hurry to go anywhere, so we stood and watched for a few minutes in silence. Finally, she led me up a separate set of stone stairs and back into the church on the opposite side.

"Come this way," she said and led the way through a doorway into what looked like another church, one that seemed more "modern"— though still plenty old—and better-lighted than the place we'd just come from. She guided me into a small garden with a statue of a man in the center and walls or pillars all around it.

"So now you've seen the birthplace of Jesus," she said.

We sat on a stone bench. "Guess so," I answered.

We sat in silence for a few moments, then Katya suggested we grab something to eat before walking back to the checkpoint and the car. I agreed, so we left the church garden and returned to Manger Square. She asked me if a falafel pita would be okay.

"I don't know what that is," I said.

She let out a tiny chuckle. "Sorry. It's pretty much a staple around here. Like, I don't know, hamburgers back home."

I shrugged and agreed. She guided me to a street vendor and bought us each a pita filled with what looked to me like huge hush puppies, along with cucumbers, tomatoes, and bean sprouts. We each walked away a moment later with a pita in one hand and a can of soda in the other.

We sat on one of the short stone walls that surround parts of Manger Square. I took a cautious bite from my pita, as Katya watched.

"What's the verdict?" she asked.

I chewed and swallowed, then answered, "It's good. What is it?"

"Deep fried ground-up chick peas," she said.

I asked her to repeat herself, and she did. "Chick peas," I said. "Whatever that is."

"Some people don't like it, but I've really come to enjoy it. I'm still not used to hummus, but falafel I really like."

We continued eating and watching the traffic around the square. Katya pulled her phone from her pocket and checked it for messages.

"Anything?" I asked.

"Nothing."

"If they don't even return your calls, I don't know why we're wasting our time with them."

"I know. We're making more progress than they are."

"At least as far as we know." I turned the pita in my hands and peeled back more of the paper wrapper.

We sat in silence for a few more moments.

"What do you think it means?" I asked.

"What?"

"What do you think it means that that man was driving Dad's car?"

She chewed, swallowed. "I don't know. I suppose if he were kidnapped or held hostage somewhere, the kidnappers would want to get rid of his car."

"They wouldn't just use it themselves, right?"

"I don't know—probably not."

"Do you think it means he's—he's still alive?"

She looked at me. "I don't know, Emma. I don't know if it tells us anything, one way or another."

"Yeah, I guess you're right."

After another pause in the conversation, she asked, "So what do you think about the Grotto of the Nativity? Does it affect you in any way?"

"Affect me?" I asked. "I don't know. Should it?"

"It never fails to affect me."

"How?"

THE QUEST

She took a swig of soda and swallowed. She tilted her head slightly to one side. "The first time I came here—same with the Church of the Holy Sepulchre in Jerusalem—I was disappointed, big time, because I hadn't imagined that when I visited the birthplace of Jesus it would be in the basement of a giant church."

"Yeah, I thought it was kind of weird."

"But after I got over the initial disappointment, I was amazed, and still am, that I can actually stand or kneel at the spot where Jesus came into this world as a baby."

I waved off a puff of cigarette smoke from a short, white-whiskered man who had just walked past. "I can see that, I guess. For me, it's interesting, but I wouldn't say it awes me. I mean, it's just a place, you know? Jesus had to be born somewhere, so it was here. It's kind of cool to visit his birthplace, just like any great philosopher, but I can't say it really does anything for me."

She nodded for a moment. "So that's how you see Jesus? As a great philosopher?"

"Yeah, pretty much."

"Nothing more?"

"No," I answered. "Why should I? I mean, to me, the really important thing is what he taught, you know? To love each other and stuff like that."

"I agree, the things Jesus taught are really important. In fact, his contemporaries said no one ever taught like he did. And no one else's teachings have had anywhere close to the impact of Jesus' teachings."

I could tell there was more coming. "But?"

She smiled. "But I think there's a serious problem with stopping there."

"What do you mean?"

"I think that simply saying Jesus was a great teacher ignores the vast majority of the facts available to us."

"Like what? What facts?"

She took a last bite of her pita, balled up the wrapper, and shoved it into one of her pockets. "Well, the preponderance of evidence indicates that Jesus claimed to be more than a teacher or a philosopher. He once even made a point of asking his closest followers, 'Who do people say I am?' When he asked that, he wasn't asking what people were saying about his teachings or his philosophy. He asked, very specifically, 'Who do people say I am?'"

I finished my pita, and followed Katya's cue by putting the wrapper in the pocket of my jeans.

"In fact," she continued, "Jesus repeatedly asserted—or implied—that he was far more than a good teacher, but was in fact the unique, divine, pre-existing Son of God. On more than one occasion, he said so in such certain terms that his fellow Jews wanted to stone him! If the words and actions of Jesus himself are to be believed, he was—and is—much more than a great philosopher."

"Yeah, but people can claim anything they want. That doesn't make it so. Just because Jesus said he was God doesn't mean he was."

"True, but if we accept the overwhelming evidence that so strongly suggests Jesus claimed to be God while he lived on earth, we are faced with two possible conclusions."

"What?"

"Either his claims were true … or they were false."

CHAPTER 53

"Okay," I admitted. It seemed pretty obvious: Jesus' claims to be God were either true or false. "So you think they were true, and I think they were false."

"Not so fast. When Jesus said, 'Before Abraham was, I am,' that statement was either true … or false."

"When he said—what?"

"He said, 'Before Abraham was, I am.' It was not only a claim that he existed a couple of thousand years earlier. It was also a reference to the name of God, who called himself 'I Am.' Jesus was saying, 'I existed before Abraham, because I am God.'"

"Okay."

"But think for a minute what had to have been the case if Jesus' claims were false."

"If his claims were false, then he wasn't God. What's so hard to understand about that?"

She smiled. "Yes, but in that case, one of two things had to be true. Either Jesus knew his claims were false, or he did not know his claims were false."

An odd, indefinable feeling came over me just then. It felt something like the way a person must feel in the first moments of an earthquake, when they sense that something is moving beneath their feet, but they don't yet know that the ground is about to give way.

THE QUEST

I think Katya suspected what I was feeling, because she more or less repeated herself. "In other words, if Jesus was a mere man who told people that he was God, then either he knew his claims were false … or he did not know his claims were false. If he knew his claims were false, and he made them anyway, what would you call that?"

I was reluctant to answer. At the time, I didn't know why I was reluctant, but I was. "Lying," I said.

"Right. If he knew his claims were false, that would make him a liar."

I didn't know much about Jesus, but I knew enough to think that didn't feel right at all.

"That means," she continued, "that you cannot call Jesus a good moral teacher, because it is not moral to lie."

"Okay, but—"

"Worse than that," she went on, "if Jesus knew his claims to be God-in-the-flesh were false, and he made them anyway, he must have been an unspeakably evil man, because he clearly told people their sins were forgiven because of him, and he clearly told people they could trust him for their eternal destiny. If he was lying about who he was, he was lying about those things, too—and if he was lying about those things—"

"He was lying to them about their souls," I said, completing the thought.

"Exactly right," she said.

"So maybe he didn't know," I suggested. "Maybe he sincerely thought he was divine."

"Okay, so let's consider that possibility. Let's suppose he sincerely thought he was God but wasn't. What would that say about him?"

"It could just say he was wrong," I answered. "He was honestly mistaken."

"Really?"

"Why not?"

She thought for a moment. "Suppose one of your professors at school started telling everyone he was a spy for the CIA and was totally sincere about it but was honestly mistaken."

"That's different," I said.

"How?"

"Because," I started, but I wasn't sure of how I would finish. "Because … that's something a person could figure out pretty easily. You know? If he really thought that, he could call up the CIA and find out the truth."

"But you don't think Jesus could have put his belief to the test?"

I pursed my lips. "Maybe. I don't really know. If I thought I was God, how could I prove it one way or the other? That's not the sort of thing you can really prove."

"You could try working a miracle or two."

That stopped me cold. She'd been setting me up.

"You could, I don't know, walk on water or feed a crowd of thousands. Maybe even raise someone from the dead. If you failed, you're not the real thing. If you succeed …"

"Okay," I said. She had me. "I guess you made your point."

"Have I?" she asked. "Or are you just trying to shut me up?"

"Why can't it be both?" I asked.

"Let me suggest one more thing," Katya said. "And then I promise I'll shut up."

I thought of a sarcastic response but quickly thought better of it.

"If you can see why it's impossible simply to call Jesus a good teacher or great philosopher and be done with it—because if he wasn't who he said he was, then he was either lying or deluded—then I at least want you to consider the third possibility."

"What's that?" I asked, though I was sure I would regret it.

"That he was who he said he was."

"Oh, that."

"Yes," she said, chuckling lightly. "That."

"I guess that's possible."

She smiled and laid a hand on my knee. "Really? That's the best you can do?"

I rolled me eyes. I really wanted her to back off, but the loving way she said things was hard to resist. "Okay, I guess I can admit ... it's probably true."

"Probably true," she said, still smiling.

"Are we going to stay here all day?" I asked, standing.

"No," she said. She stood. "Let's get going."

From the American Press website

U.S. President Prods Middle East Leaders

✉ EMAIL 🖨 PRINT + SHARE

NEW YORK—In a much-anticipated speech before the World Economic Council yesterday, U.S. President Andrew Whitman prodded Middle East leaders to renounce violence, embrace human rights, focus on economic opportunity, and participate in peace negotiations.

"The time has come for nations throughout the Middle East to abandon the failed politics of hate and violence and embrace the rights of all people to be treated with respect, regardless of regional, ethnic, or religious differences," Whitman said. The speech, delivered to an audience of economists, political leaders and business executives at Cooper Union came in advance of a five-day Middle East tour that will take the president to Israel, Egypt and Saudi Arabia. The tone of the address, meant to pave the way for his talks with leaders in those countries, reflected what the administration sees as the obstacles its diplomacy faces in pushing a peace agreement in the final year of the Whitman administration.

President Whitman addressed recent events in the countries he will visit, as well as the recurring unrest in Syria and Lebanon. But he reserved his harshest words for the Israeli-Palestinian conflict. Referring to the recent massacre of a Jewish family in the West Bank, Whitman said, "Such violent acts as these cannot be tolerated by responsible authorities. They must be not only condemned, but stopped. Any governing authority that lacks the resolve or the power to bring an end to such reprehensible behavior by its people cannot be taken seriously as a negotiating partner in the peace process." Responsibility for the massacre has not been established, but it is widely believed to have been the work of Palestinian terrorists.

The president went on to announce an unprecedented shift in policy, linking U.S. aid to the cessation of violence and terrorism, vowing to quickly eliminate all aid—even humanitarian aid—to any governing authority that "endorses, encourages or allows" the continuation of violence.

"Make no mistake. We are resolved. We will unapologetically refuse support of all who reject peace," the president said.

The speech drew immediate praise from Israeli prime minister Yoel Nachmann and condemnation from the Palestinian Authority. Spokesman Mahmoud Amar called the president's speech "disappointing," adding that the U.S. president did not propose anything new.

"What the American president needs to do is to stop spouting slogans and threats and begin to respect the rights and aspirations of the Palestinian people. The peace process cannot resume until oppression has ceased, and the president took a step backward instead of moving forward toward permanent status talks in the hope of reaching a final agreement."

The White House moved quickly to affirm the president's commitment to the establishment of a Palestinian state. But the president's three-day stay in Jerusalem, which will include tours of the Masada fortress, visits to several holy sites in East Jerusalem and a host of meetings with Israeli leaders, is already drawing sharp criticism in the Arab world, where he is accused of being insensitive to Palestinian concerns.

The Mideast trip will be President Whitman's third visit to the region in the past nine months; and his national security adviser, Hammond Spencer, told reporters that the speech was intended to "draw a line in the sand" while also "giving some hope" that progress toward peace is possible.

Some analysts say the president's rhetoric is also designed to create a sense of urgency in advance of the next presidential election. They believe the president intends to pressure leaders in the region to work with his administration instead of waiting to know the results of next November's elections.

Spencer emphasized that the president is focused on securing an agreement before he leaves office next year. He hinted that President Whitman may return to the region again before his term concludes.

"He will not rest while there is still work to be done, and it is his to do," Spencer said.

Chapter 54

We'd been walking back toward the checkpoint for about thirty or forty minutes when Katya's phone rang. She pulled it from her pocket and looked at the Caller ID screen.

"Finally," she said, and answered the call.

It took just a few moments for me to discern that it was CID calling; neither of us had remembered Katya's intention to try calling them again. I couldn't tell if it was Mr. Avraham or the other guy, whose name I still had trouble remembering, but after awhile I pretty much assumed it was the other guy. Katya told him about the tip Sarah had given us about Dad's car and then told him that we'd already been to Manger Square to check it out.

He must have tried to upbraid Katya because her next words were clearly agitated. "I'm sorry, Mr. Yadin, but we were not going to sit around the apartment all morning, waiting until you or Mr. Avraham found it convenient to return my call. If we had left it up to CID, we still wouldn't know any more than we did last night, would we?"

We kept walking, though at a slower pace than before. Our path was mostly uphill now as we drew closer to the checkpoint, and I found myself breathing a little heavier.

I heard her tell Yadin that we had seen Dad's car and engaged the driver in conversation. She paid me a few compliments as she explained how I had gotten him to reveal some information and then told how he had admitted buying the car from a settler at Ma'ale Asher.

She stopped abruptly after speaking those words. Stopped talking and stopped walking. I stopped with her and could hear the man's voice coming through the phone, though I still couldn't make out what he was saying. Whatever it was, though, he was saying it loudly.

"I appreciate your concern," she said, finally, "but let me remind you that we were unable to reach you or Mr. Avraham. And, while I know our visit to Bethlehem was not without risk, in my opinion it was quite necessary in the absence of any clear instruction or initiative from CID."

She started walking again, slowly, so I kept pace with her. She listened briefly.

"No," she said, after a moment. "I don't believe he was a settler. He wasn't wearing a kipa, and he wasn't wearing a keffiyeh. If I had to guess, I would say he was a Palestinian Christian, but I can't be sure, one way or the other."

Another pause, then: "Yes, I did. I noticed that the license plate had been changed. The Sar Shalom Institute sticker was still in the window, like Sarah had said, but the license plate was green."

He must have asked her a series of questions then, because all I heard coming from her end was a series of "No's." Then, after asking if she could expect more timely responses from CID in the future, she said, "Shalom" and hung up.

"That was interesting," I said.

"Yes, it was," she countered, a note of disgust in her voice.

"Did he have any news about what *they* have been doing while we've been doing their job for them?"

She smirked but shook her head. "Not much, but he did tell me that Ma'ale Asher was attacked recently."

"Attacked?"

"He said it's been all over the news."

"Yeah, well, we've had other things on our minds."

"Someone somehow got into one of the homes there and slaughtered the whole family: father, mother, and two children. Slit their throats while they slept."

"Do they know who did it?" I asked. "Or why?"

"It's a settlement. That's probably the 'why.'" She sighed loudly. "But they don't know who yet."

"What do you think that means for Dad?" I asked. "If he's there?"

"I don't know," she answered. "I honestly don't know."

It took much longer to get back through the checkpoint going into Jerusalem than it had before, but we made it through without any hassle, other than having to wait for the people in front of us to be thoroughly hassled.

Once we were in the car and on the road, I asked Katya what she thought our next move should be.

"We've still got a lot of money to raise," she suggested.

"And why do you think Travis hasn't called?"

We entered a traffic tunnel, moving about seventy kilometers an hour, judging by Katya's speedometer. "Don't know," she said, her eyes darting back and forth from the road to the rear view mirror.

"Is something wrong?" I asked.

She didn't answer right away but kept watching the rear view mirror. I turned around in my seat and looked behind us. "What do you see?" I asked.

She shook her head. "I'm not sure."

We exited the tunnel. Katya turned off at the first opportunity, executed a quick right turn, and then checked the mirror.

"We're being followed," she said.

"Followed?" I still sat sideways in my seat. "By who?"

"That blue SUV."

I saw it then. It wasn't close, but after a few more turns, it was obvious that it was following us. "What do we do?"

THE QUEST

"Call Mr. Yadin back."

I reached for my cell phone. "What's the number?"

She fished her phone out of her pocket and handed it to me. "Here. Once you've got him on the line, tell him we're being followed, and I'll slow down until he's close enough to read the license plate."

"Are you sure about this?"

"No," she answered. "But it's the only idea I have."

Chapter 55

"Just hit the 'call' button twice," Katya said. "That calls the last number dialed."

I've used a phone before, I thought, putting the phone to my ear. "Maybe you should just lose him."

She shook her head and swerved to avoid slowing down for a bicyclist. "No, he's following me for a reason, which means he's connected somehow to this whole thing. If I lose him, we may never know how."

A woman answered my call. I tried to stay calm and asked for Mr. Avraham or Mr. Yadin—this time I remembered his name. I told her it was an emergency. I kept the phone to my ear and told Katya, "She's getting one of them."

Less than a half-minute later, a man's voice came on the line.

"Shalom," he said.

"Mr. Yadin?" I said.

As soon as she heard that, Katya slowed down abruptly, and I had to brace myself against the dashboard with my free hand. The car that was following us had to slam on his brakes to avoid rear-ending us.

"Get the number, get the number!" Katya shouted.

"Mr. Yadin, write this down!" I shouted into the phone. "30-415-36. Did you get that?"

THE QUEST

Katya floored the accelerator then, and with a squeal from our tires, we were once again putting distance between us and our pursuer. I repeated the numbers while they were fresh in my mind and explained to Mr. Yadin that they were from the license plate of a car that was following us.

He asked how long it had been following us.

"I don't know. Katya noticed it."

"At least since we entered the Route 9 tunnel," she said, and I repeated that information to Mr. Yadin.

"We're trying to get rid of him now. It's a blue SUV." He asked what kind of SUV it was, and I had to tell him I didn't know. "But you should be able to find out who he is from the license plate, right? And then tell us why he's following us?"

"I think I lost him," Katya said.

I turned in the seat. I didn't see him. She turned a corner a bit too fast, and I banged my head against the window.

"Sorry," she said.

I kept looking out the back of the car. Still no blue SUV. "Are you still there?" I asked Mr. Yadin.

He said yes, and I asked him if he could find out who the car belonged to.

"Yes," he answered. "But it will take some time."

"Okay. Call us back as soon as you can."

He asked if we were still being followed. I said no and ended the call—then I saw the blue SUV again.

"He's still following us," I told Katya. "He's getting closer."

She turned abruptly, and we were suddenly on a narrow street. Both sides were lined with parked cars, and there was only one lane between them.

"Oh, no," Katya said.

"What?" I turned and looked behind us. The blue SUV had made the same turn.

"It's a one-way street," she said.

I whipped around and looked through the windshield. A rider on a small motorcycle approached us head-on.

"Hold on," she said. She started honking her horn and flashing her headlights. The motorcycle stopped and pulled to one side, but there still wasn't room to pass him, and our pursuer was getting closer. If we stopped he would catch us.

Katya slowed but kept honking and flashing her lights. She rolled down her window and gestured to the biker to pull over further. I watched with relief as he pushed the bike backward up the street and found a gap between two parked cars large enough to slide his bike into. Katya accelerated as we passed him and soon turned a corner onto a two-way street. But the man followed us more closely than ever.

She weaved in and out of cars, taking every opportunity to put a vehicle between us and our pursuer. She crossed a busy intersection after the traffic light turned red, and the SUV kept coming, swerving to avoid a minibus that had started into the intersection as the signal changed.

"He's still there," I announced.

"I'm doing the best I can," she said.

Katya's phone was still in my hand. I checked it, but there was no call. I wondered how long it took to look up a license number in Israel, or if that would even tell us anything. Maybe the car was stolen or borrowed.

The other driver matched us turn-for-turn and mile-for-mile despite Katya's efforts to lose him. She avoided a man jumping out of a truck on the street side and nearly sideswiped a car coming from the other direction.

Then Katya's cell phone rang. "Finally," I said. I put the phone to my ear without checking the screen, expecting to hear Mr. Yadin's voice.

THE QUEST

"Shalom," the caller said. "This is Travis Richmond." When I didn't respond right away, he added, "Emma's friend from the plane?"

Katya passed the car in front of us and whipped back into the lane just in time to avoid colliding with a small truck in the oncoming lane.

"Travis?"

"Emma? Is that you?"

"Yes, it's me—"

"I got a message that you tried to reach me."

"Yeah," I said. "A while ago, but—"

"How is your father?"

"Travis, I can't talk right now."

"Oh," he said. "I'm sorry."

A line of traffic at a red light stopped us, and the SUV was two cars behind us. I watched him. He made no move to get out.

"I have to go." I hung up. I couldn't believe that after all this time, Travis would call now, but there was no time to think about it. The light turned green.

"Hang on," Katya said. She made an illegal left turn, and the man behind us followed, delayed only a moment by a car turning the opposite direction.

Another red light loomed ahead, but Katya steered onto the sidewalk long enough to bypass the line of cars and turn right at the light into a wide street nearly devoid of traffic. She floored it, and it looked like we might lose him until a tour bus appeared in front of us. She moved to go around him, but oncoming traffic made it impossible. She slammed on the brakes, and the car stalled.

"No," she growled.

She threw the car into park, then turned the key and pumped the gas pedal, but the engine wasn't turning over. I looked.

"Katya," I said.

She looked in the rear view mirror and saw. Our pursuer was directly behind us. I could see the expression on his face—or, rather, the lack of it. He looked directly at me. Then he opened his car door.

"He's getting out."

"Oh, Lord, please," she said. She inhaled, turned the key again, and this time the engine turned over. She put the car back in drive and stepped on the accelerator as the man approached her door.

We put good distance between us and him in the next few seconds as he scrambled back to his SUV. Katya took the first turn available to her but had to slow immediately for a crowd in a crosswalk. By the time we made the next turn, the SUV was behind us again.

"Where are we?" I asked.

"I don't know."

Another sharp turn, and we were on a two-lane, one-way street. Occasionally a vehicle obstructed the lane on the right, but Katya weaved the car past obstacles left and right, increasing our lead. She came to a fork in the road and took the right fork. I looked behind and saw the SUV take the other road.

"He went the wrong way."

"No," she said. "He knows where we're going. And I don't." She slammed on the brakes, almost causing a collision with a white car behind us. After a moment—and some angry horn-honking from behind—she steered into an alley, and we were soon headed the opposite direction.

"Do you think that did it?" I couldn't see him anywhere behind us.

"I hope so. I think he was about to cut us off at the next intersection or something like that."

I turned around in the seat, leaned my head back, and sighed with relief. "What do you think he would have done if he'd caught up with us?"

She stopped for a light, and I could see her hands trembling on the steering wheel. "You saw him come up beside me. I expected him to open my door and pull me out."

THE QUEST

"And then what?"

"I don't know." The light changed, and she drove forward, still regularly checking the rear-view mirror.

We rode in silence for a few moments until Katya said she knew where she was. I turned around and checked behind us again. I watched for a while and turned back around in my seat only after I was sure we were no longer being followed.

CHAPTER 56

Just to be safe, Katya drove a circuitous route back to the apartment. We arrived more than twenty minutes after our last sighting of the blue SUV. As we angled for a parking space on the street, however, I gripped her arm.

"Katya, look!" I said and pointed straight ahead.

The blue SUV was parked on our street, half a block ahead of us.

"What do we do now?" I asked.

She didn't answer but threw the car into reverse and backed up to an empty space at the curb she had passed just moments before. We sat in silence, staring at the now-familiar SUV.

"Maybe it's not him," she said.

"Pretty big coincidence, wouldn't you say?" I suggested.

She shrugged. "Do you remember the license plate number?"

"30-415-36," I answered.

"30-415-36."

"What are you thinking?"

She threw open her door. "Stay here," she said.

She was out of the car before I could answer. I hesitated a moment, then whispered, "I don't think so."

She saw me leave the car and stopped. "I thought I said to stay there."

"Yeah, you did, but you missed the part where I said, 'No way.'"

"The keys are still in the car. One of us needs to stay with the car."

"We can stand here arguing, or we can move."

She stared at me for an instant, then sighed. "Just don't do anything drastic like you did in Bethlehem."

We crept forward, behind the row of parked cars at the curb that ran down the opposite side of the street from the SUV. We stopped suddenly as a man's arm appeared out the driver's side window of the SUV and flicked the ash off a cigarette. We couldn't yet see the license plate.

"How many people?" I asked, hoping that Katya, standing just a foot or two closer, had a better angle on the vehicle's interior.

"Can't tell," she answered.

We crept closer, until she held up a hand. "That's it. It's the same car."

She was right. The last two digits of the license were hidden by the silver Volvo parked behind it, but the first five numbers were the same: 30-415.

"He's waiting for us," she said.

"What do you think he wants?"

She shot me a look that read, *What do you think?*

"Maybe not," I offered. "If he'd wanted to hurt us, he could have rammed us when you slammed on the brakes and the engine stalled, but he didn't."

"He was following us, Emma. And now he's watching the apartment, waiting for us to show up."

"Maybe he has information."

That caught her up short.

"And he has Israeli license plates. Not Palestinian."

"What do you think that means?"

"If Dad's being held in the West Bank …"

She shook her head. "We can't assume anything. The last thing we know is that his car was sold by a settler." She turned away from me and looked at the SUV. "Maybe by him."

"So what do we do? We can't go into the apartment with him sitting there."

She gestured for me to turn around, and we headed back to the car. Once inside, she pulled out her phone, which I had returned to her after my conversation with Travis, and selected the CID number again. A few minutes later, she was talking to Mr. Yadin again and explained our situation. After numerous "uh huhs" and "all rights," she ended the call.

"He said to leave the area," she told me.

"Leave the area? And do what?"

"He said his first concern was for our safety and that they would immediately send someone to monitor the situation and watch our visitor."

"Is that what you think we ought to do?"

She hesitated. "I don't know."

"What if he leaves before CID gets here? What happens then?"

"I don't know, but what if he sees us?"

"We're watching him. He can't make a move without one of us seeing him. At least until the CID people get here."

"I don't know, Emma."

"Well, I do. And if you start to go anywhere, I'm getting out."

"Emma, we're in this together."

"I know we are. I don't care what Mr. Yadin says, there's no way we should drive away and just take our chances."

We each fell silent for a few moments and stared at the SUV parked across from the apartment as the afternoon light disappeared and evening shadows moved in.

"Don't you want to know?" I asked her.

THE QUEST

"Know what?"

"Who he is, why he's watching us, what he wants."

"Yes, of course, but not at the risk of our lives."

We fell silent again for a few minutes. I felt my eyes begin to fill with tears, but I refused to turn away from watching the SUV. "I'm just tired of waiting. After all this time of not knowing anything and not getting anywhere, I'm tired of waiting to find out where my dad is and how he's doing. Now that something's going on, I don't want to waste the opportunity."

"I know. You're right."

I thought I heard a quiver in her voice, so I turned to look. There were tears in her eyes, too.

CHAPTER 57

It took nearly a half hour for Mr. Yadin—and some other man—to appear in a black SUV, creeping along our street. We spied them when they were a few car lengths behind our position, and I rolled down my window. They came to a stop next to us.

"That's him," I said, pointing out the man in the blue SUV.

Mr. Yadin, looking past the driver from the vehicle's passenger seat, nodded and eyed both Katya and me. I thought he was going to say something about us still being in the area despite his instructions, but he didn't. Instead, he spoke a few words in Hebrew to the driver, and they slowly drove forward.

Katya and I watched as Yadin and his companion crept past the blue SUV without stopping. They sped up after passing the blue SUV, then turned at the end of the block. Katya and I shot each other curious looks.

"Maybe he's circling to come back around a second time?"

"Maybe," Katya said.

A few moments after Yadin moved out of sight, however, the man in the blue SUV pulled out of his parking spot.

"He's leaving!" I said.

"Mr. Yadin must have spooked him," she said.

THE QUEST

I turned in my seat to look behind us. Yadin was nowhere to be seen. I turned back and saw the blue SUV proceed a block farther up the street and turn in the opposite direction from where Yadin had gone.

"Follow him!" I said.

"What? No!" she said.

"He's going to get away!"

"I'm not moving," she said emphatically. "We're going to wait here until Mr. Yadin comes back around."

Within a few seconds, Yadin's black SUV appeared on our street. I stuck my hand out the window and waved frantically for them to pull alongside. When they did, I told them what had happened and where the blue SUV had turned. They sped off in pursuit.

Katya and I sat like statues as the minutes ticked by. I stared at the empty space where the blue SUV had been and wondered if we'd just lost the chance to find Dad, if we'd had an opening—and blown it. Bad as that was, what if we never even knew? What if I had to spend the rest of my life wondering if I'd had a chance? What if—

I reached for the door handle just as Mr. Yadin's vehicle appeared again. I said nothing to Katya, but I think she noticed the black SUV's approach.

Once they pulled up next to us, the driver rolled down his window, and Yadin leaned forward. Shaking his head, he said, "We lost him."

"Great! Just great!" I slammed my hand on the dashboard. "We should have followed him. I told you we should have followed him!"

Katya was as calm as I was upset. "Any idea yet who he is?" she asked.

Yadin shook his head. "Not yet, but soon."

"What are we paying you people for? So far, the only information we have, *we've* gotten," I said, indicating Katya and me. "And then we sit here for a half hour or so watching the guy, and within thirty seconds of you showing up, you manage to chase him off!"

"These things take time," he said.

"Well, I'm tired of waiting." I was done talking to him.

"Will you call me," Katya asked politely, "when you have any information?"

"Yes," Yadin said. "The minute we know anything, we will contact you."

"I won't hold my breath," I said.

We watched Yadin's SUV disappear down the block.

I rolled up my window, Katya extracted the keys from the ignition and locked the doors, and we left the car where it was parked. We walked up the block to the apartment. Both of us eyed the still-empty space where the man in the blue SUV had waited, but neither of us spoke. There was nothing to say. We had missed a golden opportunity and we might never get another one.

I entered the apartment behind Katya, who held the door open for me and then turned back to close the door and turn the deadbolt. I took two steps and froze.

Someone was there.

From the Israel News Service website

EU Backs Whitman's Call for Mideast Peace

BRUSSELS— European Union ministers said today that they supported United States President Andrew Whitman's call for peace and progress in the Middle East.

THE QUEST

EU foreign policy chief Jurgen Stein said the U.S. president had consulted the EU in advance of his address at Cooper Union in New York, and garnered a favorable response from most EU member countries. He said President Whitman and EU are very much "on the same page" in the matters touched on by the president's address.

Stein spoke as representatives of the 27 member nations in the European Union were gathering for a two-day conference on Global Climate Change. He said that, in particular, President Whitman's linkage of foreign aid to governments' intentions and effectiveness in stemming the rising tide of Mideast violence met with broad acceptance among member nations.

Palestinian Authority spokesman Mahmoud Amar dismissed the EU statement, calling it "propaganda." "The member nations of the European Union are friends of the Palestinian people, and will not desert us in our pursuit of peace. They know that any effort to cut expenses on the backs of the Palestinian people can only result in much suffering and bloodshed."

U.S. national security adviser Hammond Spencer hailed the EU statement as a "welcome sign" of cooperation and unity among the nations of the world.

The EU is the largest donor to the Palestinian Authority, providing more than €700 million in aid last year. The EU also provides aid to Egypt and Jordan. The European Union does not provide direct aid to Israel.

CHAPTER 58

I made no sound. I couldn't. My mouth hung open, but I couldn't even breathe. A man sat in shadow in Katya's prayer chair in the corner.

She bumped into me, probably expecting me to move into the living room instead of standing still just inside the entryway. An instant later, I knew she'd seen him because she emitted a growl like a caged animal and maneuvered in front of me, her arms spread out at her sides as if to bar my progress. It didn't matter. I wasn't going anywhere.

"Get out!" she roared. When I didn't move, she said, "Emma! I'm talking to you. Get out! Go!"

It took a gargantuan effort, but I finally managed to turn and reach for the deadbolt on the door. And then the visitor spoke, and I froze again.

"I will not hurt you," his calm voice said. "I am here to help."

"Emma!" Katya shouted. "Go!"

I turned back and looked at him over her shoulder.

"Who are you?" Katya asked the shadowed figure. "How did you get in here?"

"I am sorry. It was important that I speak to you alone." His English was very precise, with a hint of an accent, maybe British, maybe not.

"I bet," she said. Then: "Get out of my house—NOW."

"Please," he said. "I will go, but I beg you to listen."

THE QUEST

"You break into my house and you want me to listen to you?"

"I did not break anything," he said. It sounded like he was actually smiling. "The glass doors were not locked very tight."

Katya lowered her arms. She turned her head slightly and spoke to me. "Unlock the door, Emma."

"It's the man who was following us," I said.

She still looked like she was watching him closely. "Unlock the door, and open it. If he moves any closer, I want you to run."

"What about you?"

"I'll run, too, but it will be a lot easier if the door is open first."

I turned the deadbolt lock, gripped the doorknob, and pulled the door open. The man in the corner made no move that I could see.

"What do you want?" she asked the man.

"I have news."

"What kind of news."

"About your husband."

I heard her catch her breath. I was holding mine.

"Go on," she whispered.

"It is difficult," he said.

"Difficult?" Katya asked.

"Sensitive."

Neither of us spoke. I inched closer, so close that one of Katya's stray hairs tickled my cheek.

"Is he—" she said. "Is he alive?"

"Yes," he said.

She inhaled sharply. I thought she was going to buckle so I gripped her shoulders from behind. In the next moment I thought my *own* knees might buckle. He was alive! I felt a surge of relief and held Katya tighter, whether to hold her up or myself, or to keep me from running over to our visitor to hug him, I couldn't be sure.

"Are you sure you do not want to sit?" he said.

Katya gripped one of my hands without moving it off her shoulder. "I'm sure. Is he hurt?"

"He is slightly hurt. Not serious."

I finally found my voice and asked, "Do you know where he is?"

He hesitated. "As I say, it is sensitive."

"What does that mean?" Katya's tone was sharp. She was losing patience. I was right with her.

"It will take time to tell you."

"We're listening," she said.

More hesitation, then a sigh. "Last week, a family of four was killed in the Jewish settlement of Ma'ale Asher in the West Bank."

"Yes," Katya said.

"Your husband had visited with a different family in that same settlement until late that evening. Less than a kilometer from the settlement, he came upon an auto that had broken down and was partially blocking the road. He offered to help the men get it started again."

He stopped.

"Go on," Katya said.

"He worked on the auto for about thirty minutes, and whatever he did, it worked."

"He's good with cars," I offered.

I saw the man nod. "Are you sure you will not sit?"

"Please, just go on," Katya said.

He seemed to think for a moment, then continued. "Those men were the attackers of the Blumenthal family." He coughed. "They are … Palestinian nationalists."

"Is that what you call them?" Katya said.

"It is what they call themselves. In any case, your husband had seen them, talked to them. He could identify them. They faced a … dilemma, especially since he had seen them and their auto in such close proximity to Ma'ale Asher. When the news about their actions came out, he would certainly report having seen them, what they looked like, the color and make of their auto, and so on."

"What did they do to him?" Katya asked, her voice pierced with fear.

"He is well, I assure you, but their position was precarious."

"*Their* position?" I said.

Katya squeezed my hand tighter, signaling me, I understood, to be careful. She was right to do so. I didn't want to take a chance at stopping the flow of information or hindering—in any way—the possibility of finding my father.

"Yes, well. These men knew, of course, if they were discovered to have committed the crimes, the retribution from the Israeli government would be swift and merciless. They couldn't take that chance, so they … required your husband to go with them."

"That explains his car," I told Katya. "It was sitting there, with the keys in it and everything. Someone found it and sold it to that guy we saw in Bethlehem."

"Where did they take him?"

"They couldn't let him identify them," he continued, ignoring her question, "but they also didn't wish to kill him."

"Why?" Katya asked. "They had just killed a whole family."

"A family of Jews. Settlers, whom they view as invaders. These men believe they are at war with Israel, but more important, they identified your husband as an American and recognized that killing an American could be a dreadful mistake … from their perspective."

"But kidnapping an American is apparently okay," I said.

He paused. "I am not defending their actions. But your American president is threatening to cut off all aid—currently more than a billion dollars—to the Palestinian people in the wake of those killings. The Palestinian leadership believes it is best if this matter were to be resolved quickly and quietly—without further violence. And without any government or media involvement."

"So … this is about money," Katya said.

"To them. To me, it is about returning your husband to you. I will presently explain my agency in this affair if you will allow me to continue."

"Okay," Katya said, her tone a bit softer than before.

"As I say, these men have no wish to invite attention or to force the American president to fulfill his threat. And they also cannot allow themselves to be identified as the attackers of the Blumenthal family. As I said, the situation is sensitive."

"But my dad is okay?" I asked.

He moved his head from side to side. "He is injured—"

"Injured?" Katya said.

"How?" I asked.

"His first night in the custody of these men, he attempted to escape."

"What did they do?"

"I am told that the young men who were guarding him … broke his leg with a metal pipe."

Chapter 59

"Has he seen a doctor?" Katya asked before I could. I felt tears welling in my eyes as I pictured my father being brutally beaten with a lead pipe. "Has the leg been set?"

"Yes, that is how I entered this situation. I am a doctor."

"Is he going to be all right?" I asked.

"The leg is set, and I placed it in a splint. It should be x-rayed, though, and he will probably need surgery—certainly, I think."

"Is he in pain?" she asked.

"Some," he answered. "It is a serious break."

Katya turned to me. The room had gotten darker as we had talked, and she and I still stood in the entryway. "Should we sit?" she asked.

"Yeah," I answered. I turned to close the door, but she stopped me.

"Leave it open," she said. She walked to the couch and turned on the lamp. For the first time, we saw our visitor's face clearly. He was middle-aged, maybe forty-five or fifty years old, slim, with a full head of white hair and black eyebrows.

I joined Katya on the couch. "So you're his doctor," I said.

"Yes," he answered. "I am an Israeli Arab."

"A what?" I asked.

"Israeli Arab. I am Israeli by citizenship, Arab by language and culture, and Muslim by religion. I have family in the territories, and that is how I became involved in this situation."

"One of the men?" Katya asked.

A deep sadness flickered in his eyes until he glanced away. "My sister's firstborn."

"You can't turn in your nephew," she said.

"Not for that reason—for what would happen to her—to our family."

Silence passed between us until I asked, "So how do we get my dad back?"

"This is why I had to speak to you," the doctor said. "It cannot involve the authorities. Not Israeli, not American."

"Okay," Katya said slowly. She looked at me, then back to him. "I hired a private security company."

"Yes, I know."

"If you knew that, why didn't you just contact them? Why did you have to break into my house?"

"I do not trust them."

"Why not?" she asked.

"Do you know who the Mossad is?"

"Yes," she answered. "That's the Israeli spy agency."

"That is correct. Many private security companies in Israel employ former Mossad. I am convinced some—like the people you are working with—employ active Mossad."

"Okay," she said. "So what?"

"It makes a sensitive situation even more sensitive."

"Just tell me how to get my husband back."

"You must agree not to involve your security company or any authorities of the Israeli or American governments."

"What else?"

"You must never identify the men who ... have been holding your husband."

She leaned forward. Her eyes blazed. The muscles in her jaw tightened. "You mean the men who massacred a mother and father and children? You want us to act like that never happened?"

"Also, your husband must never identify them."

"So let me get this straight. We just promise to keep your bloody secret … and what—you'll let my husband go?"

He grimaced. "I do not have the ability to let your husband go. He is not in my custody. I am a messenger. Someone who hopes to save a life."

"So," Katya said, standing and thrusting both hands into her pants pockets, "you think the men who are holding my husband will just accept a promise from me not to say anything? I find that hard to believe."

I had to agree with her. This was sounding ridiculous.

"I can't imagine that my husband would agree."

Our visitor cleared his throat. "He has already agreed."

"What?" Katya and I both spoke the word at the same time, so that our voices were one.

"He is in agreement with our terms."

"I can't believe that. You can't expect me to believe that."

"I have not yet explained everything," he said.

Her eyes narrowed, but she didn't speak.

"My nephew's accomplice," he said. "He is a Fatah official and he runs a children's home in the West Bank."

"An official." Katya nearly spat the words.

"Yes. That fact has helped to convince your husband."

"Why?" I asked, a split second before Katya this time.

"Your husband has visited the children's home and understands that if any harm were to come to the director of the home, the children there would be in great danger."

"From who?" Katya growled.

He didn't answer.

She leaped up from her seat, and for a moment I thought she might attack the man. But she stepped over my legs and walked a few feet closer to him. "Who would those children be in danger from? Huh?"

He didn't move. Didn't speak. Didn't meet her gaze.

"Answer me!" she said, with such force it made me jump.

He turned and fastened a pained look on her. "From the director or his ... colleagues."

Katya paced back and forth between the table and the end of the couch. "So you're holding the children in that children's home hostage. In exchange for our silence about the Blumenthal murders! And if we don't agree, one of the men responsible for those murders may hurt my husband *and* who knows how many innocent children— in the home he's in charge of!"

"I must emphasize again—"

"I don't care," she said, gritting her teeth. "I don't care if you're just a messenger or the devil himself. You people are monsters, all of you, living in a monstrous culture with a monstrous worldview, using children as pawns—as shields—for your criminal activity, and you act like it's 'just the way things are'! Putting people in charge of children's homes who would murder innocent children because they're the wrong religion or simply because they're useful game pieces in some sick, sick game. Well, I refuse! Do you hear me? I refuse! I will not be bullied by people who treat children like chess pieces."

I jumped up from the couch and went to her. I thought she might soon throw something at him or turn and leave the apartment and I didn't want that. She was right, of course. I knew she was right. There was no doubt about that, but I wanted my dad back, too.

I guided her back through the entryway until we stood just outside the open apartment door. She was crying, and her tears threatened to bring tears to my eyes, too, but I tried to keep them from surfacing. I spoke her name repeatedly, softly, comfortingly.

"Katya," I said. "Katya, listen. You're right. Everything you said is right, but we may never have another chance. If we don't cooperate, what are they going to do? What will happen to Dad?"

"I don't know," she said, burying her face in her hands.

"Listen to me," I pleaded. It suddenly struck me that our roles had reversed, since I had wanted to throttle Mr. Avraham at CID and Katya had been the voice of reason. This time I had to keep the situation from deteriorating further. "What if this is our only chance? If we refuse, and this guy leaves here tonight, how will we ever find Dad?"

"But—"

"Look, I know this is a horrible choice. I don't like this guy any more than you do. But what choice do we have? What alternative is there?"

"How can we believe anything he says? Anyone who would use little children as a bargaining tool?"

"I know, but suppose he walks out of here. What happens then? What happens to Dad?"

She blinked at me and said nothing.

"Why don't we focus right now on getting Dad back? When we're all three together again, he can help us figure things out. He's so good at that." I felt a tear escape and quickly wiped it away. "Can we do that? Can we just get him home? Please?"

My voice cracked on the word *please*, and I started to lose it. She lifted her face and looked at me. She shook her head, but I thought I saw a glimmer of hope in her expression. A slight surrender.

"Give me a minute," she said. "Just give me a minute."

I stepped back but still faced her. I waited. She closed her eyes for a few long moments.

Finally, she opened her eyes again and let out a long, slow breath. "Okay. You're right. You're absolutely right."

"All right," I said. I wiped more tears from my face and straightened up. She did the same, and we walked together back into the living room. This time I closed the door behind us.

THE QUEST

Our visitor still sat in the corner chair. Katya and I returned to our previous positions on the couch. She was perched at the front of the couch, in virtually the same posture as before. I crossed my legs and placed my hands on my knee. We sat in silence for a minute or two. Katya finally broke the silence.

"I want my husband back. You know where he is and who has him. So I will agree to your terms. I will not to speak of this to anyone."

He shifted slightly and leaned forward in the chair. "They are not my terms, strictly—"

She shot him a look that was sharp enough to cut him off in mid-sentence. "But I have some terms, too."

I turned. "What are you doing?" I whispered.

She placed a steady hand on my hands. "He will be brought …" She paused, apparently running the possibilities through her mind. "He will be brought to the Kotel. Tomorrow at noon."

He opened his mouth, but Katya continued speaking, even more emphatically now. "And *you* will personally return him to me at the flagpole, in the middle of the barrier that separates the place of prayer from the plaza."

He sat motionless, wordless, for a few moments. "Tomorrow. Noon. At Al-Buraq."

Katya didn't smile, but she seemed pleased. "Agreed?" she said.

"It is agreed," he answered solemnly.

"Good," she said.

"There is one thing more."

She leaned back. "I thought there might be. How much?"

"I beg your pardon?"

"How much?" she repeated. "How much is the ransom?"

He shook his head. "There is no ransom. There is a final condition, however."

CHAPTER 60

"A final condition." Katya repeated the man's words.

"What is it?" I said.

"I must have your cell phones."

Katya stiffened and thrust a hand into her pocket. "Our cell phones?"

"I am afraid I must insist."

"You want our cell phones?" I said.

"It is the only way."

Katya and I looked at each other. If we gave him our cell phones, we would have no way of calling for help. Which, it dawned on me, was why he had to take them from us. He couldn't take the chance that we might contact the police or CID despite Katya's promises.

I pulled my cell phone from my pocket and set it on the table next to his chair. Katya kept her hand in her pocket.

"What if I refuse?" she asked.

He shrugged. "I leave and you will never see me again."

"And my husband?"

"You will never see him again."

She pulled the phone from her pocket and held it in both hands. "I don't understand. What's to prevent me from going next door to the Landaus' apartment and borrowing their phone once you leave?"

THE QUEST

"I am not leaving."

"What?" Katya and I both spoke at the same time.

"I am not leaving."

"What do you mean, you're not leaving?"

He leaned back in the chair. Assumed a nonchalant air, I thought. "I must remain with you until the exchange is made—for safety reasons."

"For safety reasons?" she said.

He responded with the tiniest of shrugs.

"So you plan to stay here all night? In *my* apartment?"

"I am afraid it is necessary."

She and I looked at each other. I couldn't believe he was serious. I couldn't believe this was happening. And I could tell she felt the same way.

"What's next?" she said.

He turned his head slightly, as though he hadn't heard her question. "I beg your pardon?"

"What's next?"

"I do not understand."

"You tell us we have to give up our cell phones, then you tell us you're not leaving my apartment. What's next? Do you have to tie us up, too?"

He smiled weakly. "That will not be necessary. I have no wish to be … difficult."

"Just tell me what else has to happen." She was clearly fed up. I was, too.

He blinked as though he was surprised. He looked from Katya to me, then back again. "Nothing. Nothing else has to happen."

"So we give you our cell phones. You stay here until we go to the Kotel to meet Daniel—my husband—and that's it?"

"Yes."

She stared at him, saying nothing.

After a long silence, I couldn't stand it anymore. "Katya," I said.

She looked at me.

"It's worth a try," I said.

She looked from me to the cell phone in her hands. Fiddled with it for a moment. Then extended it to the stranger.

He took it from her and set it on the table next to my phone. Then he took off one of his shoes and hammered her phone several times with the heel of his shoe. Then he repeated the process with my phone.

Without a word, Katya stood from the couch and picked up her Bible and journal from the table next to our enigmatic visitor. Then she moved to the sliding glass doors, through which he had entered. She locked them and wedged them shut with a single length of wood. Then she went to the front door of the apartment, locked it, and returned.

She looked at me. "I suppose we should try to get some sleep."

"Yeah." I stood, then led the way to the bedroom.

We entered the bedroom, and she closed the door behind us. "I can sleep on the floor if you like," she said.

"No, that's okay. We can share the bed."

We sat on the bed. Neither of us spoke.

My mind whirled. The events of this day—of the past several days—overwhelmed me. The ups and downs. The emotional extremes. The seismic changes. I had awakened that very morning with no inkling of where my dad might be, other than Sarah's news of the night before about his car being spotted in Bethlehem. I didn't even have any assurance that he was alive.

Now, just hours later, Katya and I had more information about Dad than we had any reason to hope for that morning. He was alive! And tomorrow might bring this nightmare to an end. I might actually see my father, God willing.

That phrase leaped into my mind with unexpected ease: God willing. What was that about? God willing? Why wouldn't he be willing? What possible reason could he have for getting my hopes up—as they were now—and then failing to return my father to his wife and me?

I shook my head. Here I was, thinking about God as if he were real. As if I believed in him. Did I? I recognized that I had done little praying since arriving in Israel. Wasn't sure exactly why. Maybe I'd been too busy. Maybe I felt more powerful than I had back home. Maybe I didn't feel the need for God as much as I did when I first learned that Dad had gone missing.

Whatever the reason, I didn't want to take any chances. I felt an overwhelming need to pray. I turned to Katya. She stared at the bedroom wall we both faced. I had no idea what she was thinking, but I decided to take a chance.

"Do you think we ought to pray?" I asked.

Katya looked at me in amazement, as if I'd just performed a magic trick. She hesitated only a moment, though, before she grabbed my hand and started praying. She prayed for Dad, for his safety through the night. She prayed for his broken leg. She prayed for our safety from the man in the living room and from the people he represented. She prayed that he would follow through on our agreement and make tomorrow's noon meeting happen. She prayed for the people who were holding Dad, and asked God to keep them from taking any action that would jeopardize Dad's release. She prayed for the children in that children's home. She prayed for the Blumenthal family and all their friends and neighbors who mourned for them. She prayed for me, then for herself. I was a little surprised she didn't pray for the people in China or Africa or something like that.

As she finished praying, I felt an enormous sense of relief wash over me. The man was still there in the apartment. We were still virtually prisoners here until we left for the meeting the next day. Dad was still a hostage. Externally, nothing had changed. But I felt different, like nothing I'd ever experienced before. I guess I'd felt like my little prayers had helped me and introduced some calm into my panic after I'd met with Rabbi Rachel, but Katya's prayers had a different effect on me. It seemed like I could actually feel my heart growing as she went on and on, until—when she finished—I felt more than relief. I think I was starting to feel … faith.

We sat again in silence for a few moments after her prayer ended until she faced me and asked, "Are you hungry? I could fix something."

Neither of us had eaten since Bethlehem. "No. I don't think I could eat."

"Me either. Think we'll get any sleep tonight?"

"I doubt it. We probably should—to be ready for tomorrow, but I don't see how."

A few more moments of silence passed between us.

"I wish we could go right now," I said.

"I do, too."

We took turns using the bathroom and preparing for bed. When we were both ready to turn in, Katya stepped over to the small bookcase against the wall.

"Help me move this?" she said.

"Move it? Where to?"

"In front of the door. I think I'll just feel better if there's something in front of the door."

We slid it into place. It was heavier than I thought. Still, it wouldn't stop anyone who wanted to get in.

Katya seemed to read my thoughts. "I know it's silly. It just makes me feel better."

After that, we both climbed into bed. I laid on my back and stared at the ceiling, while Katya lay next to me, reading her Bible and writing in her journal.

CHAPTER 61

KATYA'S JOURNAL

Thank you, Lord, for the blessing of praying with Emma—of being asked to pray with her. Thank you for providing the presence of mind and the words to pray. Even now, I'm not sure what I said, but I know you were helping me.

Can this be it? Is this really the last night before my husband is returned to me? It doesn't seem real, but I don't want to doubt. Please help me not to doubt. Give me faith and hope. Please make tomorrow the end of this long dark journey. Don't let me hope in vain. Don't let me be mistaken. Don't let anything go wrong. Please don't let my hopes be dashed.

Guard Daniel's life, Lord. Keep him through this night, and see him safely home tomorrow.

Let that man, whoever he is, keep his word.

Let Mr. Yadin and Mr. Avraham know what to do.

Let those orphans be unharmed.

Let that family's murderers be brought to justice.

THE QUEST

Most of all, Lord, give me back my husband; give Emma back her father. Give Daniel his wife and daughter, in Jesus' name, amen.

CHAPTER 62

When I awoke before sunrise the next morning, Katya was reading her Bible … again.

"You didn't stay up all night reading, did you?" I asked.

She shook her head. "I slept some," she said.

She asked me to help her move the bookcase back in place, and she left to go to the bathroom. When she returned to the room, I clearly surprised her by showing her the Bible I had been reading and asking where I could find the story of Jesus' life. I explained that I needed something to occupy my mind until we left for the Kotel, as she called it. Once she regained her composure, she told me she'd be right back and left the room.

A moment later she appeared with a different Bible. She handed it to me, suggesting I read that version instead of the one I held. The cover didn't look like a Bible at all, but she assured me it was. She even opened it and marked a page she suggested as a good starting point.

"Is he still out there?" I asked.

"Yes," she said. "Still out there." She said she'd try to fix something for breakfast … without burning it.

By the time she called me for breakfast, I had read almost all the way through the story of Jesus, which Katya said was written by a man named Mark. We talked about it through breakfast. Our visitor never moved from where he had been sitting. Katya even offered him food, but he declined the offer.

After the breakfast dishes were washed and put away, Katya and I sat on the couch and faced the doctor.

"When do we leave?" she asked.

He looked from her to me, then back again at her. For a moment, I was afraid he was going to give us bad news, telling us the meeting had been called off or something like that, but he didn't.

He stood, and then he answered her question. "Now," he said.

We had to ride with the stranger in the blue SUV, which he had parked in an alley nearby. On the way there, he explained that we would wait with him from a distance until Dad appeared at the designated spot, near the flagpole. Then we would be free to go meet him, and our ordeal would be over.

It wasn't yet 10 a.m. when we arrived at the entrance to the spacious plaza that leads to the Western Wall, what Katya called the "Kotel." She had explained on the way that the Kotel was the foundation wall of the Temple Mount, which once held the Temple, and thus was the most sacred site on earth to the Jews. I asked her why she called it the "Kotel," and she said the word was just Hebrew for "wall," but to an Israeli or religious Jew, there was only one "Kotel."

"He called it something else last night, didn't he?" I asked.

"He used the Arabic name."

The doctor led us through a checkpoint with metal detectors and armed guards. Once on the other side, I said, "Now I know why you chose this place."

She smiled. "Not just because of that, but also because of them." She pointed to the soldiers in crisp olive-green uniforms all around the area. Some were clearly armed and they were watching the crowd.

He led us up a staircase, and we stopped at a vantage point where we could easily look over the entire area. He stationed himself at the railing a few feet from us and lit a cigarette. I wondered if he had gone all night without smoking, or if he had actually had the courtesy to step out of the apartment. It seemed incongruent that he would be discussing the return of a hostage and still be too polite to smoke in the apartment.

It was only mid-morning, but there were people everywhere, walking here or there, talking in pairs or small groups, and a solid line of people faced the stone wall from one end to the other.

"What are they doing?" I asked Katya.

"Praying."

"All of them?"

She pointed out the larger men's area on our left and the section set aside for women to the right. "It's never empty," she said.

"Never?"

"People pray here all hours of the day and night."

"Is that the flagpole where we're going to meet?" I pointed at the blue-and-white flag at the center.

"Yes," she said.

I thrust my hand into my pocket, fished out my wallet, and pulled out the folded paper Artie had given to me when he dropped me off at the airport. It seemed like half a lifetime ago. I showed it to Katya. "Artie asked me to put this in the wall?" It came out as a question.

"A lot of people do that. When you get close to the wall, you'll see thousands of tiny slips of paper stuffed in every crack and crevice in the wall."

"So I just walk up and stick it in there?"

She pointed to the women's section. "As long as you're on the women's side."

I turned to the doctor and asked if I could go to the wall, showing him the tightly folded paper and explaining that I wanted to place a prayer in the wall.

He waved his cigarette. "You must talk to no one. If you do, the exchange will not take place."

"Okay," I said.

"Would you like me to go with you?" Katya asked.

"No." The doctor answered for me. "She must go alone."

THE QUEST

I descended the steps and crossed the wide plaza until I came to the opening in the low fence that marked the area for prayer. Most of the people inside the fence were gathered close to the wall, though some women were clustered at the barrier adjoining the men's area, watching something going on over there.

I spied an empty spot at the wall and walked up. Katya was right. Every possible space in the wall was crammed with a piece of paper, folded or rolled up. I looked around and finally found a spot for Artie's note. I hesitated. I hadn't thought much about it since Artie gave it to me way back at the airport, but now I was tempted to read it. He hadn't told me not to. Then again, he hadn't said I could.

I finally poked it into a crevice in the wall without reading it, adding it to the countless other prayers people had left behind. I thought, if those are all prayers, then God must be very busy. I hoped he wasn't too busy for one more, though.

I leaned my forehead against the cold stone face of the wall. "God," I said. "Please bring my father home. Please. If you're there, if you're listening, please bring him home."

After I joined Katya again, we stood together in silence, watching as people came and went. After a while, she pointed to the gold dome above and beyond the wall. "That," she said, "is the Dome of the Rock, and the gray dome is the Al-Aqsa mosque. They are both holy places to Muslims."

"Why?"

"Several reasons. Inside the dome is an exposed rock. In the Bible it's called Mount Moriah, where Abraham nearly sacrificed Isaac, which King David later acquired as the site for the Temple. Muslims believe it's the place from which Muhammad's winged horse leaped to carry him to heaven. They say the rock bears the imprint of the horse's foot."

"Huh. What about Christians?"

"What do you mean?"

"Is this a holy place for them? For you?"

She thought for a moment. "I guess you could say that, especially since we know that up there," she said, pointing to the platform where the gold-domed building stood, "was the Temple complex, where Jesus' trial was held. And just over there," she continued, pointing to the right, "are the Temple steps, where Jesus taught. About a ten minute walk behind us is the Church of the Holy Sepulchre. So for me, as a follower of Jesus, Jerusalem is filled with many holy places. The whole city is a holy place because this is where Jesus lived, taught, walked, and died … and rose again."

"Hmm," I said. I continued to watch, fascinated, as the adherents of three major religions came and went through the plaza in front of me. Bordering the Western Wall precincts was a snaking covered walkway that led from the plaza area up to the elevated platform where the Dome of the Rock and the gray-domed mosque sat. Jews, Muslims, Christians. It was mind-boggling. On the one hand, I was amazed that all these people walked—and worshiped—practically side by side. I guess my impression was that they would all be constantly fighting with each other, but that obviously wasn't the case. On the other hand, there were armed guards all around, metal detectors, and various other security precautions; these things clearly showed that the calm and cooperation could be shattered easily and instantly.

The time was passing slowly. I tried to ignore the doctor's presence while stemming my excitement at the prospect of finally being reunited with Dad, but every second seemed to last an eternity. I had no idea how I would survive the time between now and the noon meeting Katya had arranged. *Why in the world had she chosen noon? Why not now?*

My excitement began to turn to worry. The more I thought about the upcoming rendezvous, the more I wondered if it had all happened too easily. Did I really think our visitor of the night before could deliver my dad to us? Were we crazy for trusting him? What if his story was some kind of ruse, and this was a trap? What if he betrayed us? What if others betrayed *him*?

I suddenly realized—he'd shown us no proof at all that he'd even met my dad. Why didn't we ask more questions? We should at least

THE QUEST

have demanded proof of life, a phrase I remembered from some movie I'd seen years earlier. Why hadn't I thought of that before?

Were Katya and I just being naïve? Were we setting ourselves up? Was something about to go terribly wrong?

CHAPTER 63

I started to feel the old panic rising up within me, a level of terror I hadn't felt since arriving in Israel. I said a quick prayer, surprising myself, for God to calm me down and help me through this.

I turned to Katya. I needed to talk. I had to think about something else. "All these people. They're all just as sincere about their religion as you are about yours."

She smiled. "I'm sure that's true."

"But you think Jesus is the only way, don't you?"

She seemed to study my face. "I do," she said.

"How can you think that? How can you look at all these people, who don't believe the way you do, and tell me they're not going to heaven?"

"I'm not telling you that," she said.

"What? Of course you are! You just said so."

"No. You asked me if I think Jesus is the only way of salvation and I said, 'I do.'"

"Exactly!" I said. "That's what I mean."

"But I'm not the one who said that. Jesus said it. He said, 'I am the way, and the truth, and the life. No man comes to the Father except through me.'"

"That's what I'm talking about."

"My point is that you're interrogating me as though I'd made that statement. I haven't. Jesus did."

"What's the difference?"

She turned and leaned her back against the railing, facing away from the Western Wall. "I follow Jesus. I believe his words are true. That's what you'd expect of his followers, wouldn't you?"

"Well, yeah, but—I'm asking you, not him."

She laughed, and her laughter seemed to reach inside me and defuse some of my panic. "That's exactly my point. You phrase the question as if it's about me. It's not about me, it's about Jesus."

"I don't get why you won't just answer the question."

Laughing again, she said, "I'm not trying to frustrate you, Emma. Honest, I'm not. I've just observed that a lot of people, when they bring up the subject of Jesus being the only way, are finding fault with the people who believe Jesus instead of taking up the issue with the one who said those words."

"Well, yeah, because he's not around."

"I could disagree, but I won't." She winked at me. "The thing I want to point out is that a lot of people admire Jesus, and yet they use his claim to be the only way to the Father, as a way of accusing his followers. And logically speaking, you can't have it both ways."

"Okay, I guess I can see that."

"It's much easier to point the finger at me and say I'm unreasonable because I think Jesus is the only way than it is to honestly confront Jesus and what he said about himself."

"Okay, but you've got to admit, it sounds really arrogant to say that everybody else is wrong and only you are right."

"See, there you go again, putting words in my mouth."

"But isn't that what it means to say Jesus is the only way?"

"You're saying that. I'm not saying that."

"But if you say you believe Jesus is the only way, you're saying you're right and everybody else is wrong."

"No, I'm not. I'm saying only what Jesus said."

"Okay, so Jesus is saying he's right and everybody else is wrong."

She smirked, as if she'd already won the argument. "Who would say such a thing?" she said.

"I know! That's what I'm saying!"

"I think you're right."

"You do?"

"Yes. You're right," she said. "And everybody else is wrong."

"You trapped me," I said.

"Did I?" she said coyly. "I'm sorry."

"You're not sorry at all," I said, pouting just a little bit. I crossed my arms. "You're saying I'm doing what I'm accusing you of doing."

"No. I think you're doing what you're accusing Jesus of doing."

"Same difference," I said.

She shrugged, good-naturedly. "If you say so. But here's my point, Emma. You're insisting that your perspective, your position, is true. In order to be true, it must exclude positions that are contrary. So in rejecting Jesus' claim to be the only way because it's too exclusive, you are taking an exclusive position." She said those last words slowly. "If claims of exclusivity are inherently wrong, then your claim is inherently wrong."

I just looked at her for a minute. "I hate when you do that."

"Do what?" she asked, as if she was innocent.

"You know," I said.

She smiled. "I guess I do … but I'm just getting warmed up."

"I was afraid of that."

"See, Emma, Jesus' words about being the only way to the Father are offensive to many people because they seem so exclusive."

"That's what I'm saying!"

"But from my perspective, they can only be seen as exclusive if they're false."

She lost me. "What?" I said.

"If Jesus said that, and yet there are other ways to God, then it would've been the most arrogant thing anybody has ever said, to claim to be the *only* way, when in fact—in truth—there are other ways. I'd have to agree, in that case, that Jesus' words are totally exclusive and totally arrogant.

"But," she continued, "if Jesus' words about being the only way to the Father are true, then they're about the most inclusive words ever spoken."

"How?"

"Look at it this way. If Jesus is who he says he is, then he knows the way to the Father. Right?"

"Sure."

"If that's the case—and I for one think it is—then the worst thing he could do is keep that news to himself. Or to let people be confused about it. Right?"

"Okay," I said.

"And the best thing he could do would be to communicate—as clearly as possible—the way to the Father, to eternal life, to heaven."

A crowd of school children dressed in black and white came down the steps behind me and hustled past us on their way to the wall. Katya waited until they passed and then continued.

"So, if Jesus' claim to know the way to the Father was true, then it is a loving and inclusive thing for him to tell people, clearly and concisely, 'I am the way.' In fact, to do otherwise would be horribly exclusive, keeping people from knowing the one way to God. *That* would be exclusive. But to tell everyone, 'Here's the way,' isn't exclusive at all. It's inclusive. He's saying, 'Come. Everyone, come. Man, woman, child—come. Come as you are. Come with your baggage. Come with all your faults and failings. Come with your sin and shame. Come—whether you're Hindu, Buddhist, Muslim, or atheist—come.

Whatever nationality, whatever color, whatever, whatever, just come. I am the way.'"

I had to admit, she had a point. I had never looked at it that way. I told her so.

She seemed pleased. "You know what amazes me most?"

"What?" I asked.

"That anyone hearing a clear statement like that from someone with such impeccable credentials as Jesus would choose to be offended rather than choosing to follow, or at least find out more."

I watched as the group of school children crossed the plaza toward the wall. One of them started to wander from the pack, and an adult—probably a teacher—stepped aside to corral him. That's when I saw something that stopped me cold.

Katya must have seen the change in my expression. "What?" she said. She turned and faced the plaza, then swiveled back to look at me.

I glanced at the doctor, who was lighting another cigarette.

Katya lowered her voice to a whisper. "What is it?"

I shook my head. I didn't want to say anything. I didn't want to give anything away that might jeopardize Dad's safe return.

Katya wouldn't let it go. "What are you looking at?"

"Nothing," I said, doing my best to sound nonchalant.

She turned again, and carefully scanned the plaza. Then I saw her back straighten. She had seen what I had seen.

It was Mr. Yadin.

CHAPTER 64

What was Mr. Yadin doing there?

He seemed unaware of our presence as he walked across the plaza, parallel to the Wall. His head rotated slowly, apparently scanning the faces on all sides. I couldn't believe it. This was horrible. It couldn't have been a coincidence, no way. But how? How could he have known to be here? How could he have known anything? And how could he take such a chance? It could ruin everything.

I stole a glance at the doctor. He had turned to face the plaza, leaning his elbows on the metal railing and watching the streams of people walking every direction to and from the Wall. He hadn't seen Mr. Yadin, if he even knew who he was. But if he did, it was only a matter of time. Mr. Yadin was practically under his nose. Under our noses.

I stepped back to the railing next to Katya. Just as I did so, she gripped my arm just above the elbow and softly spoke my name. I looked at her. She was peering in the direction of the plaza entrance where people came through the metal detectors at the security checkpoint.

"It's him," she said.

I turned and looked. There were so many people. "You mean Dad?"

"He's heading for the flagpole."

THE QUEST

I kept looking. Our vantage point should have permitted me to see him clearly, but I couldn't find him in the press of people coming through the checkpoint at the entrance to the plaza. "I don't see him!"

"There!" she said, pointing.

I followed her gesture and saw nothing except for old Jewish men in black coats and hats, old women in scarves, a young female soldier, a father and mother and two children ... and then I saw. "I see him!" I cried, my voice too loud.

He walked alone, working a pair of crutches as if competing in an Olympic event, staring intently at the flagpole Katya had designated as our meeting place.

My dad.

"We have to go," she said, still holding my arm. She started pulling me toward the steps. I turned back toward the stranger, half expecting him to prevent us from leaving.

"Thank you," I said.

He didn't answer but dropped his cigarette on the pavement, crushed it with a toe, and turned to go in the opposite direction.

Katya and I bounded down the steps and wound our way through the streams of people crossing back and forth through the plaza on their way to and from the wall, working across the traffic.

I struggled to keep up with Katya while straining to see Dad. "Do you still see him?" I asked.

"This way," she said.

She let go of my arm then, and I gripped her hand. We navigated around a group that looked like Japanese school children posing for a picture with the wall in the background and turned, practically in unison, to look in the direction of the security checkpoint.

I didn't see him. "Where is he?" I scanned the crowd as thoroughly as I could.

Katya didn't answer.

"I don't see him!" Panic started to rise inside me, and I vowed if Mr. Yadin had ruined this—

"There!" Katya said. She pointed.

We both bolted from our spot at the same time. There was no thinking, no discussion, we just sprang in Dad's direction. I almost ran over an old woman with a cane in my haste, but I managed to avoid her at the last second. I reached him first and threw my arms around his neck, nearly throwing us both to the ground. He shifted on his crutches, trying to return my hug without losing his balance.

"Emma! What are you doing here?" he asked, obviously shocked to see me.

Before the words were out of his mouth, however, he turned and looked at Katya, reached out an arm, and pulled her in. I hugged him from one side while Katya held him on the other side. All three of us cried, without a touch of embarrassment.

If Katya had not seen him first, I may not have recognized him. He was thinner than I had ever seen him, and his clothes hung on him like on a scarecrow. He had a mottled beard of brown with flecks of gray, and the hair on his head was a bit too long, looking like it hadn't been combed in weeks. If he wasn't my dad, I might have described him as "bedraggled." But I didn't care. To me, he was beautiful.

I don't know how much time passed, but we stood together in the middle of that great, wide plaza, laughing and hugging and crying, for a good long time. As the three of us celebrated together, I glanced back in the direction Katya and I had come from. The doctor who had accompanied us to the Western Wall plaza and brought about our reunion with Dad was walking down the steps into the plaza with an armed olive-green-clad Israeli soldier on either side.

I released Dad from my embrace. "Katya. What's going on?"

The doctor and soldiers reached the plaza, and Mr. Yadin joined them. They stood there for a few minutes. It looked like Mr. Yadin was saying something to the doctor. Then they started walking again, this time toward the exit at the security checkpoint.

"Something's not right," I said.

THE QUEST

I marched over to Mr. Yadin. "What are you doing?" I asked.

"This man is under arrest," he said.

"What? No! You can't do that."

He shrugged. That was it. No answer—just a shrug.

I turned to the doctor. "I don't know what's happening. I don't know how they knew, but it wasn't us. We didn't turn you in."

The stranger shook his head and looked away.

"You don't understand," I said to Mr. Yadin. I tried to wedge myself between him and the stranger, but one of the soldiers barked a warning. I felt a hand on my shoulder and turned. It was Katya.

"Emma. It's okay."

"No, it's not. What about the children? What about the orphanage?"

"The orphanage is being raided as we speak," Mr. Yadin said, "and Abdul Qayyum is already in custody."

"Who? What?" I said.

From behind, Katya placed a hand on each of my shoulders and started pulling me away from the spot. "Let him do his job," she said.

I turned on her. "What is going on?" I felt so disoriented. Something had gone very wrong.

Dad stood next to us, balanced on his crutches, silently observing us. Mr. Yadin and the soldier left with the stranger.

"You called them?" I asked. She started to answer, but I didn't give her the chance. "You put my dad's life in danger? Without even talking to me? Without saying anything?"

She held up her hands as if in surrender. "You were there when I called."

"I was—what?"

"You were sitting on the couch when I called."

I repeated her words, bewildered. I searched my memory. "On the couch? When?"

"Almost the whole time."

"What are you talking about? You never made a phone call. And then he destroyed our phones."

"Do you remember when I stood up from the couch?"

"Yeah. So?"

"I put my hands in my pockets."

"Yeah," I said, still not understanding.

"Where my phone was."

I said nothing. I simply stared.

She sighed. "Mr. Yadin's number was the last one we had dialed on that phone. So I pressed the call button twice … and prayed that he would answer—or that it would go to voicemail—and that he would hear the conversation, or at least enough to take some action."

"So he heard—"

"Apparently enough. About your dad, the exchange, the orphanage."

"But you—they still could have ruined everything."

"Yes," she said.

"How could you do that? How could you take that kind of chance?"

"It took all the faith I had. Even though it meant getting Daniel returned to us, I didn't think either of us could live with the knowledge that we were concealing the identities of the Blumenthals' killers. But neither could I let any harm come to those children in the orphanage. So I called Mr. Yadin's number and prayed to God that he would hear our conversation and use CID and anyone else he chose to do the right thing, and he did. I didn't even know for sure, until Mr. Yadin showed up here, that he had received my call. I just had to trust that God would hear my prayers, then and all through the night." She smiled and gently wrapped her arm around my father's waist. "And the God we serve heard and answered."

I looked at her. I didn't know whether to thank her or curse her. Finally, I decided. I threw my arms around her and Dad both. "Thank you," I said.

IDF Raids Bethlehem Orphanage

☒ EMAIL 🖶 PRINT + SHARE

BETHLEHEM—Israeli Defense Force troops raided a Palestinian orphanage yesterday in a rapid strike. Landing in helicopters on the orphanage grounds, commandos secured all buildings within minutes, and disarmed orphanage staff members quickly and without incident. The raid netted three Palestinian terrorists, one of whom is reportedly a suspect in the Blumenthal murders.

The orphanage housed 123 children, both boys and girls. An IDF spokesman said the children are safe and will be immediately relocated. The spokesman also said the raid was the result of an anonymous tip.

Abu Djazair, a spokesman for the Palestinian Authority, condemned the raid, calling it "an act of terrorism against Palestinian children," and claiming that the IDF troops vandalized and looted the orphanage.

CHAPTER 65

After the whirlwind of events the previous couple of weeks, it felt strange to sit down with Dad and Katya in the garden terrace of the Little Jerusalem Restaurant. It felt even stranger to have Travis join us for dinner.

Travis and I had finally connected the day after Dad's return to us. Katya and I managed to track him down again at the archaeological site. The first few seconds of the call were awkward, but after I told him that we'd found Dad and he was okay—and explained why I had to hang up so quickly when he called in the middle of an actual car chase—the rest of our conversation went well. We talked for a long time and Travis asked how soon he could see me. I told him anytime, and he promised I'd see him the next day.

True to his promise, Travis drove to Jerusalem the very next day in a borrowed car and arrived just as Dad, Katya, and I were leaving for the restaurant. Katya and I both had been beside ourselves with joy since Dad's return, and she said she wanted to celebrate with a good meal rather than the "burnt offerings" she was likely to conjure up.

It wasn't easy bringing Travis up to date on everything. Even as we sat down to eat and ordered our food, he was full of questions.

He asked Dad, "Is your leg going to be okay?"

"My doctors seem to think so." He flashed Katya a grateful look. "We've seen a bunch of them already, and they all agree I'm going to need surgery and then maybe some rehab for awhile, but they tell me it will eventually be just fine."

THE QUEST

Travis said he was glad to hear it. "I wish I could have helped in some way."

Katya reached across the round table and patted his hand. "Thank you, but once we figured out where you were and how to reach you, things started happening so fast. I don't know what you could have done."

"I should have called sooner. Once I got to the dig, I had very little time to call."

We were all feeling so relaxed that I thought it would be okay to tease him. "Next time, just try to call before we're being chased all over the city."

He lifted a water glass halfway to his mouth. "I'll do my best," he said.

"What did you find out from CID?" I asked Katya.

"Not much. They said it's not up to them, of course, whether our doctor friend, whose name is al-Sana, by the way, will be prosecuted. They said even if he is charged, it shouldn't be too serious, though."

"I hope not," I said. "We wouldn't be here if it wasn't for him."

A thoughtful pause went around the table, until Katya said, "I did find out what CID is going to charge us for their efforts."

"Do we get a discount for doing most of the work ourselves?" I asked.

She smiled. "Unfortunately, no. But the funds from the institute will cover most of it, and the money my sister's sending should pay the rest."

"What about Artie's money?" I asked.

"Did you reach him?" Dad asked.

"Yeah, he said he still has some calls to make and things to nail down, but he had already raised a few thousand dollars."

"A few thousand dollars? Really?" Katya said.

"But if CID is taken care of, what would we use it for?"

Dad and Katya looked at each other, then back at me.

"What about reimbursing your expenses to get here? And a plane ticket home?" Dad said.

"Are you already trying to get rid of me?"

He winked at me. "You know better than that. We want you to stay as long as you want—as long as you can. Until you have to get back to school."

"Yeah, well, about that—" I said.

A waiter delivered a platter of wild mushroom and champignon appetizer to the table, and then the three of them turned and looked at me without reaching for the food.

"What about it?" Dad asked.

"I had to stop taking classes a while ago because I couldn't pay my bills." I reached for the appetizer plate. "Mushrooms, anyone?"

Travis waved the plate away. "Could the money Artie raised be used to pay off your school bills?"

"I hadn't thought of that. I guess it could," I said.

"And Beanpole, you know we'd love to help you with school again," Dad said.

So much had changed since I'd made that decision. It didn't seem so necessary to refuse Dad and Katya's help any longer.

"We got an offer on the house," Katya said.

"What?" I asked.

"Our tenants in New Jersey want to buy the house. The paperwork was already in process before any of this happened."

"Our house?" I said. The house I grew up in.

Dad said, "We figured that with you growing up and moving on and with us living here, there wasn't much point to holding on to it. And that means we're in an even better position to help you with school expenses, if you'll let us."

"So you're going to stay here?" I asked.

THE QUEST

Dad and Katya exchanged glances. "Yes," he said. He reached for her hand.

"After all that's happened?"

"Beany, I hate that it's so far away from you, but this is our home now. We believe God called us here. We still have a lot of work to do."

CHAPTER 66

After our meal—and an amazing dessert of strudel the restaurant called "Anna's Strudel"—Dad and Katya suggested that Travis and I take a walk through the gardens surrounding the restaurant, which was located in a building called the Ticho House, one of the first houses built outside the walls of Jerusalem's Old City. The menu said Ticho House was built in the late 1800s by some Arab dignitary and bought in 1924 by an eye doctor named Avraham Ticho. When his wife, Anna, died in 1980, twenty years after Dr. Ticho died, she bequeathed the house, its contents, and the surrounding gardens to the city of Jerusalem. The setting couldn't have been more beautiful … or more romantic.

"How long do you plan to stay?" Travis asked.

"I don't know," I answered. Now that I had my dad back again, I was in no hurry to leave. I didn't even mind sleeping on the couch in the living room; I had of course surrendered the bedroom to Dad and Katya since his return.

"I'll be here for three more weeks."

"Oh," I said.

"I would love it if I could see you again."

"I'd like that, too."

"My workdays are from five in the morning until one in the afternoon, and I have every weekend off."

"And you go home in three weeks."

"Right."

"Where's home?" If he'd ever told me, I'd forgotten.

"St. Louis."

"Oh," I said.

"It's probably only about a six-hour drive from Oxford, you know."

I smiled. I think I'd been smiling pretty much the whole evening. I had my Dad back. I was actually starting to admit that I liked Katya. And I was looking forward to getting to know Travis.

I couldn't believe all that had happened in such a short time. I remembered the female rabbi in Oxford saying that if God existed, maybe he would help me find Dad. I had to admit that it felt like he had. It felt like my prayers had been answered—much more so, in fact, than I could ever have imagined.

As we walked together on that beautiful Jerusalem evening, I realized that somewhere along the line, I had stopped disbelieving in God. And soon after that, I had started to believe in him.

I asked Travis if he remembered what he said to me on the plane.

"I said a lot of things on the plane. Can you be more specific?"

"You said, 'everyone's searching, but not everyone knows it.'"

"Oh, yeah. I do remember."

"I didn't think so at the time, but I think you're right."

"Oh?"

"Yeah." I stopped and turned to face him. Our faces were inches apart. I searched his eyes. "I think I'm still searching ... but I'm closer than I've ever been."

CHAPTER 67

KATYA'S JOURNAL

Thank you, Lord. Thank you.

THE QUEST

NOTES

Chapter 24

The text referenced in this chapter refers to the book, *Understanding Intelligent Design* by William A. Dembski and Sean McDowell (Eugene, OR: Harvest House Publishers, 2008), p. 104.

Chapter 35

The verses Katya looks up in her conversation with Emma can be found in 1 John 1:1, 2, Peter 1:16, and Luke 1:1–3.

Chapter 46

The parts of Job 38 Katya quotes in this chapter are the author's paraphrase of those verses.

Chapter 65

The Little Jerusalem restaurant in the historic Ticho House is located at 9 Harav Kook Street in Jerusalem.

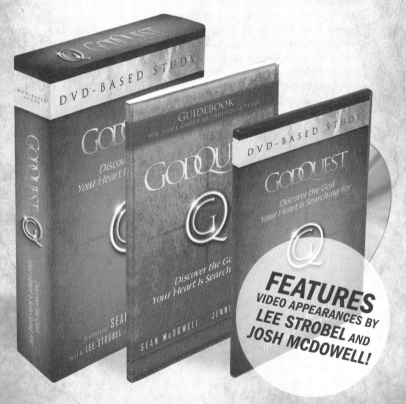

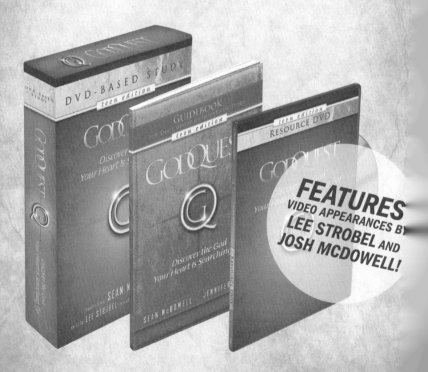